ON THE
FRINGE

COURTNEY KING WALKER

Lands Atlantic
Publishing

ON THE FRINGE
Published through Lands Atlantic Publishing
www.landsatlantic.com

This is a work of fiction. Names, characters, places, and incidents are the product of the author's imagination or are used fictitiously. Any resemblance to actual persons, living or dead, events, or locales is entirely coincidental.

ISBN: 9780982500552

Cover photo by Elena Kalis

James & Afton King and Ray & Grace Hassell
We are all connected.

ON THE
FRINGE

CHAPTER
ONE THE BEGINNING

Claire

I regretted never telling Daniel how much I liked him before that terrible night. To my credit, I was only fifteen. Not many fifteen-year-olds would admit to crushing on their best friend's older brother. Instead, they'd just act funny around him and hope no one noticed. I even spent the whole week mapping out a bunch of sneaky flirting moves in my head, with the plan to test some of my best ones really soon.

Like, tomorrow.

But tomorrow never came. At least, not a tomorrow I wanted.

The day started out pretty average; it was even on the verge of boring. Then Daniel showed up. True, he was only there to pick up my brother, Matthew, but my heart (or my nerves) couldn't tell the difference. That was why I was hiding out in my bedroom, trying to spy on Daniel, instead of going out there and talking to him like I really wanted to.

When had I turned into a stalker?

Ducking my head under the lime green curtains, I pressed my face against the window screen, debating the pros and cons of staying put versus 'accidentally' running into him on my way down to the lake for an evening jog.

News flash: I don't jog.

I pushed my glasses back up the bridge of my nose as a whiff of eucalyptus mixed with the scent of an earlier rainstorm hit me. A sneeze shot out of my mouth so fast that I dropped to the floor and counted to thirty before taking another peek.

Had he heard me? Hard to tell. But he had definitely moved.

Now he was leaning against the side of his car, still looking cool and relaxed, seemingly content to wait forever in my front yard. Behind him the fading sun was tipping over the horizon, sending out its last light across the surface of Hidden Lake, as if trying to decide whether to come or go. Just like me.

My stomach somersaulted, making me feel nervous, embarrassed, and excited all at the same time, despite the fact that I had known Daniel Holland my whole life. It wasn't like he was some hot, brooding guy who had just moved in down the street. No, not only was Daniel my older brother's best friend, but he also happened to be my best friend's older brother. I have seen him cry like a baby and dance in his underwear. For as long as I could remember, he had always been like another brother to me—one who ate too much, burped too loud, and harassed me as much as my own brother. And then, unexpectedly, he went from being my older brother's annoying friend to my very own secret crush.

Daniel

I knew Claire for twelve years, so it was pretty impossible to pinpoint the exact moment I started liking her. Don't get me wrong. I'm not talking about love at first sight or anything cheesy like that (because that would make me a real Romeo at age five). But there *was* one day that stuck out above the rest when I finally admitted (only to myself) that Claire James—*Matthew's little sister*—wasn't too bad.

It was March, and it had been raining on and off for weeks, until one random day the temperature climbed to almost 85 degrees. After three or four hours of staring out the window and ignoring my teachers, it dawned on me that I'd almost wasted a perfect day. Matthew agreed with me, so we ditched seventh period to go mountain biking in the hills behind Hidden Lake.

A couple of miles from the trailhead we veered off the rocky trail, down a muddy embankment, briefly stopping in front of a path hidden by overgrown bushes and something suspiciously poison-ivy-like. We decided to take our chance with the ivy, and shot straight through it over a trickling stream to the base of an ancient, oversized eucalyptus tree. Hanging from one of the branches was a thick, knotted rope in the beginning stages of unraveling.

That was a no-brainer.

We immediately tossed our bikes off to the side, and took turns swinging across the stream for close to an hour. Just as Matthew headed up the tree for probably his twentieth time, I heard a familiar, out-of-place voice behind me. "Hey, I want a try!"

I spun around to find my sister, Addie, emerging from the bushes.

"How'd you find us?" I asked, annoyed. The last thing I wanted to be doing right then was hanging out with my little sister.

When she spotted the rope swing, she pushed past me, and raced over to the tree. "You think you're the only one who knows about this place?" she answered with an attitude. *Typical.*

I was about to tell Addie exactly where she could go, when Matthew's sister, Claire, popped out of the bushes with mud on her shirt and a bunch of leaves stuck in her hair. I felt a smile coming on, but immediately shut my mouth and turned around because something felt off. Normally the mud on her shirt would have been plenty of ammunition for at least three or four jokes at her expense. But this time I felt a strange sensation building up somewhere inside my chest. When I realized what it probably meant, I refused to believe it. Was I *happy* Claire was there, even if it meant having to hang out with Addie?

Seriously?

Claire smiled. "Hi, Daniel."

"Hey," I said. Just like that.

When I couldn't think of anything else to say, I tried playing it cool by ignoring her as usual. But inside my head a fight was raging. I tried pretending not to care about her, but was shocked by how much I really did.

Get a grip. This whole heart-fluttering thing seemed just slightly moronic. Plus, she was only fifteen.

As Matthew soared like an out-of-control Tarzan, Claire made her way toward me until we were only a few feet apart. "Nice look," I said, plucking the leaves out of her hair, trying to keep my sarcasm in check.

"What…?" She stepped backward like she was afraid I was going to hit her, or something. When I showed her the handful of leaves in my hand, her shoulders dropped, and she seemed to relax a little. "Oh, thanks."

"Look out!" yelled Matthew before dropping right on top of us.

I jumped out of the way in time, but Claire wasn't fast enough. She screamed when he took her out, both of them slamming to the ground.

"Whoa, are you okay?" Matthew asked, still flat on his back.

Claire slowly crawled to her knees and brushed herself off. "Thanks a lot, Matthew," she said, half-heartedly kicking him in the side.

"Hey, you guys—over here!" We turned to find Addie clinging to the top of the rope, stranded above the stream. "Hurry and help me down before I fall…"

None of us could bring ourselves to rescue her because it was much more fun watching Addie in meltdown mode. Of course, she vowed revenge, but I wasn't worried; she usually picked Matthew as her target.

Finally Claire decided to give the swing a try, and slowly started climbing the trunk. She stood at the edge of a thick branch, gripping the rope with what appeared to be courageous fear, and balanced there, ready to jump. When the setting sun broke in through the trees, lighting up her face, I realized Claire looked kind-of cute, even with her funky red glasses. I tried looking away, uninterested, but *couldn't*. I was also pretty sure I was either having some kind of panic attack, or for some strange reason, I liked Claire James.

That sounded more ridiculous than I'd hoped.

We all cheered and whistled from below when Claire finally jumped off the ledge and flew through the air, straight for Addie. They both started screaming at the impending collision, as if they had no ability to dodge each other whatsoever. I was afraid to watch. It looked like it was going to be ugly, especially since it involved two fifteen-year-old girls smacking into each other. But then again, *it involved two fifteen-year-old girls smacking into each other.* Who wouldn't watch?

Sure enough, they hit hard and toppled to the ground. When their screaming turned to laughing, I assumed they were okay. Matthew and I looked at each other, wondering how we'd let our afternoon be hijacked by our sisters. But there was nothing we could do about it now. Plus, as weird as it sounded, I didn't want them to leave…well, at least not Claire.

After that, we abandoned the rope swing and took off through the trees along a shallow creek bed. Matthew and Addie quickly fell into their familiar pattern of one-upmanship, leaving Claire and I awkwardly stuck with each other, mostly in silence. I kept hoping Claire would think of something to say first. Then I realized it was the first time I'd ever been speechless on account of a girl. So, I decided to quit acting like I was twelve, and kick it up a notch.

As soon as Matthew and Addie disappeared around the next bend, I hung back to help Claire through the stream, because not only did I consider myself somewhat of a gentleman, but was also excellent at spotting a good opportunity when I saw one. Unfortunately, my nerves wouldn't cooperate with my newfound interest, and each time my fingers came close to hers, I seemed to lose all confidence.

Around the next bend, something shiny in the stream caught my eye. I crouched down and plunged my hand in the freezing water until I caught it.

"What are you doing?" Claire asked, peering over my shoulder. Her face was suddenly next to mine, and I almost jerked back in surprise.

"Hold on a sec," I said, trying to buy myself more time by leaving my hand buried in the stream, pretending to keep searching. She leaned against me, her hair dangling in front of me and tickling my neck. Finally, I took a deep breath and pulled my hand up, water dripping down my arm. "Look—I found something."

She pulled at my clenched fist. "What is it?"

I squeezed my hand tight, making her peel my wet fingers apart, and then finally gave in.

"You found that in the *stream?*" she asked, pulling my hand closer to get a better look. "Wow, that's really pretty."

Picking up the thin, silver ring I'd found, she twirled it around in her fingers, running her thumb along the beveled edge before sliding it onto her finger. We stood there silently admiring it until Matthew and Addie suddenly reemerged from wherever they'd gone. I looked up in surprise, disappointed to see them so soon.

"This way's a dead end," Matthew called. "And you guys are waaaay too slow."

"Yeah, and it's getting dark," said Addie. "Let's get out of here before we're attacked by a wild animal or serial killer. I have a science test tomorrow."

Claire shoved the ring back in my hand and turned around, taking the lead back up the stream. I didn't know what to do with it. *I* didn't need a ring, but *what if…?*

I stood there weighing my options, letting Matthew and Addie pass me. Finally, I shoved the ring in my pocket and caught up to Matthew just as Addie flicked a branch into his face, tagging him in the nose. That's how things usually went between them.

"That's for leaving me stranded on the rope swing," she said.

He rubbed his nose. "What? I wasn't the only one, you know."

"Yeah, well, it was probably *your* idea," she said, catching up to Claire.

Matthew looked my way and rolled his eyes. I shrugged my shoulders and turned away. It wasn't my fault my sister took payback so seriously.

Addie suddenly stopped and turned around, her eyes bright and animated, her grudge forgotten, just like that. "Hey! We should give this place a cool name...something mysterious. Something like–"

"Mystery Rope Swing Grotto," Claire said with a big smile, like she'd given it ten hours of thought. Maybe creative writing wasn't her thing.

"What about the *'Secret Walk*?" Addie said, ignoring Claire's suggestion, though I couldn't blame her. "That's perfect, don't you think?"

"LAME," Matthew said, kicking water up on her. I agreed, and would've probably even turned it into a perfect opportunity for a water fight, but my mind was somewhere else.

Claire placed a supportive arm around Addie and continued with her up the stream, adding quietly, "I think it's a good name."

It was almost dark when we hopped on our bikes and headed back down the trail, yet Matthew still found the need to challenge everyone to a race, as if racing two girls was even remotely challenging. Claire immediately took off close behind Addie, but held back when I called her name. She hesitated, probably convinced I was tricking her into last place, which I had been known to do on occasion.

Finally she stopped pedaling and turned to face me. "What?" she asked, not even looking at me. She seemed really annoyed.

I caught up to her, but suddenly felt like an awkward fifth-grader handing out a valentine. Embarrassed, I looked down at my feet and wondered who this wimp was that seemed to be taking over my body. "Here," I mumbled, pulling the ring out of my pocket and shoving it into Claire's palm.

She didn't say a word, but I could tell she was surprised by my gesture. Our fingers touched again, and my heart thumped like a subwoofer let loose inside my chest. "You can have it," I added, as a strange, unwanted noise escaped from my throat—something like a half-sigh, half-chuckle. I felt mortified about it the rest of the night.

But Claire didn't seem to notice. "Wow, thanks, Daniel."

She slid the ring on her finger. We both stared at it in awkward silence until at last Claire looked up at me and smiled. I brushed a strand of hair away from my eyes and smiled back, trying to extend the moment a second longer, while at the same time wishing it would end already. When I finally couldn't take it anymore, I jumped on my bike and took off down the hill in a mad dash for third place.

"Hey!" I heard her yelling behind me, trying to catch up.

Claire

Three weeks before the night everything fell apart, I fell for Daniel. Literally. All because of the rain…or lack of it.

See, if it had rained the day before, all those annoying pollen particles would have been washed away instead of multiplying en masse until they found their way up my nose; I would not have had an allergy attack the next morning, would've worn my contacts, and never ridden off the edge of a cliff.

But it didn't rain.

So, the next day I put on my helmet and glasses, and went biking with Addie because it was finally sunny and dry enough. It had also been too long since my last ride, and I was dying to get out.

But just as we were leaving, Addie's paranoid Mom dashed our ambitions by inferring that we were two helpless girls out in the middle of nowhere, refusing to let us go biking alone, thanks to the local newscast about a recent bobcat attack.

Please. We were fifteen, not five.

Still, Addie's mother would not give in, so we begged Daniel to come with us. Since Matthew was working all day and Daniel happened to be home just watching TV, we figured it was worth a shot. We definitely didn't get our hopes up, which was why we were so shocked when he agreed to come.

A couple miles and a half-hour later, Addie and Daniel were stopped at the edge of a steep incline when I came up from behind them and wildly plunged down what looked like a little hill instead of a cliff, in an attempt to impress them. I would've been much better off flaunting the sweet spin I could put on a football, or even demonstrating some of my legitimate baking skills. The next thing I knew, I was crumpled up at the bottom of the ravine, my body contorted in pain, and my bike resting vindictively on top of me, as if saying *'what were you thinking?'*

"Claire!" Daniel and Addie yelled from above.

My head hurt only slightly. Thankfully there was no blood spurting out, nor was anything that belonged inside me now on the outside.

Good. I wouldn't have to throw up.

"Are you okay?" Daniel raced down the hill and effortlessly lifted the bike off of me. He stood over me, his shadow blocking the sun from my eyes. Addie stumbled down a little more carefully, but was soon right in my face, fiercely hugging me as her smooth curtain of fruity-smelling hair slid into my face.

I tried to stand, but my ankle gave way as pain shot through my foot, forcing me to sink back into the dirt. Tears hovered inside the edges of my eyes, making my blurry vision even more blurry. But I held it all in because there was no way I was going to start crying in front of Daniel and risk him making fun of me later.

"I can't walk," I confessed, wishing to collapse into a little ball and quietly roll away.

"Seriously?" asked Addie.

"Uh-huh. I think I sprained my ankle, or something."

Daniel looked at me funny, probably unsure whether or not I was going to start crying, probably wondering what to do if I did.

"It's official," I said, trying to lighten things up a little. "I'm *super* awesome at riding my bike."

He laughed, sending the tension hissing into oblivion like a balloon pricked by a pin, and then softly punched me in the shoulder. "Nice crash, Claire."

"Yeah," Addie joined in. "Maybe later you can give us some pointers."

I could already feel the dizziness coming on, and thought I might blackout. Gripping the edge of a rock and closing my eyes, I tucked my stringy hair behind my ear, hoping the feeling would pass. Soon. When it didn't, I subtly reached for the ring Daniel had given me a few weeks ago and mindlessly twisted it around my finger.

"Here's an idea." Daniel's voice broke in through the silence. He seemed so serious, like some calculating plan was simmering inside. "I'll carry you down to the trailhead, and then Addie—you ride ahead for help."

My heart answered first. *Yes! Absolutely.*

Wait a second…what was going on, here? "No, it's okay," I protested, embarrassed by the strange emotions bubbling up inside me. "I can just wait here with Addie while you go get help."

*No, no…*what was I saying? Back up. Back up.

Daniel looked away for a minute while I tried to untangle the confusion inside my head. Did I really want to be alone with him? With *Daniel?*

"I guess," he said, lightly touching my ankle while I tried not to scream in pain. "But I still think you'll be better off if I just carry you down. It'll be a lot faster."

Addie came to my rescue without even trying to. "Come on, Claire. Daniel's right. What's the big deal?"

I wanted to hug her, but played it cool. "Fine," I said, still pretending to be put out. With an exaggerated sigh I pulled myself up on my good foot and let Addie help me climb on Daniel's back.

During the first few minutes of piggybacking down the hill, the only two sounds seemed to be my speeding heartbeat, and Daniel's labored breathing. I couldn't stand the spaces of awkward quiet hanging in the air between us, and especially wasn't used to Daniel being so serious.

"Thanks for doing this," I said, leaning in close to his face. "You probably didn't know I had such sweet biking skills."

He let out a quick laugh. "No problem."

It was quiet again, despite all the times we'd talked and laughed together like it was no big deal. I couldn't believe how nervous I was.

I felt myself slipping, and clasped further around Daniel's neck, my head inching even closer to his. He had a different, more mysterious scent than Matthew, who smelled more musky and familiar. Daniel smelled like—well, he just smelled *good.*

Around the next turn, he stopped and twisted out of my embrace, helping me onto on a moldy old log that cracked when we sat down. "Sorry," he said. "I just need to catch my breath."

"It's okay."

"We'll be down the hill in about ten more minutes. I'll hurry."

"Daniel, *seriously*. It only hurts when I stand on it. Take your time. I'm good."

We sat excruciatingly close to each other, our bare arms sometimes touching when one of us moved. I unwittingly drew his attention to my hand while twisting the ring around my finger again, its thin edge engraving a subtle line in my skin.

"So, you still wear that thing?" he asked, touching my hand.

"Yes," I said tentatively. Did he think that was a good thing or a bad thing?

I gazed up into his dark eyes as he scrutinized me, and I blushed when he placed my hand in his and slowly slid the ring off my finger, leaving my entire hand tingling when he let go. Holding it in front of him, he twisted it back and forth in the sunlight, like he was enamored with it.

"What? Are you going to take it back now?" I sabotaged the moment, suddenly afraid of my own feelings. "Just like that?"

When he turned to answer me, it felt like he knew more about my sudden somersaulting feelings than I did. A soft glow surrounded us when the sunlight slipped in through the trees, and I was convinced right then that Daniel had never been more appealing in my entire life. But I *had* to turn away from him, afraid to look in his eyes any-more…afraid for what it meant.

He squeezed my hand and finished off the moment with a carefree laugh. "I'm not going to steal it from you. I just wanted to see it again, since it was *mine*, you know." Then he slid the ring back on my finger, more quickly this time, and released me. "You ready?" he asked, standing up and turning around.

I nodded and tried to stand, but Daniel squatted in front of me. "Hop on."

"Are you sure I'm not hurting you?"

"Please. Don't insult me."

I playfully punched his shoulder, and then wrapped my arms around his neck while linking both legs around his waist. Holding me tightly, he stood up and made his way through the bushes, down the trail.

In a fit of insanity mixed with flirtation, I lightly brushed my cheek along the side of his face, and moved my lips to his ears, barely touching them. While trying to fight off the drunk, bubbly sensation tingling through my body, I inhaled his subtle aroma once more and whispered softly, "Thanks for rescuing me, Daniel."

He didn't say a word, but I was certain I could feel his smile.

***

Now, three weeks later, nothing had really changed between us, at least in front of other people. That was why I was having such a crisis in my bedroom. Because I was still afraid Daniel would reject me. It was a lot easier being daring and flirtatious when I had my arms and legs wrapped around him.

The silver ring seemed to burn through my finger, begging me to say something to the boy who had given it to me, to the boy who was still standing out there in my front yard, still waiting for Matthew…still alone.

I wondered what was taking Matthew so long.

Well, okay, I had a guess. It had something to do with a girl and the fact that tonight's party was supposed to be *the* party of the year. I was not cool or old enough yet to be invited. It was just for juniors and seniors—well, the popular ones like Daniel and Matthew, and of course all the girls who followed them around everywhere like a bunch of ditzes. Addie and I vowed to never let each other turn into a ditz, no matter how much we claimed to be in love. EVER. *Stalker,* okay, but *ditz,* forget it.

I pulled my hair into a ponytail and released it again—nervous habit, thanks to hair that always seemed to be having an identity crisis. Not only was it forever stuck somewhere in between reddish-brown and strawberry blonde depending on the day and the color I wore, but it also couldn't seem to choose curly or straight. It insisted on lingering forever in a wavy in-between that was always getting in the way.

Your hair? You are obsessing about your hair now? What is wrong with you? Get out there already. Fine.

His back was toward me when I finally reached the edge of the porch.

"Hey, Daniel," I called, the cool breeze relaxing me a bit, giving me a little confidence. When I couldn't come up with anything else to do with my hands, I nervously fingered the corner of my glasses, and then finally dropped both hands to grip the porch railing.

A strand of Daniel's dark hair fell across his dark eyes shadowed by the porch light as he turned toward me, smiling his playboy smile. He wore jeans and a snug, grey t-shirt pulled across his chest just right. When he brought his hand up to brush the hair away from his face, the butterflies in my stomach began their migration north, straight toward my heart.

"Oh, hey, Claire." He said my name calm and easy, like he was expecting me (or so I imagined). For a second I was speechless, and felt my face go warm, but then managed to pull it together.

"So, you guys are going to a party?" I asked, flipping back my flyaway hair, trying to be smooth. I wondered if he could hear my heart pounding.

"Yep," he said coolly, seemingly content to stay where he was, just staring at me.

And then I couldn't think of anything more to say. My brain shriveled up, leaving me mute and defenseless. Daniel seemed to wait for me to speak, like it was my turn, but I was too busy trying to locate the earlier confidence I had somehow misplaced.

Concentrate. Concentrate!

Just when I started to stutter out something (probably something really lame, too), Daniel smiled his famous dimpled smile that had nearly every girl at school under his spell, including me. "Matthew wants to check out the new girl. So as his best friend I'm supposed to go, too. You know how that goes." He laughed a little, throwing his hands in the air for effect. Then he looked around, like he was checking to see if we were alone.

We were.

Before I knew it, he was walking toward me. I held my breath and looked around, wondering if anyone else could see us. *Oh, my.* He was still coming…

"Addie and I are going to a movie. You guys should come with us," I blurted.

What the…? Did I just ask Daniel out on a date?

I suddenly felt queasy.

What was I thinking?

While debating whether to run back inside and take cover behind my curtains again, I noticed Daniel had made it to the bottom of the steps and was now looking up at me. Something seemed different now. *His eyes?* Yes, his eyes had definitely changed. They didn't look as flirtatious, or quite as confident anymore.

"Sounds fun. Maybe I'll meet you there," he said, more quietly than usual. "If I can get away."

I didn't know what else to say. Was Daniel Holland nervous? Was that even possible? His dimples about did me in, and before I knew it, I was wandering down the steps, like something was pulling me. Our feet and eyes met, and I nearly froze when I felt his fingers reaching for my hand. Sure, they were barely touching, but still, Daniel's hand was right next to mine, and it was even kind of warm. I had to tell myself to breathe.

"Claire." His dark eyes found mine. I dared look up at him, to the outline of his lips. His face seemed so close and I felt my heavy eyelids falling…

Breathe.

"Letsssgooo!"

The front door burst open as Matthew tore out of the house. Without even looking at me, he bounded down the steps, right through us, interrupting our perfect moment. Daniel jumped back at the intrusion, like he was about to get in trouble.

He turned and followed Matthew to the car.

I couldn't move, *almost* couldn't breathe. All I could do was watch Daniel walk away from me. Before disappearing into the dark, he briefly turned his head and smiled.

That was the last time I saw him alive.

CHAPTER
TWO THE END

Claire

About an hour after I watched Daniel drive away to his very important party, I was sitting in the dim theater with Addie, waiting for the previews to start. When Addie started texting Daniel, I casually looked over, trying to read the screen while trying even harder to hide my interest in all things Daniel. Addie still had no idea how I felt about her brother, and my plan was to keep it that way.

"Are they coming?" I asked in my best casual voice, though secretly I felt like bursting.

"Nope. They can't," Addie said, matter-of-factly, her fingers still working.

My heart sank. "Why not?"

"He says they met some friends at the party. They're going to stay."

Dang!

"What's so great about that stupid party, anyway?" I griped, resigning myself to a lousy mood for the rest of the night.

Addie whipped her head around and rolled her eyes in usual Addie fashion. "Who cares, Claire? Get over it."

Okay, so I was usually fine with the attitude. Occasionally, it got on my nerves, but Addie was my best friend. We'd known each other since we were three, so I was willing to overlook a little moodiness here and there, accepting it as part of the package deal. Tonight was no different, though it didn't help my mood any.

As the lights dimmed, so did my excitement for the rest of the night. No matter how much I tried to clear my mind and think of something else, it was impossible trying not to picture Daniel getting comfortable with a bunch of clingy girls, while I'd been left behind in a stupid movie theater.

"*Everyone's* going to be there," I pouted again. "I wish we could go, too, instead of hanging out all by ourselves like losers at a dumb movie."

"Which was *your* idea," Addie answered dryly.

Convinced my life could not get any worse, I sunk back into the spongy headrest and closed my eyes until my phone buzzed from somewhere at the bottom of my purse. After fumbling in the dark for a couple of seconds, I finally found it. My heart jumped as soon as I saw the text. "It's…it's Daniel," I announced too eagerly.

Addie turned. "Why's he texting *you*?"

I couldn't help smiling, but still tried to hide my excitement. Addie would never let me live it down if she knew how much I dwelled on thoughts of her brother.

"He says he'll see us after the movie," I said very coolly, though inside I felt like a combination of Diet Coke and Pop Rocks.

"He couldn't just tell *me* that?"

He could. But he didn't.

The next ninety-three minutes *crawled* by. I tried to watch the movie, but didn't care at all if the girl got the guy in the end (of course she did, they always do). I even checked my phone during the slow parts just to be sure Daniel wasn't trying to call.

But he wasn't.

Dang, again.

When the credits started rolling, Addie and I made our way through the crowds to wait outside for our ride. We shivered in the misting rain at the edge of the sidewalk, wishing Mom would hurry up. I began wondering what was taking her so long since she was usually pretty OCD about that kind of thing.

After tucking my hair behind my ears for the thousandth time, I realized any attempts to tame it were useless. The wind and rain would never stop shrinking it into a wavy, frizzy mess. That was just how things usually turned out for me.

I glanced over at Addie with her smooth, dark hair flying all over the place, wondering how she always managed to look impeccable, even in the rain. She wore almost no makeup, yet her dark skin and thick eyelashes seemed merely an accent to the better parts of her—deep topaz eyes, subtle dimples that emerged when she smiled, and thick, mane-like hair extending down to her waist. Except for the scowl on her face, Addie was a striking image of natural beauty.

When the mist turned into fat raindrops, Addie used her oversized purse as an umbrella while eyeing me again, this time with a look I took to mean *my mom, my fault*. Which was kind of true, but *still*. I turned the other way and pretended to ignore her as images of Daniel continued to invade my mind, images of a familiar smile that nearly crippled me, of dark hair falling into dark eyes.

Cars came and went. Ten minutes more...

Feeling rejected, I fell into a daze watching the swirling patterns of white, orange, and red car lights through my rain-spattered glasses, wishing Matthew and Daniel had come with us to the movies. I secretly hoped their party was a bust so they'd be as miserable as me.

"Where *is* she?" Addie grumbled again, breaking into my thoughts just as Mom's blue Audi pulled up.

I started to move until I saw my mom's red, hollow eyes staring out at me, even through the dark passenger-side window veined with rivers of rain. I was hesitant to get in the car. I didn't want this, whatever *this* was.

A car honked behind her, and an irritated Addie quickly slid into the backseat. "Get in, Claire," she said, already getting comfortable.

The car honked again. Finally I moved, sliding in next to Addie. Instead of driving off, Mom pulled into the closest parking spot, prompting Addie to ask what was going on. Turning around in her seat, Mom took one look at Addie and started to cry.

Daniel

The night had gone from boring to deadly in about two minutes.

Before I knew what had happened, there was shouting and breaking glass as a rush of bodies flew around me, everyone climbing on top and over each other, trying to get out of there as quickly as possible.

Then I saw the gun, and froze.

Everyone froze. As if that would keep a killer from pulling the trigger. I even thought about ducking. But it was too late by the time the thought reached my brain.

The bullet reached it first.

Surprisingly, it was nothing like the movies where everything happens in slow motion as the victim helplessly watches fate mow him down. No, Matthew just stared at me blankly as the crack of a surreal blast tore through the air, and then I felt myself jerking hard to the left before falling against the bookcase, my head oozing warm juice.

Claire

"What's wrong, Mom?" I was terrified of the answer. "What *happened?*"

Mom sniffed loudly. "It's Daniel."

"*What?* Is he okay?" Addie asked. But the interior of the car was already beginning to spin, and I felt my own head falling into my shaking hands. I closed my eyes, afraid to look up, because Mom couldn't seem to answer Addie's question.

It was a simple question.

Addie gripped my knee. "Where is Daniel, Mrs. James?"

"There was an accident… But I need to get you home now, honey. Your grandparents are waiting for you."

"Grandparents? What about my parents? Where are *they?*"

"They're taking care of everything."

I still couldn't lift my head, even as I heard Addie's voice tipping into delirium. "Taking care? *Everything?* I don't understand. Where's Daniel? Where is he, Mrs. James? What happened to Daniel?"

"Addie… Daniel's…" Mom choked. "Daniel's been shot–"

"SHOT?" she gasped. "*How?* Wait. Where is he?"

"He…Daniel didn't make it, Addie. He's…"

What?

"What?" Addie wailed. "No!" she pleaded, pounding her fists into her lap. "No, NO!" she screamed, hurling with precision the same words I was thinking, but couldn't find a way to release them.

Daniel.

How could he be gone?

A numbing blackness invaded my vision. Even with my eyes squeezed shut, everything inside me felt broken into pieces. I tried holding my breath to stop myself from crying, but it didn't work. Nothing worked. Never again would I see or hear or touch Daniel. *Ever.* It hurt like a knife carving into me, ripping out my insides, twisting and cutting. I wanted to scream out loud but could only seem to scream in my head.

Not knowing what else to do, I reached for Addie and squeezed her hand as she lay in my lap, sobbing all the way to her house. I could barely watch as Addie's grandfather gathered her into his arms and closed the door behind them.

If only they had come with us to the movie, I kept repeating in my mind. But no, Matthew and Daniel had gone to the party instead. *Everyone was going to be there,* I had whined. Now all the what-ifs were starting to eat at me, and the more I thought about it, the faster I seemed to fall.

Mom was still talking and driving, but I didn't hear most of what she was saying... something about the party and a fight...and a gun. *Why was there a gun?* We lived in Hidden Lake. It was a safe place. Now all I knew was that Matthew was really hurt. But *he* would eventually get better. Daniel wouldn't.

My brother watched his best friend die.

At some point I ended up in Matthew's hospital room, though I couldn't remember how. His head was wrapped up like a mummy with a pair of purplish, puffy eyelids peeking out through the bandages. There was swelling, pressure, and a concussion; but my brain was drowning in a confusion of medical terms that meant nothing to me. Peering out of the rain-spotted window, I listened to the voices outside Matthew's stuffy room while Dad stood next to Mom. She was slumped over in a chair next to Matthew, humming a consoling, but unfamiliar tune. The silver ring Daniel had given me kept me company as I twisted it around my finger over and over again.

Matthew stirred then went still again. Around him, loud machines beeped and blinked, rhythmically dripping liquid through the IV tube into his hand. I had no idea how he would be able to wake to this nightmare.

How would I?

Daniel

I didn't die instantly, though it probably looked that way. I heard myself screaming, but now wonder if the sound ever left my throat. Matthew was strangely quiet, the outrage of it all probably shocking him into silence. I remember trying to look around, being unable to tell the ground from the walls or my hand from the background. Everything was melted together into a muddy blur, faded color dripping all over the place like a messed-up painting.

The pain. Was there even a word or a way to describe it?

It felt like a vise compressing my head. I could no longer think or move, unable to see or hear anything. Somehow I managed to scream out until everything around me shut down to black. I searched through the dark in my mind, trying to find a way out. Just when I thought I found it, the pain stopped.

At last.

Finally I was free from pain and confusion. In fact, I was numb–then the realization of what that meant hit: the bullet in my brain had killed me.

I turned to look at Matthew holding a bleeding head in his lap, and wanted to look away. I didn't want to see the bright red soaking into my best friend's shirt, or listen to his familiar voice begging for me to wake up.

"Matt—" I yelled, trying to touch his shoulder. But my hand passed right through him.

The screaming erupted a few seconds later. Instinctively, I put my hands to my ears to block out the noise, but the voices only seemed to get louder. I turned to the left, then to the right, and then leapt over the couch, ran down the hall, and was out the door in half a second.

I knew I was dead and that the body back there was mine. That part was easy. But I wanted to know why I was still here, *wherever* this was? Where was my life after death?

Where was heaven?

Trying to avoid the parked cars scattered haphazardly along the curb, I ran down the driveway into the dark street, and realized my legs were moving along clumsily like I was still alive. I jerked to a stop in front of the next empty car, as if someone had hit pause. Everything instantly stalled as I waited there gazing into the dark windows, wondering....

Without moving my feet, I tried willing myself to go forward.

It's all in my head, I kept telling myself when nothing happened, even after some intense concentration. Still, I kept at it, trying to make my mind conquer my legs—again, *and again*, almost giving up, until the slight pull of something gently nudged me forward.

I could feel it…like a gasp of air being sucked out of me, followed by a kind of pressure squeezing my body (or spirit, or soul—whatever I was now). Next thing I knew, I was floating in the middle of a grey pickup truck, my neck and head sticking out above the roof, my torso and legs right near the stick shift.

I told myself to move again, this time away from the truck. It was jerky at first, and then I was traveling smoothly, floating…drifting away from the house…down the road…through a thick cement wall, across a muddy field as the distant sound of sirens and haunting echoes of human voices screaming bloody murder followed my retreat, permeating my mind.

Claire

Even though Addie was my best friend, it was torture being around her because of how much she reminded me of Daniel. At first, just looking at her was like another knife digging deeper into my heart. But the day of the funeral changed all that. I had to step it up no matter how much it hurt because Addie was on the verge of losing it any second. Not that I was doing any better, but at least I still had a brother.

It was a calm, sunny morning at the cemetery, and everyone sat quietly in orderly rows of metal chairs facing a mahogany casket topped with a hundred and one colorful flowers. The air smelled clean and new, like the beginning of a perfect summer day, which it was not. We were all trying to listen to words that were supposed to comfort us, all squinting in the morning sun that could care less we were wearing black. I thought it was supposed to rain at funerals, anyway. That was how it seemed to work in the movies.

Addie suddenly reached for my hand and gripped it tightly. I had known her long enough to tell it was not a regular squeeze. Not this time.

Her dad was standing at a makeshift pulpit in front of the crowd. It was his turn to speak. He looked like he was trying to be brave. We were all trying to be brave, but let's face it—courage does not count if you feel like you're dying inside. Right then, *not* crying would have been pointless…and impossible.

"…was such a good son," he was saying. "Daniel would always drop everything to help someone out…always put everyone else first…to his own detriment–"

Matthew suddenly jumped up as a strangled sob tore from his throat. His chair fell forward, its folding legs trying to latch onto his feet. But he took off down the grassy hill, into the road, through a line of cars.

Addie really lost it then. Another gasp escaped her mouth, and she stood, too, like she wanted to follow Matthew. But I wouldn't let her. I was afraid she wouldn't come back. Instead, I held onto her sweaty palm like my life depended on it, and pulled her back to me.

"Addie," I whispered in her ear, pulling her head close to mine. Her eyes were squeezed shut, and she was shaking.

Her dad had already stopped mid-sentence at Matthew's departure—confused, conflicted, not sure what to do or say while her mom leaned forward in her chair, her body bent in half, her back and shoulders shaking up and down as nearby hands rested on them, attempting to soothe her. More crying erupted left and right, in front and in back of me, surrounding me.

It was a disaster.

Addie's eyes popped open and looked around when she realized everyone was watching her. I nudged her head back down to mine and told her to close her eyes. Her hand still squeezed mine. My fingers felt numb as I wrapped my arm around her, whispering into her ear everything I was sure she needed to hear, even though it felt like a lie. I almost felt guilty about how easily those words came out of my mouth.

"Addie, it's going to be all right. Some day it will. I promise, like we used to make pinky promises when we were ten. Remember that? It's okay Ads…"

She sobbed. Her dad sank down on the ground. No one could do or say anything. I rubbed her back, smoothed her hair, told her lies. "He's not gone forever, Addie. We'll see him again, we will," I said, trying to convince us both. Of course that was when my voice caught, her dad's words repeating themselves in my mind over and over again, *"He was such a good son…would drop everything to help someone out…always put everyone else first…"*

Every word was true, and I couldn't stop thinking about how much I had lost by losing him. Not *just* Daniel, but all that made him Daniel. All that made Matthew and Addie love him and whatever it was inside him that made his eyes light up every morning. I felt like I'd just discovered a massive iceberg beneath the tip of Daniel Holland, yet, I hadn't even come close to knowing who he was. Now I would never have the chance.

When I felt the sob making its way out, I tried holding it in, but every bit of strength I'd counted on had evaporated. Addie somehow found the frame of mind to hug me. I hugged her back, not caring about all the people who were staring at us. By then, we were just trying to hold each other up. And failing miserably.

Daniel

After wandering around for days, or maybe it was weeks, trying to figure out why I was still here, I finally found my way back to Hidden Lake and stretched out inside a canoe. Drifting around beneath the black sky, counting each star over and over again, I wondered about the *whys* that wouldn't leave me alone.

I should've been somewhere else by now—in some quiet, perfect place, relaxed and forgetting all my problems. I certainly hadn't done anything in my life that would banish me to that *other* place. I was a standup kid, and rightfully had high expectations.

It seemed like I had insomnia, like hordes of ants were tunneling through my head, making it impossible for my mind to be still. Where was the dark tunnel or bright light? That's what they teach you to expect when you die, right? Instead, I found myself back at Hidden Lake, like it was my own personal waiting room.

Problem was, I didn't *want* to wait. I wanted to get away from here and move on to someplace else. Especially since I couldn't shake the notion I had left something behind and couldn't go any further without it.

Whatever *it* was.

Cue the ants.

At around star number 2,002, I began to have an idea of what *it* was, despite trying to shake the feeling *it* had something to do with Claire.

What was that about?

No matter what I did, her image, voice and scent seemed to attach themselves to me. She crept up around me, swirling and floating her way into every inch of me until nothing remained untouched. I even attempted fighting thoughts of her with logic. I mean, it wasn't like I was in *love* with the girl. Can someone really be in love at seventeen anyway?

I vowed to stay put in the canoe until all thoughts of Claire vanished, hoping by then to have found the dark tunnel and bright light, or at least some place with an 'up' button. My plan failed almost immediately, though, because the more I tried pushing the vision of her away, the more I couldn't stop thinking about her. It was a vicious cycle.

Maybe Claire had a message for me. Something to give me closure so I could move on. Time to find out. I got my sorry butt out of the canoe, and went to look for her. But when I saw the date on a newspaper and realized I'd been dead for two weeks, I wanted to cry. Seriously. I can admit that now, I'm man enough. Two weeks had felt like only hours to me. Next week was graduation! It was terrifying to realize life goes on without you.

As I drifted unnoticed through the crowded halls of my school, everything looked just like I remembered. Rows of dented, metal lockers faced each other, lining the narrow hallways as all the kids, some my friends and some not, pushed through each other to make it to their next class. They all passed through me while I stood in the center of the commotion, staring out at everyone, trying not to care.

It was strange how all the noise seemed so much more distracting now that I wasn't part of it—the clanging locker doors, the shuffling of feet, the ringing bells, the buzz of conversations all trying to be heard; it was jarring. I had to remind myself that none of it mattered anymore because as soon as I found Claire, I was never coming back here. *Ever.*

The first bell rang and all the kids filed into class. I looked for Claire by poking my head through the classroom walls. At first it felt weird, a little bit like losing your breath when someone socks you in the gut...but after twenty or so times, I finally got used to it.

When the tardy bell stopped ringing and the last door swung shut, I exited B-Hall and floated across the empty quad toward the gym. The giant octagon was surrounded by a bunch of old benches and sorry-looking planters holding a couple of half-dead bushes. I wasn't used to seeing the place look so empty. I should've been stuck behind Matthew in first period economics, not floating around out here like a cloud taking note of all the bad landscaping.

About halfway across the quad, I got the chills—a strange phenom-enon when you're dead. I zoomed back and forth, trying to shake the sensation off, but that didn't work. Frustrated, I stopped near a tree and hovered above a bench, wondering what the deal was. That's when I saw her—a crazy-looking lady with unruly hair, leaning against a vending machine by the cafeteria. I could tell she was dead because she was actually looking at me. Plus, she happened to be wearing a ratty pink robe and fuzzy slippers. High school girls aren't really known for letting something like that slide.

Still, it wasn't her outfit or even the crazy hair that had me staring, but my own curiosity of meeting another ghost for the first time. Obviously this being stuck thing didn't happen to everyone who died, or else there'd be a lot more of us bumping into each other. So what was *her* deal? Why was she here?

I gave her a nod, hoping for some sort of response, but she just looked away, disinterested. *Fine.* I ignored her and kept looking for Claire as the chills faded along with any interest in my fellow ghost.

After two more classrooms without any luck, I finally found Claire in room E-9 sitting at her desk and looking off in the other direction. But she didn't look like the Claire I remembered. Something was definitely wrong. She was gazing out through the towering wall of windows reflecting the morning sun, past the bald, blabbering teacher and the ticking clock, beyond the present and off to some other place. She seemed stuck…just like me.

Her face said it all.

That was when I understood there was no message for me. At least, not one with some magical spell capable of sending me off to heaven. No, Claire was broken. *Lost.* Alone. I'd never seen her eyes look so tired. I could feel her emotions like heat from the sun as they bounced across the room toward me and soaked into my soul.

Outside the classroom, I sunk down beneath the pane of windows next to a yellow rosebush and a busy anthill, wishing to wring out this swelling sadness inside me that had suddenly appeared without warning. But nothing could be purged without a body—no crying, no exertion, no pills to take away the pain or calm me down. *Nothing.* Instead, something ballooned inside me until I felt like I might explode. All I could do was sit there and drown in it, wondering why Claire affected me so much, wondering if she always would.

CHAPTER
THREE THE FOG

Claire

Matthew, Addie and I tried acting normal around each other, but everything felt strange and different and wrong. How could we have expected anything else? It was like I lost everyone that day, not just Daniel.

Addie floated away in her own bubble of counterfeit composure, fooling everyone else but me, refusing to let anyone see her in pain. She seemed unreachable, at least for anything more than the current configuration of the school's popularity chain. It bothered me to watch her act so alive and unaffected knowing it was just that: an act. I felt much better shut up inside my self-made pity cocoon instead of faking happiness in front of the world. Of course, Mom and Dad were not happy with the way I chose to cope. They kept comparing me to Addie, asking me why I couldn't turn to them or to my friends for support instead of keeping everything inside. I told them it was none of their business, and to get lost (okay, that part I just said in my head when I was really mad at them).

Pretty soon, Matthew was hanging around us less and less, until he vanished altogether into a new group of friends who had never even known Daniel—friends who had no idea that the old Matthew had been swallowed up by a new, guarded one, by someone unrecognizable to the rest of us. We all tiptoed around him for months, not sure what to say or do…how could any of us understand what he was going through?

I had a pretty good idea, because even months after that awful night, I still felt paralyzed. Although I tried not to dwell on Daniel, it was impossible to push him out of my mind. Ever since the funeral, I kept thinking about the Daniel I thought I knew but obviously didn't. Sure, he was cute—especially with his perfect smile and the way he made everyone else happy just by walking into the room. But I was starting to see that the ache inside me persisted mostly because I was just learning who Daniel *really* was beneath all that charm.

Which was worse—regret or grief? Because I could feel *both* carving themselves into my heart, and the pain only seemed to get worse as the months dragged on.

Toward the middle of August, Mom and Dad organized one last family outing together before the start of the new school year. Matthew was going off to college in a few weeks, so I guessed it was their way of prolonging his childhood. We both went along with the plan, not really caring where we were going as long as they quit bugging us about life and everything in it.

Silently, Matthew and I sat together in the back seat, having since lost the ability to act 'normal' with each other after that unspeakable night. Now, it seemed that Matthew was always plugged into headphones—a permanent accessory to his blond-buzzed head. As he gazed out the window, I peeked at him, surprised by the sadness that seemed to be radiating from his blank, glossy eyes. They were still strikingly blue, but now seemed to be missing the intensity that used to take me by surprise. I wondered if I'd ever see his smile again.

Once Dad veered off the highway, I knew exactly where we were headed as we climbed up a steep hill that wound its way into the forest. Matthew was still stuck in a passive trance, but my eyes were wide open, bouncing back and forth while trying to peer through the dense fog that wove in and out of the trees. It looked like a ghost had dressed up the forest in tulle.

After parking, we climbed the stone steps leading up to the front of the planetarium, and made our way through the glass-walled lobby. At the risk of sounding like a science nerd, I had to admit that the planetarium was pretty cool, especially for not having roller coasters or fried food. There was something mysterious about the way it sat nestled up among the haunting pines and redwoods—a bit magical, if you ask me.

Once inside, Matthew immediately abandoned us, silently slipping away into one of the dark theaters. Following his lead, I left my parents and their credit card at the front desk, ignoring Mom's protests that we all stick together as a family. That was the last thing I wanted to do right then. I could hear Dad trying to pacify Mom, who was already complaining about the family's inability to stick to the plan (*her* plan), but their voices were fading quickly. All I knew was I needed to escape.

After slipping away from the noise up three flights of stairs to the top floor, I stumbled upon a massive row of floor-to-ceiling windows that transformed the billowy fog into stunning rectangular pieces of art.

Even without the sun, it was amazing how bright everything was up there, and I made sure to slow down a little and try to take it all in.

Just beyond the windows was the door leading out to the observatory deck. I pushed through it into the chilly fog, and followed a narrow walkway leading out to a viewing platform. Wishing I'd brought my jacket, I did my best to stop shivering by wrapping my arms around myself. Yet, despite the cold, my heart was flying. I felt like a tower perched high above the trees, surrounded by a thick battalion of fog—a breath of fresh air after months of depression. For a second, even thoughts of Daniel's death left me.

My glasses fogged up as usual, so I shoved them in my pocket and kept on going. What was the difference out here, anyway? Everything looked blurry, but maybe that was the point, wasn't it? To cloud out the world around me, and forget everything?

Reaching out to the low, cement wall in front of me, I gripped the metal rail running along the top edge, and slowly followed it to the far end of the platform. Since I'd been here before, I knew the fog was hiding a hundred-foot drop to the ground below—but that didn't keep me from leaning out over the wall. With my hands firmly gripping the rail, and my knees locked in place, I leaned forward and let the upper half of my body go.

I felt free, almost like flying as I gazed out over the translucent expanse. The cool air floated through my lungs, making me feel bold, even careless, like staring death in the face and daring it to take me like it took Daniel. A flash of anger shot through me when I thought about how fragile we were, and for a second, I wondered if anyone would even notice. All it would take was one final breath as I let go of the rail and dove into the void....

Peace.

Quiet.

My heart sped up, and it felt like someone was sneaking up behind me.

Quickly, I pulled myself back to solid ground and spun around, nervously looking around for any sign of a visitor. But nobody was there. Just white. And quiet. And the sound of my own breathing.

Ignoring my racing heartbeat, I turned around and leaned over the edge again. But a faint voice inside my head held me back. "Stop, Claire. You're going to fall."

I hesitated, listening for more, and then inched out a little further. "Don't be stupid, Claire," the voice warned again, resonating inside my head like I could feel it, like it had its own presence within me. "Get away from the edge."

Instantly I obeyed, cautiously shuffling backwards until a door handle brushed up against my back.

I scanned the deck again. But I was still alone.

My mind went quiet.

Positive I'd heard a voice, a real voice deep and soothing, even though I had no explanation, I stared blankly out into the white expanse with my back to the door, wondering what had just happened.

As the quiet lingered, my heart slowed, and the fog thickened around me.

Daniel

Who would've thought I'd end up being Claire's guardian *ghost?* The idea was laughable. I'm not even sure how it worked that day with the fog, except for the fact that Claire acted like she could hear me—and somehow I'd kept her from falling.

I never even really warned her; it just happened to be what I was thinking when she started leaning over the edge of the deck. Next thing I knew, I heard myself telling her to move. And she listened.

Right then it felt like I'd found my purpose. Claire was safe, and for once, I was content. *Finally.* After so long, I felt at peace.

Maybe Claire didn't have answers for me like I thought.

Maybe Claire *was* the answer.

CHAPTER
FOUR SWEET SIXTEEN

Claire

Thoughts of Daniel continued to consume me the rest of the summer and on into the new school year, no matter how much I tried to "move on." So, when my sixteenth birthday came around, it was bittersweet. However, my family insisted on a celebration.

That warm September night, Addie, the future wedding planner, took over the party by inviting a few other friends for a day of organized crazy, eventually ending in a sleepover under the stars. Forget that I just wanted to go to an expensive restaurant with fancy desserts. I didn't even like camping, so I had no idea what Addie was thinking. Still, she set up camp on my front lawn that, like an unfurled picnic blanket, practically spread right down to the lake. According to Addie, it was the perfect spot, because once the porch lights were off, it was dark enough to see the stars and quiet enough to hear the crickets. Basically, it was like camping without the bears and porta-potties. I couldn't argue with that.

Of course the whole night Addie kept begging us to play stupid games like Capture the Flag and flashlight tag, like we were still in elementary school. Before long, everything about my birthday was starting to feel like fifth grade all over again, minus the braces and truth or dare. I was about to tell Addie to forget the lame entertainment and just let us go to sleep, but when I looked at her and saw in her animated eyes something I hadn't seen since May fifteenth, I realized that for the first time in months, Addie looked genuinely happy.

Reluctantly, I drummed up some enthusiasm and crawled out of the tent with a flashlight, ready to play Addie's game, grateful it was only tag and not something really embarrassing like skinny-dipping or strip poker, both things to look forward to as she got more bored and less creative.

Everyone took off running in different directions, and I headed toward the lake. No one seemed to make a sound. All I could hear was my own breathing and the steady shuffling of my footsteps along the gravel as I moved down the hill, trying to decide where to go next.

Veering off the path, I tripped over an old log hidden in the grass, and dropped the flashlight on my big toe. Instead of screaming out in pain, I held my breath and watched the flashlight roll away from me, down the hill toward the lake. I listened for it to hit the water, but could only hear my own thumping heart.

Annoyed that I was stranded in the dark beneath a useless moon, I kicked the stupid log for tripping me up, and then started back up the steep hill. A few steps later, I slipped and lost my balance again. As the ground spun beneath my feet, I careened backward. A sharp pain shot through my head at the same time the shock of water splashed over me. Instinctively, I held my breath as the cool water seemed to hold me. For a moment I drifted in a daze, and then felt myself beginning to sink.

It was almost impossible to see anything under the water. I had no idea where I'd fallen in the lake or why I couldn't push myself up. It was like a haze of darkness had settled over my mind, preventing any part of me from cooperating. No longer able to hold my breath, terror shot through me as reality hit. *I was going to drown.*

A sickening sensation arose in my stomach, pushing past the searing pain in my head and the burning in my lungs. I couldn't get past the flood of panic overtaking my brain, telling me over and over again that I was about to die.

Daniel

As soon as Claire hit the water, I looked around and shouted for help, but Addie and her friends were off somewhere else. Not that they could hear me, anyway.

I didn't know what to do. Claire was drowning, and I couldn't move a pebble if I had to, much less pull someone out of the lake. Instantly, I shifted under the water, and found her limp body sinking away from me in slow motion. I watched in disbelief. Was this really it for Claire? I couldn't believe I'd been compelled to stay behind for, *what*…just to watch her die? So soon? This couldn't be right.

Bits of rocks and dust followed after her in a stream of bubbles as she reached the bottom. She tilted her head forward and looked at me, confused, like she knew I was there, like she could see me. *Could she?* I reached for her, but watched my hands pass right through her body. I was useless; her arms just bobbed up and down in the water through me.

As her eyes closed, I thought she looked peaceful, maybe even beautiful. It reminded me of that day months ago at the rope swing, when I'd first realized I liked her. I could admit it now, but of course confessing my feelings did nothing for her.

What was I thinking?

There it was again—that same burning sensation radiating from my chest like the last time we talked, just before I died. I could remember it now. She'd asked me something, but I hadn't really paid attention because I'd been trying to figure out what I was going to do about her—about us. And then Matthew appeared, and I'd left her standing by the porch…

Now, something else was happening inside me, right where my heart should be. I didn't know what it was or where it came from, but it felt like a sharp jolt of electricity, followed by a pounding in my mind that directed me to reach for her again. The water suddenly felt thicker, like syrup, and I fought through it, touching the very tips of Claire's fingers. Somehow, I could feel the cold, smooth surface of her skin; it was like I was *alive* again. Grasping her hands in mine as another explosive current shot through us, reminding me to *move,* I pulled her to me and shot up through the water, breaking through with surprising force. The air felt light and warm as I dragged her out of the lake to the muddy shore. There, I knelt beside her, trying to ignore the pulsing waves of voltage burning through me.

I seemed to be jumping with electricity, but at the same time felt distracted, overwhelmed and confused. Yet, somehow my mind knew what to do. I leaned over Claire and brushed the hair away from her face, letting my lips touch hers while blowing air into her mouth. Despite the strange feeling of my own breath, I pushed aside my runaway emotions, and blew again. After the third breath, I waited and watched.

Nothing.

Her skin was turning blue and she still wasn't moving.

"Claire." I shook her. "Claire," I said a little louder.

She stirred briefly, turning her head from side to side, and then her eyelids fluttered. I held my breath—amazed I had breath to hold. Then she squeezed my hand and looked up at me with surprisingly bright eyes. I smiled, just in case she could see me. But her eyelids fell and she was still again. I didn't move, for fear of breaking her. She seemed to be on the edge, and I didn't know which way she was going to fall.

Her eyes flew open again and she gasped for air. I released her hands and held her head, instead. She reached up toward my face, her fingers running down my neck to my arm, her fingertips digging into my skin, gripping so hard it almost hurt.

I *loved* the feel of her touch.

And then it was like someone snapped their fingers, and everything between us melted. Claire let go of me at the same time my hands fell through her body to the ground, the electric connection vanished, just like that. She looked up and all around, then turned over to her knees and started coughing up lake water. I thought she might never stop.

As the lingering electricity inside me fizzled out, along with my mortality, I withdrew into the shadows. Claire tried to sit, but was too weak, and fell back into the grass where she lay staring into the darkness, like she was looking for something.

Maybe me?

"Claire," I said, hoping. But she didn't seem to hear me.

"Claire!" a deep voice called from somewhere up the hill.

Claire turned her head toward the voice. "Dad," she said, her own voice weak, just louder than a whisper. But her dad had heard, and was already running down the hill. He pulled Claire into his arms and carried her up the hill. As the mortal world took care of her like they were supposed to, I drifted across the lake to the edge of the dock, wondering if that was even something I was supposed to do—interfere with life and death like that?

If only someone had interfered for me.

Wading into the shallow water, I ached to feel the cold on my ankles, wishing more than anything to be able to pick up a rock and skip it across the lake like Matthew and I used to do.

I suddenly felt so alone, missing everyone: Matthew, my parents and Addie.

And now I missed Claire even more.

Claire

At first there was only black…and then a soft light starting around the edges of my vision, spreading inward as the night around me seemed to vanish. I could feel myself dying, like I was being torn in two. One part of me floated to a bright, quiet place, while another could still feel the sensation of being pulled out of the lake and carried along through the mush to the shore.

"Claire."

Who was saying my name?

I was in some faraway place where nothing was pressing or hurried, and I adored this newfound sense of peace so different from everything I was used to. It was a total sense of freedom, like I was alive through every living thing; I could feel, breathe, think, hear and see everything in the universe all at once.

Watching from above, I saw Daniel leaning over me. His eyes looked tired and heavy, like he was having a hard time keeping them open. I remembered how happy and carefree he had always been when he was alive, and sensed the weight of his worry. I even thought about going back down there to let him know everything was okay, that I was perfectly fine—except, my mind and body didn't feel connected.

Daniel cradled my limp body in his arms, brushing away the mop of wet hair covering my face. His tenderness sent chills through my heart. When he grasped my fingers, I tried to go to him, to feel his strong hands squeezing mine like I used to only imagine. But some sort of invisible barricade prevented me from reaching him. Daniel was right there, but it felt like a whole planet separated us.

"Claire," I heard his soothing voice whisper in my ears, sending icy tingles through me, even up here. *His voice.* I had not heard Daniel's voice in months.

"Daniel," I called out to him, but my own voice was silent.

I wanted to feel his arms around me and even felt some kind of twisted jealousy toward my own body as he held it there in his arms. *I* wanted to feel his touch, not just hover up there and watch from above.

I wanted to be with Daniel.

As soon as those thoughts left me, I sensed a loss of control as the light ebbed, and I floated like a feather down to my body.

Down...down...down....

Soon, everything felt warm, limp and foreign, although a sense of sadness lingered inside me—until I realized Daniel was still holding me. My heart jumped. I opened my eyes to find him inches away, his dark eyes above that familiar, dimpled smile, and I nearly blacked out again in intoxicating relief.

My fingertips brushed his face below his dimples then drew a line down his neck, along his arm, my fingers pressing into his skin. His eyes followed the movement of my hands, lingering on the spot where I gripped his arm.

In the distance, voices called my name, all echoing from different directions. I kept quiet, though, unable to stop staring at Daniel's face. Daniel was *alive*—right next to me—holding me. I wanted to speak to him, but was afraid to interrupt whatever dream I might be having.

"Claire," he said, holding my hand, his fingers intertwined with mine.

Something electric pulsed between us, and a surge of water exploded from inside of me. I coughed and sputtered until my aching lungs starting working again, but then realized I could no longer feel Daniel holding me. He was still there, still in front of me, but his hands had disappeared through mine. We stared at each other, his eyes mirroring the confusion I felt.

Dad's voice was getting closer. I looked up the hill, weakly calling out to him, and when I turned around, Daniel was gone.

What was happening?

I tried to stand, but my body was uncooperative. The dark sky swirled in circles above me, little white stars shooting through the sky, and I lay back down in the muddy grass, waiting.

Dad rushed to my side. I looked around again, replaying in my mind what had just happened, trying to understand. Daniel *had* been there. I knew it. But where was *there?*

Daniel

After her dad carried her away from the lake, I followed Claire to and from the hospital. Once they'd been home for almost an hour, I left her alone and drifted down by the lake to a spot beneath the creaking eucalyptus tree. It was my haunt, I suppose—where I liked to hang out and keep an eye on everything.

Hours passed, light changed. I never moved. Time was nothing to me now, and I had since learned patience. That was how the days usually passed for me.

Usually.

A thick, summer fog started creeping in from the bay and spreading across the lawn, its ghost-like movement almost putting me to sleep. Then I remembered I didn't sleep anymore, and snapped myself out of it just as the pin-pricked sensation of spiky goose bumps erupted all over me like a fever, making me restless.

I began roaming through the neighborhood to scope the place out, drifting up the hill and across the lawn to Claire's front porch, and then back again to the end of the dock. The chills seemed to come and go, making me feel foolish, like I was playing hide-and-seek with someone who wasn't even there. A few months ago, I'd have said I didn't have time for this…but, as it so happened, I had all the time in the world.

When I drifted back to my familiar spot under the tree, the chills came back even stronger, like ice water on the back of my neck. A wispy thread of fog started circling up my legs and spiraling around my throat, like it was trying to choke me. I gasped and brushed it off, then shifted away from the tree, out to the dock. The sounds of crickets and lapping water broke the silence as I turned in circles at the edge of the lake, my eyes scanning the darkness.

Who was out there? *What* was out there?

"Hello?" I called.

Something came up behind me.

I spun around to find the small, black eyes of a ghostly intruder watching me, just inches away. I held my non-existent breath.

"We finally meet," he said with a deep, but surprisingly soft, voice.

At first glance, he didn't look much older than eighteen or nineteen. He was unbelievably pale (like *growing-up-in-a-cave* pale), with a mass of black hair piled on top of his head like a Mohawk. His black eyes kept darting back and forth, like he was trying to focus on my face, but didn't know how. I immediately sized him up, and figured he wasn't any bigger or stronger than me (from what I could tell in the dark, the fog, and without a mirror for a decent comparison). Although I wasn't scared of him, there was still something about him that gave me the creeps.

"I've been waiting so long for this," he spoke again, pointing a finger at me.

I leaned away from the offending gesture and kept my mouth shut, but watched him curiously, since this happened to be the one and only time another ghost had ever spoken to me. I probably should've been taken aback, but was mostly just confused.

He crossed his arms in an apparent display of machismo. "Twelve years is a long time. As a matter of fact, do you realize you and I both died at the same age?"

Okay...

He paused, looking at me like he wanted me to say something, then started up again. "Are you bewildered and confused? Does that simple mind of yours run helter-skelter with possibilities you didn't know existed? You want to know how you came to be here on the Fringe?"

He shoved his head through mine, our foreheads obscenely overlapping. *Whoa.* Everything seemed to meld together into one dark blur, bringing on a bizarre claustrophobia. I felt like throwing up.

"Fringe?" I said, pulling away from him before the dry heaves started.

But he was already onto the next subject. "Do you want to know how I found you?"

I wasn't sure if I should ask, having not taken the class on *crazy* yet. Hoping the guy would get the hint and leave me alone, I turned away from him and floated out over the dark lake.

"Don't you know who I am?" I could hear him calling after me, almost desperately.

Of course I didn't listen to my gut and just disappear. No…I stopped halfway across the lake and turned around. I *did* want to know who he was, and took the bait.

"Who are you?" I asked, trying to throw in a little attitude, attempting to act tough.

"Come *on.* I don't look familiar to you? *At all?*"

I cruised back and studied him more closely, but nothing was ringing a bell. I shook my head, wondering what I was missing. Just as I opened my mouth to respond, he rushed at me, his face scowling like he was struggling to suppress a scream or a laugh. I suddenly felt like a character in a Batman movie, face to face with the Joker. He stopped within inches of me, and I jerked back at the intrusion. Personal space is all you can call your own around here.

"Look at me!" he yelled, shoving his hands through the mound of hair on his head. "Don't you remember when I died? Come on! Dig into that thick mind of yours for once."

"I don't know what you're talking about!"

He threw his arms high into the air, and then stiffly drew them back to his sides. "How could you forget? There was thick, red blood everywhere. After you killed me, you LOOKED. You stood there and stared at me wide-eyed just like you're doing now. You laughed inside when you saw what you did. DIDN'T you? I SAW YOU there. YOU KILLED ME!"

His eyes were bulging, and I considered the possibility that he may very well fold in on himself and cease to exist.

But I wasn't so lucky.

When Claire's porch light flicked off and we both turned to look, everything about him transformed; his scowl faded and his eyes lost their fire, replaced by an icy, calculating coolness, like he had just regained control of whatever force was boiling to get out. Like he now knew what to do with his anger.

He drifted purposefully backward toward Claire's house, stopping just outside her window. His arms smugly folded across his chest, he turned to face me. "So, *she's* the reason you're here. I've been following you, wondering why you watch her the way you do. That's it, isn't it? You *love* her."

Love? Um, that was definitely a matter of debate for another time. "What do you want?" I asked.

"What do I want? I want lots of things, just like everybody else. Problem is, we can't really have what we want, can we? But I do believe this is getting fun. There may be some point in this sad, pathetic story, after all…or at least a way to make things right."

"Will you start making sense, for once?" I yelled, this time trying to put a little more edge in my voice. Confrontation had never been my strong suit. "I don't *remember* you!"

He flew at me.

"You fool, you stupid kid. YOU KILLED ME!" he screamed again, giving way to the flood of anger shooting through the red that seemed to glow in his eyes, shutting me up.

We glared at each other until I pulled back a little, hovering in silence in front of a ghost who appeared to be insane. Afraid to shift away from Claire but not knowing how else to escape this lunatic, I darted to the other side of the lake. Of course, he immediately caught up, and threw himself in my face.

"What do you want from me?" I asked.

"What. Do. I. Want. From. You," he repeated, each word as if each was a single sentence. "You cost me *everything*. I don't want *anything* from you now."

"Then, go. Away."

"But she is *everything* to you, isn't she?"

My mind started to spin. *No,* I wanted to say, but couldn't.

The ghost gazed out across the lake, a faint smile forming on his lips. "And now, I believe she's *everything* to me."

"What are you talking about?"

"This will be fun." He turned away from me like I was no longer part of the conversation. "Not exactly what I envisioned, but probably a lot more entertaining."

"Stay away from her," I warned, trying to act like I actually had some way to follow through. But the ghost only smiled at my bluff, staring at me while fading out, never looking away until he was gone.

I didn't know whether to cry or cheer or fall over in exhaustion when he disappeared. What I *did* know was that I had to get away from Hidden Lake, to clear my mind of the chaos I felt. Right then, all I wanted to do was forget Claire...forget this place, *the Fringe*...forget caring...forget about everything so I could worry only about myself, like it used to be.

Was that too much to ask?

Concentrating on going somewhere else, I ended up at Big Sur watching the sun peek out over the hills, lighting up the ocean as the deafening waves crashed through my mind, clearing out the remains of an unwanted voice lingering in my head.

Claire

I hardly slept that whole night, figuring almost drowning was a pretty decent reason for insomnia. All attempts to convince my parents I was fine had failed, and they insisted on taking me to the hospital, where I spent a couple of hours under observation.

It was embarrassing having everybody stare and talk about me like I was an anomaly, and I wondered if they expected me to suddenly drop dead. It was the only explanation for why I found myself stuck in a little blue piece of cloth undergoing way too many tests in the middle of the night. I was definitely not a fan of so much attention.

We got home around three or four in the morning, but I could only stare up at blurry shadows on the ceiling. Even worse, the insomnia gave me anxiety; the more I wanted sleep, the further it seemed to drift away as I tried to remember *exactly* what happened in the lake, but couldn't seem to recall all of the details.

After a couple of hours, I gave up sleep altogether and sneaked down the hall into the dark living room. For a while I lay on the couch and gazed out the window at the little spot of moonlight trying to break through the fog. Still unable to relax, I opened a window and snuggled beneath a blanket, letting the cool breeze tickle my face as my mind drifted.

I still couldn't believe it. Daniel, *who was dead*, saved my life. How was that even possible? There was no explanation.

My head wouldn't stop throbbing. It was probably begging me to quit thinking so much—but I couldn't seem to rid the image of Daniel's face from my mind, or his touch from my skin. I felt consumed by his presence, even though he'd disappeared hours ago.

Of course, I could never tell anyone what really happened down in the water. They'd assume I hit my head too hard and take me back to the hospital for reevaluation.

No thanks.

Even as the fog helped the shadows linger, nighttime vanished too quickly, and was already fading to morning. Trying not to wince, I touched the tender spot on my forehead where I'd hit the rock, and then pulled myself upright.

Something thumped against the wall down the hall. It made me jump, but then I realized it was probably Dad, up bright and early as usual, already getting ready for work.

My stomach growled, calling me into the kitchen. After sliding a piece of bread into the toaster, I waited at the mahogany table, staring at a too-perfect arrangement of yellow tulips, letting the bright color hypnotize me. When I felt my body finally starting to relax, the toaster popped, and I jumped as if the *ding* had been a bomb. The sudden movement seemed to initiate a dull, steady pounding in my head that ricocheted through my body, bringing on an ache that made me want to scream. I closed my eyes, massaging my temples until I could breathe again, and then headed for the counter to retrieve my toast.

Just as I dug my knife into a butter tub, a quick flash of something darted past my left shoulder.

I turned.

Dad?

But nothing was there.

My heart continued beating faster than normal, despite my attempt to ignore it. I snatched my toast out of the toaster and started spreading butter in a circular pattern until it looked like a work of art. I turned my head again just in time to catch a glimpse of a dark, shadowy shape jumping into the half-open pantry…it looked like the tail end of a black, flowing scarf.

Not Dad.

My nerves exploded to life as a tingling, simmering heat hovered just above the surface of my skin, like a fresh sunburn. I gripped the butter knife trembling above the toast, and ran through a mental checklist of every possibility—unexplained smoke, a wild animal, a raving axe-murderer—as if any of those suggestions made reality less frightening.

Peering from side to side, I made sure nothing was about to sneak up on me before I figured out an escape route, just in case. *Escape?* Not when I couldn't even move. Fear had thwarted any possible plan of action, my heart protesting as loudly as the clock on the wall.

Whatever it was, it seemed to be waiting for me behind the frosted pantry door. This was so much worse than a spider, which meant there was a huge possibility I might faint. What to do? *What to do?* As scared as I felt, I really *needed* to know what that thing was. With the greasy knife still clutched in my fingers, I stood perfectly still, tense and terrified, trying to gather up enough courage to face the unknown before it got me first.

Six deep breaths and four carefully maneuvered shuffles later, I was close enough to touch the pantry door. I gulped, and then peeked around the corner. Inside, a wide, black, pulsing, ribbon-like thing about the length of the door was twisting back and forth, disappearing and reappearing every few seconds like the air was smudged with black chalk. It was silent, but seemed almost self-aware.

Still grasping my useless piece of flatware for a weapon, I stepped closer. The ribbon thing paused, as if contemplating its next move, and then dashed further into the pantry, almost stuffing itself into the corner. A chill raced up my arms, even after I reassured myself it wasn't some bloodthirsty madman with a bigger knife than mine. I tried to hold still, my hand just barely touching the doorway, but I couldn't stop shaking. After contemplating running away and hiding in the safety of my bedroom, I finally braced myself for the worst, and flung the door wide open.

The ribbon shot right into my face. I clamped my eyes shut and screamed, turning and running toward the sink. A grinding, metallic noise hissed all around me, echoing through my ears as it seemed to wrap itself around me like a giant coil, cold against my skin, hard and sharp.

"Claire!"

I screamed again, spinning around with the buttery knife held high for my attacker, but found myself engulfed inside my dad's arms. He held my wrist above my head until the knife fell to the floor with a metallic clink. The ribbon thing instantly unwound itself from my body, darted past Dad, and disappeared through the wall.

"What are you doing?" asked Dad, nearly shaking me. "What's wrong?"

"What *was* that?" I asked, afraid to look.

"What was what?"

I peered around Dad's shoulders, but there was no evidence of my tormentor.

Dad held me tight, rubbing my back and smoothing my hair. "Claire," he said again, his deep voice soothing. "Was it a nightmare?"

I looked up into his eyes. "Serious? You mean, you didn't... No. I...I'm fine. I just... But, didn't you see it, too?"

"What?" he asked, looking around the kitchen. "See what?"

How could he have missed it? "You didn't see it, Dad? That...that *thing*?"

He placed a hand on each of my shoulders and looked at me. "I didn't see anything. Just you, Claire. And you were acting like you'd seen a ghost, or something."

"Ghost?"

He nodded his head. "Are you sure you weren't dreaming, or sleepwalking?" Dad asked as I pulled away and found my way back to the table, slumping low in one of the chairs.

He seemed reluctant to let it go, but finally fell into his normal routine of Frosted Flakes alongside a glance at the sports section. Closing my eyes, I rested my head on the table, listening to the commotion, still wondering why Dad hadn't seen or heard anything. How was it possible?

After Dad finished his breakfast, he stood behind me, tickling my back. "You know, you hit your head pretty hard last night. Maybe the doctor should have another look at it." He lifted my chin with the tip of his finger until I looked up at him to find his familiar smile. That was one thing I loved about my dad—he always managed a smile, whether happy or not.

"No, Dad," I protested. "I *really* hate hospitals and doctors. Especially now."

He kissed the top of my head. "Are you still taking the medicine they gave you? Maybe this is some kind of side effect."

"Dad, *really*," I sighed. "It's not the medicine. You *seriously* didn't see anything?"

He shook his head and started walking away.

"Nothing?"

"Why don't you go back to bed? Maybe you need more sleep."

"There was something there, Dad," I said, noticing the frustration breaching his patience. He stopped and leaned against the doorway, observing me with an irritated look combined with his unique smile. That was what he was good at, what he was trained to do—to listen, observe and solve problems. But he couldn't solve this one.

"I'm going to talk to Mom about taking you back to the doctor," he said. "Just to be safe." Then he walked out of the kitchen, down the hall.

"Come on, Dad," I called after him.

He was already gone.

I rested my head back on the table and let my eyelids droop. Despite the lingering vision of ghostly ribbon wrapping itself around me, I found myself finally drifting off to sleep.

CHAPTER
FIVE MOONBEAMS

Claire

The demented ghost thing didn't return that day…or the next, or the next. I finally decided to call it a "ghost" because I couldn't think of anything else it could possibly be; my imagination was pretty lame. Daniel hadn't come back, either. He'd vanished along with reality. Sometimes it felt like I was living inside the head of someone else's dreams.

I took a risk one day, and asked Addie how often she thought about Daniel. She didn't answer right away, but kept turning pages of a magazine we'd been flipping through for the last half-hour. We were lying in my family room in our pajamas, having just finished doing our nails after a ton of homework. Mom and Dad were in the city for a Giants' game. They invited me, but I never liked baseball once the popcorn and drinks disappeared, which usually happened after about ten minutes.

"What if he's somehow still out there, still connected to our world?" I asked as we sunk deeper into the leather sofa.

"I don't believe in all that stuff," Addie said, looking the other way as she dragged her hand through her smooth hair.

"What's there to believe? I mean, just ask yourself if it's possible. Isn't anything possible?"

Addie still wouldn't look me in the eye, and I was starting to regret saying anything. "Fine. *Anything* is possible," she said, finally looking at me. "But I'm talking about what's *probable*. Can you honestly say you believe there is something after this life? What would be the point?"

"What would be the point of living at all if everything just…vanished? I just can't believe it all ends at death. I can't imagine not ever seeing him again."

Addie stood up and walked to the window, peering out into the dark. Her back was to me, but I could tell she was crying. *Dang.*

"I'm sorry, Addie." I rushed over and put my arm around her. "I'm sorry. It's just…hard trying to make sense of what happened. I'm obviously not doing a very good job."

She turned to me. Her always-brilliant eyes looked dull and heavy. *I am so sorry*, I thought weakly, my eyes drooping like hers. She made an effort, finding a smile inside her, trying to pretend she was okay. Grabbing my hand, she led me outside to the front porch. We sat down on an old, paint-peeled bench and huddled together under a blanket, silently listening to the frogs and crickets. She rested her head on my shoulder, her long, chamomile-infused hair draping across my arm.

"I just want to stop missing him," she whispered, her voice cracked and broken up. "It hurts so much to think about him, that it's easier to block him out entirely. It isn't so bad that way."

I didn't know what to say.

She continued, her voice getting weaker as she whispered, "But then I feel so sad, like I'm losing him. It's like no matter what I do, I'm stuck somewhere in between."

Somewhere in between.

When Daniel died, I thought he went off to some vast, happy place beyond the clouds—but maybe he didn't. Maybe I had it all wrong. After my drowning incident, I didn't know what to think anymore. If he wasn't *there* and he wasn't *here*, then *where* was he? Maybe he was just standing in an open door with a view in both directions.

As I stared out into the darkness, my mind explored the possibilities, eventually sending me off into a world of semi-dreams. I almost fell asleep with Addie resting on my shoulder, when a slight movement down by the dock caught my attention. At first, I thought it was just the fog, which had started its nightly drift inward—but after looking more carefully, I realized whatever it was seemed to move *through* the fog, not with it.

I tensed, my nerves reminding me of the unwanted aberration in my kitchen. I had no interest in meeting it (or anything like it) again. I moved Addie off my shoulder, trying not to wake her, but her eyes still shot open.

"Oh…" she gasped, disoriented. "Wha–? Did I fall asleep?"

"Let's go inside, okay?" I suggested, looking behind my back. *Please don't let it be something horrible,* I repeated again and again in my head. As we walked back inside the house I expected some black, vaporous shape to attack us at any moment. My heartbeat continued to escalate, making it nearly impossible to remain calm.

"Addie, you go to bed and I'll lock up," I said, trying to be brave.

In a zombie-like trance, Addie made her way down the hallway. I turned off the lights and locked the front door, pausing at the window, wondering what was out there. Finally turning to go to bed, I froze, convinced something outside had moved beneath the hazy moonlight, something that looked like a person. I placed my hands on the chilly windowpane and peered at the dock, trying to focus on the movement...

I gasped.

Across the street, at the base of the hill, was a figure encircled by the fog, standing beneath a tree. I leaned closer for a better look, but my breath fogged up my glasses and the window, and I had to pull back to wait for the little cloud in front of me to fade away. When I looked a few seconds later, a section of the fog had thinned out long enough to reveal a face—a seemingly familiar one.

I pulled open the creaking front door and slipped outside into the fog that floated here and there in varying thicknesses, creeping through the air like it was alive. A pounding exhilaration shot through me as I sneaked forward, looking and listening, wondering how or when I'd lost my mind.

Crazy. You are crazy, I kept telling myself.

Not crazy? How about stupid? Definitely stupid.

Even then, I had the strange desire for a giant butterfly net to catch whatever was out there, as if *it* could be captured so easily.

My heart pounded in my ears as I hesitated, wondering which way to go. I felt completely vulnerable, like a classic horror movie victim trying to decide whether or not to go back inside. It was way too dark for me to be creeping around, especially only a few weeks after practically dying out there, but I had to find out if the face belonged to who I thought it did…just in case.

Trying not to trip again, I slowly walked toward him. The closer I got, the more nervous I felt, and the air around me seemed to grow heavier upon each step.

Twenty yards, then fifteen… About ten more, then six…three…

Two feet away I stopped, repeatedly blinking. I considered pinching myself like they do in cartoons, because right there in front of me, beneath the tallest eucalyptus tree in the neighborhood, stood someone who appeared to be Daniel. It *looked* just like him…but was it *really* him, or was I just *really* delusional?

When we made eye contact, the expression on his face changed from passive interest to complete surprise. I took a step closer, and he jerked upright and froze, as if questioning whether he should stay or go.

"Daniel?" I whispered, but my voice caught, coming out all hoarse and scratchy. I tried again, but only managed, "Da–."

He seemed nervous, and pushed his hands into his pockets as he watched me. His chocolate hair fell in layers around his face, resting over his left eye, looking the same as the day he died, his skin still olive-tan like Addie's. His shoulders broad and arms long, his eyes, lips, chin, neck and everything all still just right. He wore a black, short-sleeve t-shirt, jeans, and a pair of black Vans.

I fought the urge to scream out loud or throw my arms around him. Instead, I just stood there, paralyzed with uncertainty. Do I touch him, or talk to him, or *what?* Daniel didn't move either. It seemed like he had merged with the tree trunk, and all I could do was watch him, despite my mind telling me this was impossible.

The next thing I knew, he was smiling at me, his dimples as charming as when he was alive. I took a quick breath and smiled, my heart burning as I stepped closer. He took a step, too, until we were only inches apart. But when I reached for him, my hands passed through his torso, like he was a part of the fog. I couldn't feel anything when he reached for me, either—not even the slightest indication that his hand was resting directly in the middle of my head.

I looked up again into his familiar, brown eyes—eyes that used to make my heart skip a beat, that *still* did. They drew me into him, causing my heart to leap, twisting and soaring like a kite fighting the wind. That was the moment I was *positive* I loved him. That I always had, and always would.

"Daniel," I said, this time like it was the only word I knew.

His lips moved in response, but I couldn't hear anything.

"What?" I asked, wondering why it seemed like a mute button had been pressed. I shook my head to let him know, and his smile withered as the light in his eyes disappeared. A kind of sadness seemed to fall over him. He dropped his head and looked the other way…away from me.

"What, Daniel?" I repeated, stepping closer. But he stepped back from me, shaking his head in defeat as the tree trunk swallowed him up. "I don't understand," I pleaded, moving toward him. I wasn't going to let him leave. Not yet. "Please…" my voice quivered as I reached for him.

Daniel turned away from me and walked through the tree. I chased after him, but there was nothing to catch. He had disappeared. Still, I peeked around the tree and looked all around, hoping to find him, hoping he was not really gone.

He was.

I rested my hands and forehead against the tree trunk and fought the tears, overwhelmed with euphoria and confusion. My breathing slowed, the rhythm loud and deep as I inhaled in… exhaled out…in…out… But I seemed incapable of moving.

It wasn't until I heard the sound of Dad's car coming down the street that I pushed myself away from the eucalyptus tree, and reluctantly dragged myself home.

Daniel

I had no idea she could see me until she walked over and looked *at* me instead of through me. All reality was shot to pieces then, and I insanely forgot something greater than a few feet separated us. Something like death.

But that changed the instant I spoke and realized she couldn't hear me.

What was I thinking?

Talk about rejection. Not only was it frustrating, but it also looked like I'd made her cry. *Way to go.* It was one thing to play hard to get with a random girl at school. It was totally different now that the girl was Claire.

I felt awful.

Right then I vowed never to let her see me again. I would keep my distance, only getting close to her when she was distracted, or if she needed saving again.

But as it turned out, things didn't really work the way I'd planned.

Claire

After seeing Daniel in the fog that night, the grief I had absorbed since his death started oozing out like a radiation leak. I felt myself unraveling. The only logical explanation was that I was losing my mind.

But I knew I wasn't

There was no question I saw Daniel that night beneath the tree, but *why*? Why had he come back? Why, of all the whys had he looked at me like a war had been lost, before disappearing?

The only certainty was when I looked into his familiar eyes, my whole world changed. Again. The strange feelings, the grief, the confusion all merged together into one sense, fueling a determination to somehow see him again. I started wondering if Daniel was somewhere out in the dark *every* night, watching me.

As soon as the sun would disappear, I'd postpone sleep night after night, hoping to catch a glimpse of him. Meaningless distractions such as homework or television completely failed as my thoughts got tangled up in plans to lure him back to me. There had to be a reason he returned more than once. But no matter how many nights I sat out on the front porch or wandered alone down by the lake, he didn't come back. After countless days of hoping and waiting, I finally admitted to myself that it was time to give up. The sane part of me concluded that it was a lost cause.

But I was about to learn that forgetting Daniel was not meant to be.

Two weeks after seeing him under the tree, I went on a date with a guy from school, named Drew. The idea was to get my mind off of Daniel, which was surprising, considering I had lived as such a recluse for so long.

Drew's idea of flirting was sneaking up behind me as I walked across the school parking lot to find Addie for a ride home. I jumped, and he laughed while running his fingers through his curly blond hair. Then he asked me out, and I surprised myself by saying yes.

When he picked me up on Friday at seven o'clock, he seemed much more nervous than I was. He was good-looking (in a tan and beefy sort-of way), friendly and popular, I still didn't "like" him enough to be nervous.

After saying our goodbyes to my overly excited mother, Drew drove us to a seafood restaurant out on an old wooden pier by the bay. As we devoured a basket of fish and chips, the sun settled down behind us into a salmon-colored horizon over the water. When we finished, he drove us up a winding road into the hills for a ride on a little black steam train beneath the stars. The scent of redwood fused with woody eucalyptus created a calming, almost medicinal fragrance. I inhaled the aromatic breeze and fought off the chilly air as we huddled together in an open box on the train chugging along through a moonlit forest tour.

Just as we rounded a corner, the steam engine whistled. I looked out to my right as the sparkling bay and distant lights flooded into view. At that dramatic moment I felt Drew shift and subtly put his arm around me. Although I liked the warmth he radiated into my freezing body, I was not exactly sure about this move so soon. But, I'd always shied away from awkward confrontation, and even though I didn't lean into him, I didn't move away, either.

When the train came to a stop, I hopped out, perhaps a little too quickly, and waited for Drew as he exited along with everyone else. But instead of heading back to the car, he wanted to take a walk up a small, grassy hill. I was starting to think the date would never end, and made sure to keep my hands busy the whole time by wrapping them around myself as we walked side by side.

I could hear music before we reached the top of the hill, and admittedly was curious. I looked over at Drew, but he just shrugged innocently. As we crested the hill to find a kaleidoscope of spinning lights, I gasped. An old-style carousel, housing a dozen brightly painted horses, spun around and around. The entire platform lit up beneath thousands of miniature lights. I turned to a smiling Drew, who was proudly waiting for my reaction, like he had dreamt up the entire place, himself.

Okay, not a bad touch. Maybe it wouldn't kill me to at least hold his hand.

Together we walked inside the blue and white painted archway onto the platform, and checked out the vending machines stocked with postcards, toys, giant lollipops and mounds of cotton candy. The whole place smelled like buttery popcorn, sweets and peanuts, as if we'd stepped back in time and were visiting some traveling carnival. Everything looked and smelled somewhat familiar—and then I vaguely remembered having come here once when I was little.

After paying the cashier, Drew immediately attacked a mass of neon blue cotton candy, while I fumbled to unwrap a rainbow-spiraled lollipop the size of my hand. He seemed oblivious to me, his face still buried in the fluff. As I tried to find some acceptable way of licking my giant-sized sucker without getting sticky all over my cheeks, my heart sped up for no reason.

Sugar rush?

The air felt heavy, pressing me into the ground, reminding me of the night I saw Daniel under the tree. I was pretty sure my sucker had nothing to do with it.

Could it be? Again?

I looked around, scanning the crowds for a familiar face in a sea of strangers. Drew eyed me curiously, now, his eyes popping out over the cotton candy. He looked like a cartoon—a cute one, no less, and I quickly took another lick while hiding behind my monster lollipop, struggling to act normal while my mind seemed to be playing tricks on me.

Smiling faintly at Drew, I did my best to ignore the strange sensation, to convince myself that it was nothing. But no matter what, I couldn't shake it, which made me even more annoyed at myself for dwelling so long on thoughts of Daniel. I'd already spent enough time obsessing over him, and the fact that I was out on a date was proof of my resolve. Or, so I thought.

I finally gave up on the sticky monstrosity and tossed it in the trash, then hopped on the carousel with Drew, mounting an ivory horse with an angry face, nostrils flaring and golden streamers trailing down its mane. It was mid-gallop, and without question in the midst of a particularly intense race. It fit my mood perfectly.

A few kids and teenagers joined us. Drew straddled a pink pot-bellied pig and made a goofy face while swinging his arms up and down, like he was racing. I smiled, but the show was mostly for the little kids, who were laughing hysterically at Drew's every move. He seemed to eat up the attention.

Music blared as we jerked forward, the lights blinding us. As it picked up speed, I let my head fall backward, trying to allow the lights, music and movement take hold of me like I was floating along a mesmerizing current, the wind softly blowing my hair.

After a few turns, I glanced over at Drew, who was now wearing a cheesy grin with a bit of cotton candy stuck to his chin. That was when I knew for certain there was nothing romantic there. Sure, he was cute, and even gentlemanly—but it just wasn't going to happen.

The carousel began to slow, and I swayed as it pulled me along, the blurred scenery coming full circle again and again and again. About the fourth time around, a familiar face caught my attention, and my heart sped up when I realized it was Daniel.

I watched him each time we spun by, but tried not to be obvious, mostly for Drew's sake, but also for fear Daniel might bolt again if he knew I'd spotted him. But it was nearly impossible to look the other way. How could I *not* look? He was off in the far corner away from the bright lights, leaning against an out-of-order popcorn machine. This time he wore a pair of tan shorts and a different t-shirt with some sort of graphic pattern across the front, but the colors were muted and grey, making it difficult to pick out much detail. He seemed to blend into the wooden-planked wall behind him, like a camouflaged shadow.

The carousel leisurely slowed into its final rotation as a shrill series of bells rang and bodies rushed everywhere, all trying to get off. Even though Drew had already stepped off the platform and was waiting for my hand, I couldn't move. Not with Daniel right over there.

How… why… *what* was I supposed to do?

I looked over at Drew, who stood there smiling, apparently more and more clueless as the night went on. I didn't want to disappoint him, not with that permanent grin on his face, so I took his hand and jumped off the carousel, even though my heart was still racing and my mind was trying to balance reality with, well, *with Daniel.*

We made it halfway down the hill, near an old decorative lamppost and a wrought-iron bench, when I made my decision. I stopped and asked Drew to wait there, telling him I needed to go to the ladies' room. He looked a little embarrassed at the request, but obediently sunk into the bench and started playing a noisy game on his iPod. The minute he looked down, I took a detour.

Daniel was still planted inside the platform by the popcorn machine. He hadn't moved a muscle—a cliché that was literally true this time. I contemplated turning around, of leaving the vision of Daniel secured safely in my mind where it belonged. But I couldn't turn away after considering the facts: I was not sick. Daniel was not a hallucination. And I was definitely not on drugs. Every aspect of my life screamed normalcy, which could mean only one thing. Daniel really *did* exist in some other sphere...only, for some reason he occasionally decided to visit me.

Why?

Well, tonight I planned on figuring that out.

Daniel

When I saw Claire out on a date with *Drew,* of all people, I lost my resolve to keep my distance. Not like Drew was a jerk, or anything. He was just, well...not her type, although pinpointing who *was* her type seemed impossible. I might venture out on a limb and suggest that maybe *I* was Claire's type, but then that would be a little self-serving. Let's just say I was one thousand percent positive that some dude from the football team was definitely *not* Claire's type.

I sensed a change in her energy that night as I hung back a few cars, following them to dinner, then up into the hills for some kind of nature excursion (Nice move, Drew. I didn't know he could be so…romantic). It was actually relieving to watch Claire finally enjoying life again, even with this guy. She seemed to be okay for once.

At first I watched them from far away, feeling slightly irritated, possibly even jealous when she smiled because of him. I really had no intention of letting her know I was there watching them, and that was the truth. But before I knew it, Claire had ditched her date and was already walking toward me, almost cornering me.

And then it was too late.

Claire

Inhaling deeply, I walked toward the platform where Daniel stood frozen like a photograph. Once he realized I was coming right for him, he took a step backward, like he was about to leave.

Don't go, I silently begged.

He shifted sideways toward one of the rear entrances leading out into the trees. But I didn't take my eyes off him. Past the whirring carousel, through the music and crowds and sweet smell of candy, I continued my pursuit down the steps and into the shadows of the unlit park grounds. Just as I nearly reached him, he was another fifteen feet away from me. Somehow he had instantly shifted backward, and now watched me from behind the carousel platform. A feeling of vertigo swept over me, and I stopped. Nothing had moved, yet in a blink, Daniel had shifted away from me again.

Where was he going?

I followed him out there, down the steps to the fresh air and a starry sky. Once out from beneath the glaring lights, I pulled my sweater around my shoulders and crept along in the dark, making my way through the shadows to him. I could see he was wearing flip-flops now, and I shallowly wondered how often he deliberated footwear.

Only a few feet apart now, we faced each other. He seemed hesitant, like he was debating whether or not to stay. I stopped and reached for him, my fingers hovering near his chin.

He looked in my eyes, like he wanted to say something.

I smiled.

His eyes seemed to brighten at that, and he smiled, too. Lifting his hand up near mine, he extended his fingers wide as our hands overlapped, absurdly occupying the same space. A sudden look of irritation swept over him, and his hands quickly fell to his side.

"What?" I asked, whispering.

He started to speak, but hesitated, looking at me apologetically.

I wanted so much more, and could feel my frustration beginning to seep through, overpowering my awe. "Why do you keep coming?" I said over the beat of my pounding heart.

When he didn't respond, unwanted tears gathered inside my eyes. Daniel looked away, seemingly hurt.

"Wait…" I said, already regretting my outburst. "It's okay, Daniel. That's not what I meant. Don't leave yet. *Please,*" I begged.

He looked up, but his eyes were so dismal. I was afraid I'd blown it.

In the distance, a deep, reverberating rhythm of a clock began to chime, the bonging drowning out my voice. It reminded me of the date I'd ditched. When the tenth chime finally dissolved into a soft echo, I turned around, scanning the crowd behind me. No sign of Drew yet.

Daniel—what was I going to do? Even though I couldn't stand the thought of leaving him, I also knew he could never be a part of my life, either. How could he? He was *dead*. Yet, Daniel Holland stood before me with a smile that seemed to melt my heart.

Except, now he was stepping backward, away from me.

"Don't leave," I said. "Not yet."

His eyes told me he had to.

"Claire!" Drew's voice called for me in the distance, though I was convinced I still had a few more minutes.

Daniel seemed to be drifting away from me, but I wasn't ready to let him go. In protest, I lunged at him. But, instead of my hand gliding through him like before, it stopped against the solid mass of Daniel's arm—an arm that was warm, and real and alive.

I gasped.

He froze.

I could feel his skin, and clung on to him with surprising strength, afraid to let go. My shocked face duplicated Daniel's. I was dumbfounded. *Thrilled*. Confused. Had I once and for all really lost it—imagining this because something in me finally snapped?

Daniel held still, fixed momentarily in a daze that had obviously stunned him like it did me. He reached for me with his other hand, touching my shoulder. The feel of his skin sent electrifying chills up and down my arms, like icicles dancing with firecrackers. I could feel every one of his fingers gripping my skin.

"What…happened?" I asked, looking for answers. "*What…?*" But I didn't know how to finish.

The sound of the crowd behind me seemed to disappear, leaving only the leaves rustling in the creaking trees.

"Claire…" he said deeply, slowly.

His voice. I could *hear* it—a deep, soothing voice I loved more than anything. It was foreign, yet familiar, as deep as it was gentle, one I had known my entire life.

I closed the gap between us and wrapped my arms around his neck, pulling him to me. "I can hear you." The whole time I'd known him, we had never once hugged, not deliberately, not like this. Daniel held me comfortably, his hands pressing into my back, sweetly suffocating me.

"How can you hear me?" he whispered in my ear before letting out a little laugh. I pulled back to see his smile.

"You're *alive*," I said, my fingers pressing into the base of his neck. I loved the feel of his hair.

"I can't believe this," he whispered, his feathery breath dancing across my skin. "This is crazy!" He released me to scrutinize his own arms and hands. "You don't know what it feels like to…to breathe, and to *feel* again, Claire, after nothing for so long…to feel something, to feel *you*." He pulled me to him again, his fingers pressing softly into my skin, as if touching me for the first time.

"*Are* you alive?" I asked.

"I don't know. Nothing makes sense."

"You mean this has never happened before?"

"Are you kidding? *No*! No, this is insane!" he said, lifting me off my feet in one giant swoop, spinning me around until I was dizzy.

"Daniel!" I laughed.

He put me back down, still holding my hands tight, when a lock of hair swept down into his eyes. He brought his hand up to push it away, then paused. "That used to bug me."

"What did?"

"My hair. I always hated how it fell down into my face."

"You did?"

"Yes. But now it just makes me feel more alive."

He grew a little more serious then, having slipped a bit from his high.

"What's wrong?" I asked, grabbing his hands again.

"I just feel so strange right now, like I'm crawling out of my skin. Like I can't get enough of life, but don't really need it anymore, either. Does that make sense?"

Not really. "I guess."

Drawing me to him again, his arms crushed me as his cheek gently brushed against my face. But the sound of the carousel seemed to find us again, sabotaging our embrace and reminding me of my abandoned date. Strangely, I felt like I could sense Drew approaching, and the panic hit us both at the same time.

Daniel let go of me as I took a painful step backward. "He's coming," he said.

"Let's hide," I whispered, looking around for a good hiding spot. But Daniel wouldn't move with me as I tried pulling him with me into the trees.

"We can't, Claire. Not now," he said, standing firmly, refusing to follow.

"Why? Daniel?"

"I need to tell you something," he said, "about your—"

I suddenly couldn't hear him anymore, even though he was right there. His mouth was still moving, like someone had pushed a mute button, and when I reached for his hands, nothing was there.

We stared at each other in defeat. Whatever connection we had shared was lost. Whatever brief life Daniel had experienced was gone. I stood there in disbelief as he shook his head.

"Claire?" a voice spoke from behind me.

Of course I jumped *and* screamed. It was Drew. He looked at me like I was mental.

I pretended to be thankful he'd found me lost in the woods, but sensed he wasn't buying it. He led me back down the hill to the car without saying a word or breaking a smile.

I turned to look for Daniel one last time, but he had already disappeared into the night.

CHAPTER
SIX BOO

Daniel

I felt bad. Well, just for Drew. I could already tell Claire was going to be fine, which was pretty much how I felt, too. I couldn't wipe the smile off my face.

The trees flew by me as I shot into the sky above the tiny city, eventually slowing down to take it all in—not the distant city lights below me, but the shocking fact that for a few minutes I had somehow come back from the dead. Not only that, but I couldn't seem to take my eyes or hands off of Claire, either.

I didn't get it. How did I go my entire life without even noticing her—until it was too late? I never believed in fate, or true love, or anything like that, but *did* wonder if there had been signs along the way—some sort of early indication she meant more to me than I'd realized.

Maybe it was time to hit the rewind button in my head, time for a dive into the ol' Memory Trace, something I'd recently discovered. It was kind of like flipping through an electronic photo album—except instead of watching the blur of images flash by until I found what I was looking for, *I* was the one zooming through a three-dimensional tunnel of my own life, sometimes for hours or days at a time, just exploring my mind like a deep-sea explorer searching for treasure. It was easy to get lost in there if you didn't pay attention, though. Just last week I got stuck for three days in a body surfing memory. I couldn't help it. It was so relaxing.

There had to be something inside there, some long-lost Claire memories hidden in the back of my mind that might explain this ridiculous, post-mortal crush I couldn't seem to get under control.

I closed my eyes and let myself sink into the tunnel, wondering how far back I could go, wondering if I'd even find anything worth visiting. Pretty soon, my life was surrounding me, and I started to look for glimpses of Claire, wondering where she might be hiding...

Backward... *holding Claire behind the carousel...* Backward... *the sound of a gunshot...* Back... *playing basketball in the driveway with Matthew...* Faster... *waterskiing in Tahoe...Christmas day with Grandma...* Faster... *swimming in the lake... poison ivy... Boy Scouts... skateboarding...* faster... *Disneyla... camp... pai... a... g... ... ...* Slower... ... *tr... bike... hospit...* Slower... *rainstor... fog...moving day...*

Slow.

Stop.

The hot sun broils me as I stand out in the driveway, staring down the street at the moving van. I'm pretty sure the old guy with the big nose who used to live there died in his sleep, and now a new family is moving in. The driveway is filled with a gazillion boxes, and just when I turn to go back in the house, I hear voices and footsteps coming toward me. Addie comes out of the garage with another girl who also looks like she's three or four years old, and they are already holding hands like they've been best friends their whole lives. Figures. Girls are way too lovey-dovey. Gross. The first thing I notice about the new girl is her glasses. The second thing, her hair, since I can't decide whether it's blonde or brown or red...

Too far.

Go.

Fast-forward... *broken leg at school... st... bre... grounded...a parade...* Stop.

Colors exploding in the sky. Fourth of July. Sparklers everywhere. Claire and Addie are chasing Matthew and me down the hill to the lake. Their laughter catches up to us, and we stop and turn to face the white sparks shooting out from their hands.

Skip ahead.

Side by side we float on our backs beneath the stars, my arms stretching outwards while I kick my legs through the cool water. I feel like I can stay out there all night in the lake just by myself, although Claire isn't bad company, either. Every time I'm around her, things always feel calmer, which is such a nice break from Addie.

Sailing by her, I reach out for the canoe and untie it, then lunge into it while Addie and Matthew skip rocks from the dock. I laugh as Claire tries to pull herself up inside the canoe, without any luck, of course. She gives me a dirty look and pretends like she knew what she was doing. Finally she succeeds and flops beside me. As she stares up at the sky, I secretly watch her familiar silhouette until she jabs me in the side. In return, I pop her on the forehead and dive back into the water, leaving her alone to bring the canoe in all by herself. Serves her right...

Go.

Fast-forward... *ice... ho ... Washingt... grape jello... haircut... scared of...* Skip.

Stop.

Claire thinks she's so funny for pushing me into the lake with all my clothes on. I can't get her back right now because she's already wet, but I'll make her pay. She definitely has something coming to her, that's for sure.

Pause. This was funny—I could feel it approaching before the images were even in front of me. I laughed.

I sneak in when everyone is sound asleep. The house is dark and quiet. The frog is slippery, so I drop it twice, but he's too slow, and I catch him before he disappears under the table. Claire is snoring when I tiptoe up next to her. She looks funny sleeping, and I want to laugh, but keep to the plan: drop the frog on top of her head and get out of there. I hear the scream when I reach the kitchen, and I bolt for the door. Man, I wish I could see the look on her face right now. Matthew will have to describe it to me later.

Stop.

Skip Forward...*Claire pitches me the whiffle ball and tags me smack in the eye... I throw up in the bushes on the way home from school and Matthew and Addie run away from me, but Claire stays behind and holds my backpack for me... we're running through the sprinklers... going to the movies... mountain biking... carpool... football games... pizza night...*

Stop.

Unwind.

Breathe.

I couldn't believe how many Claire memories I had forgotten over the years. I never realized how much she was such a part of my life. Sure, at the time, most of the details seemed as routine as brushing my teeth or tying my shoes. Who remembers stuff like that? But now I knew what made Claire so much more interesting than most of the girls I'd liked or dated—which was probably why I still couldn't get her out of my mind. It had something to do with all those crazy, funny things that made her unique, like the sound of her low-pitched laugh, or the way her neck got splotchy-red when she was embarrassed, how she stuck with glasses most of the time despite advances in modern technology. Or the way she screamed whenever someone snuck up behind her (it could even be a babbling baby and she'd still freak out), and all the other strange, funny, dorky, unique things that made her Claire....

It felt like she had snuck in the back door and crawled right up inside my head without me ever knowing. There were probably a hundred more memories, but I was already feeling the weight of the Memory Trace. It was exhausting searching through my mind like that, like reliving hundreds of hours of thoughts and feelings all at once in a short amount of time. It even made me feel kind of sleepy.

And it was time to wake up and go back home.

To Hidden Lake.

To Claire.

Claire

The drive home was mostly silent. Obviously, there would be no explaining to Drew why I had wandered off alone in the dark. What would I tell him, anyway? That I was playing hide-and-seek with my dead crush? Rather than make up some far-fetched story, I kept my mouth shut as he drove, the stereo blasting through the strain. I just hoped he wasn't the gossipy type.

When Drew dropped me off, I mumbled a sort-of apology, unable to look him in the eyes. I didn't know exactly how to say sorry, so I gushingly thanked him instead, and then he left me alone beneath a cascade of moonlight.

The porch light flickered on much too quickly as the door creaked open to Mom's cheerful face. She probably had insanely high hopes that Drew would solve all of my problems. I was sorry to disappoint her, but still offered a weak smile, pretending. She really had no idea how far from despondency I truly was. *If she only knew.* Then again, I was pretty sure she would send me off to the shrink she'd been threatening for the last three months if I told her how my evening really went.

"How was it, hon?"

"Fine." I found it nearly impossible trying to play casual while bursting inside.

"Did you have fun?"

I sunk to the empty bench and sighed in frustration, wishing I could tell her the truth, but knew that was out of the question. How could I tell *anyone* I wanted to be with someone who was dead but occasionally came back to life? Chills trickled down my arms and legs when I replayed in my mind the moment Daniel swung me around and said my name. I *loved* the sound of his voice.

"Not much to talk about?" Mom asked, putting her arm around me.

"Not really. It was fine," I said, though I was beginning to sense some sort of premeditated lecture.

"Did you like him?" she asked too eagerly. "Was he nice?"

"Sure, Mom. He was nice. Not my type, though."

"Claire, you've got to try–"

There. She'd said it—the one thing I was sick of hearing everyone tell me—that I needed to "try harder," that my loneliness was all my fault, and if I would just give more guys a chance, I might actually end up liking one. I was so done with that guilt trip.

"Mom," I stopped her, sitting up straight.

She quit mid-sentence, but hesitantly placed her hand on my leg, as if her gesture would make up for what I knew she was thinking about me.

"Drew wasn't my type. It had nothing to do with anything. I'm not depressed. I'm not on the verge of suicide or anything. *Please* don't lecture me about it again."

"I'm sorry, Claire." Mom stood, apparently annoyed at me as she tucked her rusty brown curls behind her ear and looked toward the lake. I turned away from her, hoping she'd let it drop. "Well, at least you went. That's better than nothing," she said, then went back inside and left me alone on the bench with the quiet.

I dozed off twice because I was too lazy to get up, but finally managed to drag myself inside to bed. An antique clock on top of the tall chest of drawers ticked at me, along with a too-loud chorus of crickets coming in through the open window. I could feel myself drifting, but also kept thinking of Daniel. I wondered where he had gone. Was there some special place where he bided the time? I doubted he slept or ate, or did anything temporal like that...but then again, maybe old habits persisted there, too. Maybe he traveled the world, gliding in and out of all the impossible and forbidden places he always wanted to go like the Middle East or Bangkok. Did he somehow know more now? Was he sad about dying? Is that why he'd returned, or was some great mission preventing his departure?

My mind eventually drifted away into the mysterious place that captures all of us every night, holding us prisoner until the great sleep ransom has been paid. Tonight, I welcomed imprisonment without resistance, though just before defeat, a single question echoed through my mind like the persistent, ticking clock.

When will I see Daniel again?

Daniel

She was asleep now, though I didn't watch her through the window or anything. That would probably freak her out. Instead, I hung out on her front porch and stared out at the lake, watching for patterns made by the moonlight. Sometimes I wished to be able to fall asleep again and wake up the next morning, refreshed—eight hours vanished, just like that. Instead, I had to patiently wait the night out minute-by-minute, second-by-second.

The wind was blowing now, though I couldn't feel it myself—not even the sense of something pushing on me, or moving a strand of hair. But I still remembered the way it felt on my face. Trying to imagine again, I closed my eyes at the sound of fluted chimes hanging from the eaves of the house next door. They stopped and started over and over again through the night as the breeze hung on.

These were things I noticed in the absence of living. I couldn't help it. *Details.* Maybe if I'd paid more attention when I was alive, Claire would've come under my radar sooner than a couple of weeks before I died.

Chills started climbing up and down my arms and legs like little biting spiders, burning into me so that it almost hurt. I drifted across the grass, then up the street and back again, trying to find another ghost. "I know you're here," I called out while hovering over the porch railing, swinging my legs. "Come out, come out, wherever you are."

But there was only silence.

I hadn't heard from that other ghost since that confrontation in the fog weeks ago. I'd even forgotten about him until now. Hopefully, these goose bumps didn't mean I was in for a repeat visit.

"Why don't you grow up and show yourself, already," I said to the mysterious intruder while tapping my fingers along the peeling rail, trying to figure out my next move.

Claire. *She* was my next move.

I shifted into her room to make sure she was okay. But there was no need for alarm. She was fine, all curled up in her covers, okay for now, even though the chills kept climbing up my limbs. To be safe, I spent the rest of the night skimming every inch of the dark house, rotating from one room to the next.

Just before the first speck of sunlight popped up over the horizon, I returned to check on Claire one more time, hovering impatiently in her doorway while brainstorming ways to get rid of an unwanted ghost. What was left of the moonlight drew a soft outline of her elongated shape, making her look so peaceful there as she probably dreamt about normal, safe things not involving ghosts and dead boyfriends. I inhaled unnecessarily, realizing I wanted to hold her and hear her say my name again.

She sighed and turned to her other side while mumbling something I couldn't understand. Then she let out a gigantic snore. I burst out laughing, though I felt guilty for watching her sleep. I could only imagine how red she'd turn if she knew I was there, so I drifted back to my spot on the porch to be hypnotized by the wind chimes all over again.

While gazing out across the lake, I saw someone—a woman, this time. She was hovering above the surface of the water, her dark hair flying all over the place, watching me. She looked slightly familiar, but I couldn't remember why. Tonight my mind was being uncooperative.

When she realized I'd spotted her, she looked surprised like she'd been caught, and then turned around and drifted away through the trees.

Who was she?

I drifted across the lake toward her, wondering what she wanted, following her through the trees, in and out of backyards and neighborhoods, across the freeway, then downtown to the mall. She kept leading me along, like she wanted me to follow, but never stopping long enough for me to catch her.

At first I was curious…then confused…then bored. I finally left her when she drifted into an empty Starbucks and pretended to order something. She even stood at the counter and looked up at the menu on the wall, like she was trying to decide what to get.

Claire

Something woke me. I leaned up to my elbows to look around the room, trying to find the source.

The window was still open, welcoming in the faint music of wind chimes. The tune felt haunting—it was a perfect combination of highs and lows at all the right times, and sent a wave of chills up my back just as I heard a soft thumping noise somewhere in the distance. But it was so low and faint, I assumed it was just part of the music.

Already feeling the restless leg dance coming on, I flipped to my other side. My bare arms shivered beneath the cool breeze, and I pulled my covers up to my neck, wondering why it was suddenly so cold. I tried closing my eyes, but they refused to cooperate, like they knew there was something waiting for me in the dark.

The curtains blew inward, but not like anything I'd ever seen before. They seemed to hover in mid-air, lasting for a couple of seconds, like some invisible force was pulling them across the room. It was absolutely longer than what a normal wind could do—kind of beautiful, but mostly creepy.

I stared at the ceiling, trying to close my eyes so I wouldn't have to see or imagine anything else that might be going on around me. Ignorance was definitely an acceptable remedy for all things that went bump in the night, especially when images of a dark, ribbon-like ghost began to enter my mind.

My heart began pounding. *Hard.* And the room seemed to be coming alive as normal early morning noises suddenly seemed so much more terrifying—a creaking ceiling, a shrill scraping, a rustle in the bushes outside...

The curtains blew inward again, but this time something followed through them—something thick and black like an inky shadow floating across the room, twisting and revolving. I gasped, throwing the covers over my head, praying for it to go away. A huge gust of wind slammed the door shut, and I screamed, certain my heart was going to pound right through my chest and jump onto the floor.

Within seconds, the door burst open and the light flicked on. "Claire, what's wrong?"

I peeked through the covers to find my dad in his underwear, standing over me. He looked worried. I leapt upward and threw my arms around his neck, pulling him close to me. He held me tightly while calmly running his fingers along the back of my head. "It's okay," he said. "It's just a bad dream."

That was when I realized I still couldn't tell him the truth. He had already chastised me for screaming like a maniac in the kitchen, and if I told him I'd seen a ghost, he would certainly send me back in the hospital for another round of testing.

"Claire?" he asked again, smiling patiently as his blue eyes rested on mine.

"I'm okay, Dad," I finally said, feeling the air coming back to my lungs.

"You sure?"

I looked around the room and saw nothing. "Yes. I'll be fine. But can you close my window."

"You dreaming about aliens again?" he asked playfully, messing up my hair. I laughed, a little, remembering how as a kid I used to have recurrent dreams for years about dinosaurs peeling off my skin or aliens transforming into my Grandma. Seriously.

Dad finally let me go, even though I wanted him to stay until I was certain nothing was coming back to get me.

As soon as the light was out and the door closed, I shut my eyes again and counted down from fifty, taking deep breaths the whole way down. When I got all the way to one, I started all over again...and again...and again...

CHAPTER SEVEN FOUR AND A HALF MINUTES

Claire

I never fell back asleep that night, and the rest of the weekend I fared even worse. Insomnia is a tricky little devil, making it impossible to sleep when you want to, and even more impossible to stay awake when you have to. I had to force myself out of bed Monday morning and almost missed my ride with Addie. She didn't let me forget it the rest of the day, either. My Algebra teacher even caught me nodding off and called me up to work out a problem on the board. He knew I'd been sleeping, which was proof that he's evil, or at least a big jerk. Not only did I majorly bomb the problem, but I was also pretty sure, thanks to the sound of people laughing behind my back, that I'd probably been snoring, too.

But I made it through alive.

That evening after dinner, Addie called me for a break from homework, which usually meant a raid through my pantry (since her parents only ate diet stuff like protein bars and hummus) and then a walk down to the dock to hang out and talk. It was already dark when we got there, but the moon was bright and the porch light was on, making the chance of me falling in the lake more remote.

While snacking on Hot Tamales, a bag of Sun Chips and a Diet Coke, I listened to Addie go on and on about her personal drama for at least twenty minutes, until a lull in our conversation had me daydreaming again. I was purposely trying not to think of the creepy thing in my bedroom the other night in order to more specifically remember what happened before that, when Daniel held me in his arms. I was beginning to wonder if the moon held some magical power over us, and I couldn't help looking for him, wondering if he was off in the shadows right now, watching us.

"How's Matthew doing?" Addie asked, pulling her knees to her chest as she turned to face me. The moonlight lit up her face, which of course made her look unfairly stunning in the silvery light.

"I guess okay," I said. Matthew rarely called home anymore, and I didn't know the last time he'd come for a visit. I missed him.

Leaning on my elbows, I stretched out across the splintery planks as a soft breeze tickled my face. My mind returned back to thoughts of Daniel, because thinking of Matthew was too depressing.

Addie started rummaging through the half-eaten bag of chips. "I really miss him."

I sighed in agreement, "Me too," but immediately realized she was talking about Matthew, not Daniel, and I sat up like a light had flicked on. "You miss *Matthew*."

"Yeah. *Your brother*," she said, shoving a handful of chips in her mouth. "Whoojuh think I meant?"

"Oh. No, that's what I thought," I said quickly, wondering where I had taken a detour. Daniel was plastered all over my mind like a billboard, and the more I tried to detach myself from him, the more mixed-up I got.

Addie finished munching, but eyed me suspiciously while slowly licking each finger one by one. I tried to ignore her, but was becoming more and more convinced she could see right through me—that she knew I was hiding something. I waited, not knowing what to say, wondering if she would call me on it.

The wind whipped my hair across my face and snatched the bag of chips from out of Addie's hands, carrying it through the air like a kite being tugged on a string. She screamed and chased after it just as I felt a warm bank of air settle in around me.

Daniel.

I looked all around us, but still didn't see him anywhere.

"Got it!" Addie yelled triumphantly as she grabbed the bag from out of the air. She then crumpled it into an impossible little ball and shoved it in her pocket. "I better go," she said, pulling me to my feet. "I still have tons of homework to do."

I followed her up the hill to the street, looking everywhere for Daniel's face blending into the shadows.

"See you in the morning," Addie said, leaving me in the street as she made her way to her house. "But set your alarm this time. I don't want to be late again!" she yelled from her driveway.

After skipping up the steps, she disappeared inside her house. I headed up my own driveway, thinking the night seemed unusually quiet. Sensing someone behind me, I turned around to find Daniel grinning at me. I felt my face grow warm. I smiled, but found myself looking down at my feet before glancing up again, almost like a first date.

"Hi," I said out loud, forcing my hands into my pockets.

He looked as solid and vivid as if he were alive, but when I tried to touch his arm, there was still nothing there. He didn't respond, but pointed to my wrist, or maybe my fingers. Confused, I held my hands up in front of me, trying to figure out what he wanted.

"What?" I asked.

He mouthed something, which was when I discovered how incompetent I was at reading lips and shook my head in defeat. "I'm sorry."

I think he gave up then.

After a car passed, I looked down the street to make sure we were still alone. When I turned back around, Daniel was ten feet away. I followed him, but he kept heading backwards down the hill, toward the lake. Finally he waited for me at the edge of the dock, where he looked like he was relaxing, just hanging his feet over the side.

I caught up and sat beside him, staring out across the lake, not knowing what else to do. It seemed like he could hear me, even though I couldn't hear him. But I still felt funny and awkward talking out loud.

"I'm not really sure how this all works," I finally said, still staring straight ahead. "You can hear me, right?" I turned to look into his eyes.

I think I blushed again when he nodded with a dimpled smile, *'Yes.'*

"Good. At least that's something," I laughed, trying to ease the tension. He mutely laughed, too, but stopped short with a look of irritation when he tried talking. It was uncanny how convincingly alive he seemed, and it made me sad.

"I really miss you, Daniel," I blurted out, but then felt vulnerable for saying something so blunt.

His arm slipped away from me, and he looked down at my lap, his hand hovering atop my wrist again. I glanced at his hands crossing over mine, and realized he was pointing at my watch.

"My watch?" I asked.

He smiled and nodded in agreement.

"My watch…" I repeated. It was 10:01. The second hand silently ticked its way around the face, and Daniel appeared to be holding his breath, anticipating something.

Fifteen more clicks.

Then *it* happened. *Again.*

Daniel grabbed my arm, and like before, I could feel the pressure of his fingers on my skin. His subtle warmth soothed me, and I held my breath as he drew closer, his lips nearly touching my ear. My skin tingled with what felt like a thousand little feathers dancing all over it when he leaned into me and whispered, "Four and a half minutes."

Daniel

Four and a half minutes was not enough time to tell Claire everything. I squeezed her arm, still freaking out that I could *feel* again.

"How is this happening?" she asked as I reached for her hands.

I was surprised she was still wearing the dulled, silver ring I'd given her. I twisted it around and around her finger while trying to figure out what to say and where to start, wishing she could just read my mind because I didn't have enough time to tell her everything I wanted to.

"I have a couple of questions for you," I said, but she already seemed too far away. I pulled her closer, with her head just under my chin so I could inhale her familiar scent. "Do you remember anything about your birthday—about the night you almost drowned?"

I expected her to think for a minute, or to gather her thoughts or something, but she didn't even take a breath. "Yes," she said, her eyes suddenly alive. "I remember *you.*"

"Me?" I asked, pulling back.

"I'm pretty sure I saw you right before I passed out…or drowned… I still haven't figured out exactly what happened yet. I think I actually *died*, at some point." When I didn't respond, she continued. "Right before you saved me. I was off somewhere else in some calm, peaceful place, and I didn't want to leave."

"Why *did* you leave?" She had me hooked now, despite the ticking clock.

"Because of you. I think you said my name."

"You heard me?"

"Yes! That's what woke me up—*your voice*. When I opened my eyes, you were right there. I even grabbed your arm, didn't I?"

I nodded, recalling that night, wondering if Claire had ever thought about it before now.

"I wish we had more time," I said.

"Wait. How do you know how much time we have?" she asked, her hands squeezing mine.

I took a deep breath, trying to absorb the cool air into my lungs as her big, brown eyes watched me eagerly, looking for answers. "I don't know if this makes sense, but I think something happened between us the night you drowned. When I brought you back, it was like it is right now—like I was alive again, right? So I'm guessing you must've brought something back from the dead with you, something that lets us connect like this."

"Seriously?" Claire asked, looking doubtful.

"Yes. I think something happens to us every night at the *exact* time you drowned, which was right after ten-o'clock, according to your watch."

Hearing it from my own mouth sounded even crazier. She acted like she was going to speak, but didn't know what to say. I couldn't blame her.

"It's like a four-and-a-half-minute breach through a barrier, or something," I said.

"A four-and-a-half *what?*"

"How long we can communicate. At least that's my guess. I think it's how long you were dead before I saved you."

"*Really?*" she said, shifting slightly. "Four and a half minutes? Talk about…I don't know…strange, crazy, unbelievable." She let out a little laugh. "I guess it's better than four minutes."

I didn't know what else to say, especially when I realized how much I just loved being next to her.

"Wait—what happened Saturday morning?" she asked, her whole body stiffening. "Were you there in my room? Did you see it? It was something…something creepy…like a *ghost.*"

"Ghost?" I asked, confused.

"I don't know, but it's the same thing I saw in my kitchen right after I drowned…you don't have any idea what I'm talking about?"

I must have been shaking my head.

"I don't know how to explain it, Daniel. I thought you'd know. But since you don't, maybe next time, if there is a next time, which I'm hoping there isn't, you can see for yourself. Because something keeps coming into my house, and whatever it is, it's keeping me up at night and I'm a basket case at school. Not to mention snoring, in the middle of class–"

"Claire," I said, worried but trying not to let on, wondering if Mr. Psycho Ghost had somehow reached her without me knowing. "Don't worry about it. I'll figure it out. Okay?"

She did look exhausted with big, gray half-circles underlining her eyes. What was she talking about? What happened? I wanted to ask her to describe it, but didn't want to waste any more of our four and a half minutes.

Smiling, she tilted her head up. "Four and a half minutes is all we have? That's it? Maybe I should've stayed dead longer."

"Funny," I said, pulling her to me, feeling once again all those emotions that reminded me how much I missed being alive. Would this teeny slice of happiness be worth the upcoming letdown lasting fourteen hundred some-odd minutes? I wasn't sure. Not yet.

Claire still seemed to be searching, her mind running a million miles an hour. No wonder she couldn't sleep. "Can you see me all the time?" she asked, like she just randomly skipped to another chapter.

"Yes."

"Are you *supposed* to watch over me, like are you my guardian angel, or something? And where do you hang out all the time? How do you get around?"

I wanted to laugh at her—for the sudden impression of being at a job interview. It was kind of cute. But when I looked down at her watch and saw our time almost gone, I started to panic...and without even thinking, I felt my head slowly moving toward hers.

Back when I was alive, I would've never made a move on Matthew's little sister. He'd have killed me, for sure. But death had already changed me. Now I really couldn't care less what anyone else thought.

I brought my fingers to Claire's cheek as an unfamiliar sensation of nerves and emotions twisted inside me...

And then I kissed her.

Claire

I held my breath and willed the world to suspend its rotation when his lips touched mine. I'd just been thinking of my next question, when he kissed me so suddenly, I gasped. It was soft and serene, like a whisper to the lips. When I realized what was happening, I had to pull back a little to breathe. He looked surprised and disappointed at my pause.

Wait, hold on!

Before he could complain, I leaned back into him, eagerly finding his lips again. His hands cradled my head, intertwining his fingers through my hair, pulling just hard enough to hurt a little, and just soft enough to feel good.

Just as I clasped my hands behind his neck, he pulled away from me and rested his forehead against mine. His hands fell along the sides of my face, crawling down my neck to my shoulders, and finally to my bare arms. Softly, slowly, his lips brushed mine one more time, and then he smiled at me.

I smiled, too.

Our connection broke in the next instant, but he was still there.

Still warm from his touch, I brought my hands to my lips and tried holding on to the lingering memory of his kiss. Behind me, the porch lights flickered at my house, reminding me of my normal life without

Daniel—the life with rules and consequences for breaking the rules. Reluctantly I stood up.

"My mom's probably wondering where I am," I said, explaining my departure.

He nodded, watching me drag my feet up the grassy hill. I faced him while walking backwards, smiling as the feeling of elation bubbled all around me. Right then I wished he could say something else to me—*anything*. Even reciting my phone number would have felt romantic. I already missed hearing his voice.

"You're not going to watch me sleep are you?" I teased. "Not like some creepy ghost-stalker?"

He smiled and shrugged his shoulders, meaning, no...or maybe? I wasn't sure, but he definitely looked guilty.

"Well, you better at least give me some privacy, you know. No peeping-tom business from you," I said, half kidding, half serious. It was a little freaky knowing he could watch me whenever and wherever.

He laughed at me, and I think mouthed the word "Okay." I felt a little guilty after that, because Daniel was obviously not some psycho voyeur just because he happened to be dead. Still, I felt better getting it all out in the open.

Walking up the steps, I imagined his eyes penetrating my back, and wondered how long he could just stare at something. What was it like to have nothing to do all day long?

When the front door clicked behind me, the air seemed to instantly dissolve into nothing, my heartbeat relaxing into a quiet rhythm.

"Where've you been, Claire?"

I looked up to find Mom sitting in the living room, casually watching me over a book she was reading. She had a pair of those teeny glasses resting at the edge of her nose, ready to slide off. Her dark, curly hair fell into her face after a long day at work. She looked like a librarian, the way she sat there eyeing me.

"Sheez, Mom," I gasped. "Were you *trying* to scare me?"

"You said you'd be home before ten. I was really starting to worry, you know."

"I was just… just taking a walk…trying to think. Stuff like that," I lied, walking right past her through the arched entrance leading into the dark kitchen.

She closed her book and followed me. "Taking a walk? It's pitch black, Claire–"

I stopped and turned to face her wary expression, waiting for a lecture.

"It's not smart for you to be out this late by yourself. Especially down by the lake."

Was she spying on me?

"I know, Mom. I was with Addie…most of the time." It was true, really.

"*Please* be more careful from now on." Mom had probably re-hearsed this very conversation in her head at least twenty times tonight while she was waiting for me. "You *have* to let me know where you are so I don't sit up and worry all night. I thought we went over this already."

That was Mom's specialty, ever since Daniel had been killed— *worrying with a vengeance.* Both of my parents were always on alert now, always watching and obsessing about my safety. I understood. But it was still annoying and inconvenient. Especially now that Matthew was away and I was their only target.

"Okay, sorry," I said, trying to get around her without another lecture about my dating life.

"Claire, don't you think–"

"'Night, Mom. See you in the morning." I yawned and practically dove for the dark hallway to make my escape.

Daniel

What was I thinking? Obviously I wasn't.

After that kiss, I watched Claire climb the steps to her house, and then shifted away. I needed to concentrate for at least two seconds before my runaway emotions took over again. What was I doing?

I took off running—except it was more like jumping through time as everything passed by me in shifts and spurts. It was mind numbing, exciting, and relaxing all at the same time, and it was exactly what I needed. Blaring lights and the unique sounds of San Francisco greeted me beneath the dark sky. I flew alongside the crowds and blank faces, all of them unaware of me racing by. It was like being the only one on a moving sidewalk, while the rest of the world strolled along at a snail's pace.

At the end of a busy street, I walked smack into an oncoming semi-truck. It was as easy and intuitive as blinking, and I felt invincible. It was a familiar sensation—one I'd felt when I was alive, too, up until the moment someone shot me in the head. Now, the rush of danger was still exhilarating as I stood in the middle of the street and let the traffic tear through me over and over again. After getting bored of that, I moved away from the road and glided through a greasy brick wall, plastered with decaying paper. I closed my eyes and shot up through the clouds, leaving the city behind. Soaring across the bay and over the congested roads, I ascended into the shadowy foothills to a mountain that seemed to prop up the moon.

Even there, I still couldn't stop thinking about Claire. I'd lost all sense when I kissed her, and now I was doomed to torture myself over and over again with memories of that kiss and her touch. How could I give that up? Would four and a half minutes, one day at a time, be my only chance at all with her? Would it just end up torturing me? I was starting to realize seeing her again would only end up making me want *more* time with her—time that was not even guaranteed. *Hello?* I'm dead. Remember?

But what was time at all without her? That was the point, wasn't it? To spend time with her? No, that was *not* the point. *You're just supposed to watch over her, not fall in love with her.* How could "life" still be so complicated after death?

Done flying through the sky, I descended to a snow bank while checking out the world, feeling so small compared to the rest of the universe. My problems were nothing next to everything else. Who was *I?* Who was I *kidding?*

As I stood there drowning in confusion, a strange, cold sensation started intruding into my thoughts, making it impossible to think straight. It felt like I was being pulled away from this place, like my mind was being stretched in two different directions. I closed my eyes and tried to ignore it, as if that would somehow block it out. But the feeling only grew stronger.

What was going on?

And then, before I even said her name, I knew.

Claire.

In a second I was back at Hidden Lake on the front porch next to the haunting, fluted chimes. Sharp chills shocked me like electricity, and my first reaction was to search the neighborhood, then the lake, and the street—just like last time. But the further I drifted away, the fainter the chills became.

That was when I realized something was inside the house.

Claire

Sleep evaded me as usual. Once again, I couldn't stop thinking about Daniel. His voice echoed in my ears and mind, the feel of his hands and lips still overwhelming me. This time, I consciously fought sleep just to be able to relive being with him again and again, and as the euphoria flooded through me, I found myself smiling in the dark.

Until the night took a horrifying detour, and my eyes suddenly popped open.

"*Ssssrooophhhh.*"

What was *that?*

I held my breath, listening, but the only sound I could hear was the *tick-tock* of the clock across the room—that was, of course, if you didn't count my own heart thumping loud enough for the whole neighborhood to hear.

"*Ssssrooophhhh.*"

Now it sounded like a deep, throaty snake. I held still for one tortuous, extended, moment, waiting…waiting…

"*Ssssrooophhhh.*"

It was getting closer, and I didn't know what to do. Peeking over the mountain of pillows I'd piled on top of me, I surveyed the room.

Nothing.

The clock continued to tick. Outside, an owl hoo'ed or hooted or did whatever they do, which was when I realized I should get up and close the window. But I was too scared to move. A shivery breeze wafted in through the open window, capturing and randomly entangling the long flowing curtains. But this time it just looked like normal wind. My muscles relaxed a little as I waited and watched, deliberating whether or not to risk leaving my bed to shut the window.

"*Sssrooophhhh,*" it hissed again, now sounding less like a snake and more like the blubbering squeal of a deflating balloon.

Was it back again? The ghost...that *thing?*

I jumped up, only making it to the end of my bed, my knees protesting the entire time. Fear seemed to be seeping from me like slow poison, preventing me from thinking clearly. I felt like I was stuck on an island, sharks swimming all around me, just waiting for me to slip up.

"*Sssrooophhhh.*"

This time the hissing noise was much louder, and not only sent shivers up my spine, but also seemed to send those shivers, like daggers, straight into my back.

Forget the window. All I wanted now was to get out of my room. But when I turned around, hovering in front of me was another revolving ribbon-like smudge of black, but much bigger and darker than before. It pulsated through the air like something out of a science fiction movie as it made its strange sound, hissing and sucking, almost like it could see me—like it was *watching* me.

I waited for a scream to find its way out of my mouth, but it never came. Instead, I held my breath and watched the ribbon expand and lengthen like taffy being pulled. I was mesmerized by its eerie motion, immovable like in a real nightmare where your legs refuse to work. I wanted to run away, to scream out loud, to turn on the light and make whatever it was go away, but some unseen power seemed to hold me in place, binding me with invisible cords. My mind had shut down, like some kind of darkness was overtaking my senses. I could feel myself wilting as an icy hand began to wrap itself around my throat...

"Claire," I heard my name, though it sounded distant and far away.

I couldn't see anymore. My room seemed to disappear, and all I knew was a black, cold, pain taking over, climbing up my neck.

I gasped.

"It's okay," the voice spoke again, this time more in my head. It seemed familiar and warm, but still beyond my reach. "I'm right here."

But the darkness was still too thick, until I heard music in my head. It sounded so familiar...a melody repeating itself over and over again, reminding me of my childhood. And then a simple thought emerged from the muddy depths of my mind, forming a clear impression that told me to listen more carefully.

I managed to match the music with a person, then zeroed in on a face; a face with dark hair falling into darker eyes, a pair of dimples, a mesmerizing smile, and a smooth, calming laugh...

Daniel.

Soon, a dim light was crawling out of the shadows, casting the rest of the darkness away. I felt myself starting to regain control, able to breathe again, and my eyes opened just as the shadowy ghost started to fade. I went to the light switch and flipped it on, the yellowish hue overhead nearly blinding me. By then, the dark ribbon had thinned down to almost nothing, and finally disappeared into the wall.

I felt like I'd been crying, but was too tired to even wonder why, and climbed back into bed, burying myself in the covers. After a few minutes, I flipped to my other side, and was slightly startled to find Daniel sitting on the edge of the bed, his hand next to mine.

So he had been here, after all. Somehow, I knew he must have helped me.

I reached for his hand, even though it sailed right through, into the pillow. I wanted to talk to him and ask him what happened, but was too tired. Maybe tomorrow, after my mind had a chance to untangle itself from the confusion that was now a normal part of my life. Right then, I felt mixed-up because even though Daniel was right there beside me, I felt painfully alone.

Daniel

Chills attacked me when I shifted into the house. Something was there—something stale and rotten like the stench of garbage. I followed the trail of decay down the hallway and into Claire's room.

She wasn't asleep or even under the covers, but was clinging to the edge of the bed, transfixed in the moonlight, its pale glow falling across her face and through the room, illuminating an unwanted visitor. Her eyes seemed glued open, shocked at the psycho ghost drifting toward her and calling her name. I could feel her terror floating toward me, filling the room with fear.

Yet, I wondered if Claire was seeing something different than me, because I didn't really think there was anything *scary* about him—even after our encounter at the lake. Sure, he rambled nonsense and wore way too much black, but right now he looked about as threatening as I did, except maybe he was even a little shorter. Really, he bore no resemblance to any of the ghosts in horror movies—no hanging skin or protruding bones, nothing like that. So what was the deal? What did Claire see?

As the ghost watched me out of the corner of his eye, I went to her. At first, he seemed surprised to see me, but then a smirk formed on his lips, almost like he was glad I'd arrived. I tried sliding in front of him, blocking his way, but he ignored me, focusing all his attention on Claire.

What was he doing?

I was too fresh, too green to know what to do. Still, I wasn't about to give up. I *had* to figure out how to help her, even if it meant just staying with her no matter what happened. What could happen? He was just a ghost, right?

A mental ghost with a grudge.

His eyes narrowed, and he suddenly turned his focus to me. I begged for Claire's attention by waving my hands in front of her eyes and trying to throw my arms around her, like a shield. But nothing worked. She was unreachable, under some kind of spell.

I looked in her eyes. "Claire." Her gaze went right through me...to *him.*

He was laughing.

I ignored him and concentrated on Claire. "You're okay," I said to her, trying to cup her face in my hands, wishing to be able to force her to look at me. I could *almost* feel her skin and even smell the subtle floral scent in her hair, like a garden.

"That's right," the ghost whispered in her ear. "You're scared of me, aren't you Claire?"

She sunk to the floor and started shaking, gripping her knees and squeezing her eyes shut as the ghost hovered over us both.

"Claire," I said again.

She buried her head in her knees and released a muffled sob, her hands clenched into fists. The ghost then placed his index finger at the middle of Claire's back and slowly dragged it up her spine, all the way to the nape of her neck. His hand tensed as he pressed harder, and I felt sick when I saw her hair move to the side. She screamed. I tried pulling her to me, but my arms slipped through her.

"It's me, Claire. Don't look at him anymore. Stop listening to him. Think of me. *Look* at me. Remember last night?"

Her eyes relaxed and she smiled for a second. The ghost drew backward a little and scowled at me. I wasn't sure how my words were helping, but kept at it, convinced I was on to something. "Remember the carousel, Claire? Think of the music and the lights…think of me…how I held you. Remember that?"

The ghost shot toward me, stopping right in front of my face. The darkness in his eyes raged like two black hurricanes. "Shut. UP," he demanded before bringing his hands to his head and thrusting them through his hair.

But Claire's eyes had already popped open. She was wiping her tears, and we both turned to watch her take a deep breath as she pulled herself up. Without saying a word, she went directly to the doorway, flipped on the light switch, and then turned around and leapt to her bed, diving into the covers.

Over by the window, the ghost glared. His words came out slow and calm, though they seemed to be filled with some kind of controlled rage that had been tempered over the years. "This is just the beginning," he seethed, before disappearing through the wall.

The room was quiet.

I went to Claire, mouthing the words, "I'm sorry."

She looked exhausted. I wanted to tell her everything was going to be okay, but had no idea if that was true.

Instead, I sat on the edge of the bed as she fell asleep, wondering how I was going to stop this nightmare from happening to her again.

CHAPTER
EIGHT TWENTY QUESTIONS

Claire

I awoke to the sound of Addie's honking, and knew I was in trouble. Despite my insistence, she refused to leave without me. "You've been acting like a complete basket case for the past week, and I really doubt you can pull yourself together without my help."

Not true.

But I kept my mouth shut and rushed to get ready while she drilled me with a million questions, asking me three times why I'd been acting so bizarre lately.

She was overreacting. Sure, I was a little scatterbrained at the moment, but it wasn't like I'd been ignoring her. We still hung out together every day, and I hadn't stopped listening to all her worries or all the latest gossip. I was just a little more tired than usual, thanks to weeks of insomnia since my birthday—since Daniel came back.

Even after all that ghost business, I still felt dizzy with excitement remembering Daniel's kiss. I kept thinking about how his lips felt on mine, when his hands pulled through my hair and drew me into his chest…

"Claire!" Addie had her hands on her hips, glaring at me.

"Sorry," I said, pulling my hair in a ponytail and grabbing my bag. Maybe Addie had a point. Maybe I did need her help.

We were not horribly late—ten minutes definitely earned us a tardy (not my first), but at least I didn't miss my first class. I also managed to stay awake the whole morning, even during Algebra.

At lunch, Addie and I ate mostly in silence, probably because my snoring debacle yesterday had already trickled down the gossip line, and now she was embarrassed to be seen with me. After awhile she left me alone at our usual bench to dump her tray, and then stopped to talk to some other friends. I barely noticed her absence or return because I was still stuck inside my daydream, perfectly removed from reality.

"Claire," Addie's voice butted in.

"Huh?" I asked, my mouth still full.

She frowned at me with an evil eye, immediately bringing me back to the present. "*So?*"

"What?"

She just stood there, waiting for a response. But what was I supposed to say? There was no way I could tell her about Daniel, even if I wanted to. The last time I brought him up only made her cry. Telling her the truth was definitely out of the question.

"You've been acting kind of weird today. Are you mad at me, or what?"

She was way off base for once. I started laughing, which turned into coughing after I inhaled a piece of granola bar. She rushed to my side and started patting my back until the hacking stopped.

"Are you okay?" she asked, putting her arm around me. That was what I loved most about Addie—it was the best part of her. Although blunt and full of energy, she had a soft side that instantly connected to everyone around her. Most of the time she seemed so two-dimensional, and then out of the blue she would do or say something sweet and caring.

"What?" she asked when I didn't answer.

"It's nothing, really." I wiped the tears from my eyes as she squeezed me again. I wanted so badly to tell her what was going on—to tell her *something*. But what? That I was with Daniel last night? That he was probably right here, right now?

I looked in her bright, blue eyes, smiling at my best friend who knew everything about me, and nothing at all. "I..."

"What?" she asked, smiling, like she already knew my secret and was just toying with me. It was hard to ignore Addie when she smiled like that. Just ask the whole school. "Are you in *love?*"

What! How did she know?

"Come on, Claire, it all makes sense now. Who *is* it?" She practically knocked me over, begging for information.

"No! I'm not in love," I lied, looking the other way.

"Yeah, *right.*"

Her protective wall reappeared, and she turned her back to me while combing through her purse, pretending to be looking for something she would never find. Surely I'd hurt her feelings, and now she was probably convinced I secretly had a crush on some boy at school and was probably even more furious at me for refusing to tell her who it was. Too bad I couldn't just lie about it and say it was Drew or something. But I sucked at lying, at least to Addie.

Thankfully, she let it drop. I never heard a word about it the rest of the day and hoped she'd forgotten about it altogether. With Addie, you never know.

After school, the wind blew in a dreary cluster of charcoal-blotted clouds, obscuring the sun and putting me in the mood to ignore my homework. I wrapped myself in a blanket and vegged out on the back porch with my iPod, watching the rain pour down until the rushing sound drowned out my thoughts and carried me away where nothing could intrude....

It was dark when I woke up, and I was guessing I'd been asleep for at least an hour. The air smelled musty and clean at the same time (was that even possible?), and it was still raining. I pulled out my earphones and threw off the blanket, ready to finally face my homework, no matter how torturous.

"Hi, Hon," Mom greeted me inside. She was taking off her heels and looked tired, like she'd just gotten home from work. "Where were you?" She gave me that worried look again.

"*Relax*, Mom. I just took a nap on the back porch."

"A nap? Really?"

My defenses were up and ready. "Yeah, what's wrong with that?"

"Nothing." Her eyes shifted from me to the counter, where a couple of paper bags lay. I was suddenly starving when I realized they contained my dinner, and as if on cue, my stomach growled.

"Go ahead and eat," she said, pushing the bags toward me, and heading down the hall. "I'm just going to change out of these clothes."

It seemed like I was eating by myself a lot lately, especially now that Dad was working on some huge acquisition or merger or something. I reached into one of the bags for the chicken burrito I could already smell, and plopped it onto a plate along with a handful of tortilla chips and a wedge of lime. I turned to sit down, and squealed, nearly dropping my dinner, because Daniel was sitting across from me at the table, silently strumming his fingers over the smooth surface, smiling at me like he had a secret.

Mom rushed in half-dressed—one leg in, one leg out of a pair of jeans. "What's wrong, Claire? Are you okay?"

I tried to iron out my smile in order to appear a little more serious for Mom, since she'd rushed back half-naked and all, but Daniel kept waving at me from the table, giving me a very cute, slightly cheesy grin. A stubborn giggle kept inching its way out of my mouth, almost spilling into total laughter. Mom just gaped at me, her bare leg still hanging out of her pants, like she was trying to figure out which swear word to throw at me. Daniel made a quick little motion with his fingers, which I took to interpret as a spider crawling across the table.

Right, spider…good idea.

"Sorry, Mom. I thought I saw a spider. A big one."

"What are you? Four? You scared me, Claire!" she barked at me while hopping into her jeans.

I shrugged my shoulders, wondering why she was always so uptight. I felt like telling her to relax, but decided against it with Daniel right there.

After getting situated at the table, I was about to take a bite of my dinner, when Mom sat across from me, right in Daniel's lap. I tried not to laugh when he made a funny, distorted face and then faded away, only to reappear in the chair next to her.

"Wazso funny?" she asked, her mouth full.

"Nothing." I immediately stuffed my mouth to keep from laughing.

It was tough eating dinner *and* having a decent conversation with Mom while trying not to stare at Daniel, who seemed to be watching my every move. Talk about self-conscious. I tried telling him with my eyes to knock it off so I could eat in peace. But either he couldn't understand, or he was ignoring me for fun.

As was always the case, Mom bored me to death by talking office politics, which was, I think, when Daniel finally got the picture and drifted into the TV room. Being dead did have some perks—I wished I could float away when things got dull, too.

My mind and eyes wandered all over the place while Mom did her talking. I took note of Daniel's attire. Today he was wearing long black and grey plaid shorts and a white t-shirt. Gosh, he looked cute. Was he actually lying on the couch, or did it just look like it? Maybe it was a very controlled float…I made a mental note to ask him later.

Eventually Mom ran out of things to say, and she started cleaning up while I dove into my homework. Was Algebra really that necessary? I could feel each one of my brain cells dying a slow death, and I gave up before even making it to the second problem. I needed my brain more than I needed math. Why did they insist on torturing us like this?

I looked up from the table at Daniel, but he'd disappeared. *Dang it.* Now where'd he go?

Mom settled into the sofa to watch some cheesy soap opera drama, and I headed to my room for some peace and quiet. When I opened the door, Daniel was sitting cross-legged on the floor at the foot of my bed. Curious, I walked right through him to my dresser, wondering how it would feel. Surprisingly, it felt like nothing.

After pulling a fuzzy green sweater over my head, I joined him on the floor with my back against the wall and my knees pulled tight to my chest. He was kind of like a 3-D movie—directly in front of me, but without any substance. I couldn't resist pulling my hand through him like a cloud.

"So, now what?" I said, resting my hand in my lap, then nervously tucking my hair behind my ear.

He responded by shaking his head slowly and deliberately, obviously trying to tell me something.

"What?" I asked, confused. Then I thought I understood. "Oh, I get it... You're kind of like a dog—"

He wrinkled his brow in confusion.

I laughed, explaining, "I mean, since I can't hear you, I'll ask you a question and then you nod *yes* or *no*...or wag your tail...or I can throw you a stick...*you know*."

He laughed.

"Okay, then. But, talk about a one-sided relationship. It's not fair," I complained, settling down into a couple of purple pillows from off the bed. "First things first." I tried not to laugh, but a smile kept slipping out. "Do you *miss* me?"

He squinted his eyes and smiled while shaking his head. I threw a pillow at him, but he didn't even flinch as it sailed right through him, smacking into the opposite wall.

"Wow, you're *good*," I praised. "It must be nice not having to comb your hair or think about what to wear."

He laughed.

"Okay. Time to get serious."

He nodded.

I knew what I wanted to say, but was afraid to get right down to it. I pulled off my glasses and cleaned the lenses with a pillowcase while trying to think up the correct wording. I'd always been better at writing my ideas down on paper rather than speaking them out loud. It was so much easier when no one was looking at you, waiting on your every word.

Taking a deep breath, I replaced my glasses then turned to face Daniel. At first, I found myself studying the fringe of his dark eyelashes, until the pull of his gaze drew me to his rich, chocolate eyes. They seemed so vivid, so alive, as they focused on mine, never blinking. It was impossible to keep the wave of my own self-consciousness at bay.

"Okay, I've been thinking about you. A lot." Because he couldn't respond, it felt like I was talking to myself even though he was right in front of me. But I kept going, determined not to let my flushed cheeks or racing heart stop me. "About last night. I have a ton of questions, if that's okay."

He was so attentive, his eyes never looking past me, or at the clock, or distracted by anything else.

"Let's see…" My mind felt all fuzzy and flustered, littered with a bunch of mental blockers strewn all over the place like an obstacle course. It was what usually happened when I had too much going on in my head all at once. "Can you hear my thoughts?" I asked, finally, stupidly. What a dumb question.

No.

I moved on to the next question, feeling a little more confident. "Are you actually sitting on the ground, like me, or are you floating on top, like a cloud?"

He looked confused, and I realized I hadn't stuck with yes or no.

"I mean… can you feel anything when you're sitting like that?"

No.

"Do you feel pressure?"

No.

"So, what? Do you just float? Without moving? Is that how you do it?"

Yes.

"Interesting."

Okay, now what? That wasn't so bad, but it also wasn't too deep, either.

"Do you remember when you died?" I asked, afraid to jump to serious so quickly.

Yes.

I suddenly felt very melancholy. "Do you know who it was? You know, the guy who shot you? They never caught him."

He shook his head and closed his eyes for a second. I felt a lump of regret forming in my throat. What was I thinking?

Daniel looked up again, staring straight ahead at the wall, and then he placed his hand over mine like he was trying to hold on. I got lost for a second while studying his profile, following the outline of his distinct jaw—rugged, but strikingly beautiful. When he turned and caught me watching him, I felt embarrassed, and quickly refocused.

Next question. "Do you ever watch other people? Like your family, or Addie?"

Yes.

"And, Matthew?"

Yes.

"How's he doing?"

Daniel half nodded, half shrugged. He must know about Matthew, about how he had pretty much disappeared. It depressed me even more, realizing how sad Daniel must feel about it, even more than the rest of us. But I pushed on, anxious to change the subject.

"What is it like? I mean, are you happy where you are?"

Yes.

"Was it scary? Dying?"

No.

"Do you miss living?"

No. Yes.

"Did you whisper to me up at the planetarium?"

He sat up with a look of surprise. I looked down at my fidgeting fingers, playing with my ring again, a little embarrassed, afraid to be wrong. But I was right. He didn't deny it, and his surprised expression revealed the truth. I *knew* it.

"I felt you there," I confessed. "And I heard a voice tell me to move. It was you, wasn't it?"

Yes.

As I stretched out across the floor, resting my head on one of the pillows, the questions kept coming. I couldn't stop thinking, and I forgot to be nervous. It felt good.

"Did you see that thing in my room last night?" I asked.

He didn't respond yes or no, but kept watching me closely, like he was trying to be careful.

"Do you know what it was?" I finally asked, afraid for the answer.

Yes.

"What?" I demanded.

He didn't answer. He even seemed a little preoccupied.

"Is it something horrible?" I re-phrased.

No.

"Well, okay. I guess that's good, I think. Is it part of *your* world?"

Yes.

I hunted for the next question, trying to get to the bottom of my living nightmare. "Is it something I should be afraid of?"

No.

"No? Then why is it so *scary?*" I laughed nervously. But Daniel remained serious. If I didn't need to be afraid, then why the long face?

There was a knock on my door.

"Claire?" It was Mom.

"Yeah?" I jumped to my feet as she peeked in through the door.

"Addie called. She said you weren't answering your phone."

"Oh, sorry. It must be off. What does she want?"

"She says she *has* to come over and borrow a book or something."

Shoot! It better be sooner and not later. "Okay. Thanks, Mom."

"I'm leaving now, okay?" she said.

"Where?"

"To the movie, remember?"

I'd blocked out most of what she was saying at dinner while Daniel was making faces at me. "Oh, yeah, *right*. Who are you going with again?"

"Dad. I *told* you already."

"*Dad?* He's actually going to a movie with you? Wow, it must be a slow day at the office."

I guess she didn't think that was very amusing because she just stood there staring at me with those deep creases she gets between her eyebrows when she's annoyed.

"You're not going anywhere, are you?" she finally said.

"No, I'm a slave to my homework tonight."

"So dramatic."

"'Night, Mom."

But instead of leaving, she remained in the doorway for a couple of seconds, and then suddenly stepped in a little further. *Great*. When I looked around for backup, Daniel had disappeared again. Why did he keep popping in and out like that? It was making me nervous.

Mom was now sitting on my bed, making herself comfy. Oh no.

"Are you going to be okay, Claire?"

Was she serious?

"Mom, it's just a couple hours. I'm sixteen."

"I don't mean tonight," she said. "I mean, generally."

The lecture. I hadn't even seen it coming. She had ambushed me when I was weak with Daniel on the mind.

"I just can't stand to see you so alone all the time," she said, her voice cracking a little. "It's been over four months, Claire. I think it's time to move on."

I took a deep breath and walked to the opposite side of the bed. "Everyone wants me to pretend that Daniel never died. I can't do that, Mom. It isn't magic."

"How does Addie do it then?" she asked, all flustered. "He was *her* brother, not yours."

Ouch.

I didn't want to look at her anymore, afraid of crying or screaming or admitting I loved Daniel, and that I always had. I held my breath and fell backward on the bed, hugging a pillow like it was my life preserver.

"Claire…I'm sorry. I just watch how Addie and Matthew–"

Oh *no.* I threw the pillow against the wall and pulled off my glasses, wiping the tears that were starting to form. "Matthew? You want me to be like Matthew? Mom, do you have any idea what you are saying?" She looked offended, like I'd slapped her. "Matthew is *gone*, Mom!"

"Well, of course he is gone. He's at college."

"No. That's not what I mean. Just because Addie has a social life and Matthew isn't around for you to check up on all the time doesn't mean either of them are doing any better than me," I said, standing. "If you ask me, I'm the sane one. I'm the only one who still believes Daniel is out there...that he's not...not...oh, never mind. You just need to let me deal how I need to deal and quit bugging me about it."

Of course she just sat there and stared, probably wondering where she had gone wrong. When the silence lasted too long, she stood and glanced at her watch. "I have to go, or I'll be late."

"Have fun," I mumbled without looking up.

She walked out the door. A couple of tears sat at the edge of my eyes as her footsteps faded down the hall, and for the first time *ever* I turned to my homework for relief.

CHAPTER
NINE RAIN

Claire

It took me over an hour to do five problems. FIVE! When finished, I leaned forward, rubbing my temples, feeling like I'd just run a marathon. The house was too quiet. I looked around the room. Daniel had not reappeared yet, and Addie was still a no-show. I should have probably called her, but didn't feel like risking a thirty-minute conversation.

"Daniel?" I whispered, wondering why. It wasn't like he'd be hiding under the bed or inside the closet, or anything. Still, where did he go this time?

As I was putting away my homework, the doorbell finally rang. I opened the door to find Addie huddled inside the porch overhang, drenched from the rain.

"Why didn't you drive, or at least bring an umbrella?" I asked, letting her in.

"I couldn't find one that worked, and Mom took my car to the store because hers is in the shop, and I didn't want to wait for her to get back because I have to borrow your Spanish book, I forgot mine at school, and..." she took a giant breath as I closed the door behind her. "That entire worksheet is due tomorrow but I'm only halfway done, and I'm borderline B+ in Spanish. Who wants a B+?"

Me. "You know you're totally dripping water all over the place, Addie."

I grabbed a towel from the bathroom and sopped up her footprints leading down the hall. By the time I caught up to her, she was already changing out of her wet clothes and rummaging through my closet for a dry outfit.

I looked at the clock. 9:47. Fifteen minutes, give or take. It *was* possible. But with Addie...

"So, you *do have* your Spanish book, right?" she asked.

"Yes, it's over here. Just a minute." I pulled it from my bag and handed it to her. "Just give it back tomorrow morning on the way to school."

"You're all done?" she asked accusingly, a mixture of shock and jealousy.

"Yes. But you probably don't want to copy me," I said, joking.

"Don't worry, I wasn't planning on it," she answered, completely missing my joke while flinging her hair around and ringing it out on my floor. *Nice.* "I really need to start on this, Claire. Do you think you can give me a ride home? I know it's like only four houses away, but I don't want to get all wet again."

"Sure, of course. Now that you're in *my* clothes."

"*Funny.*" She rolled her eyes—a special talent of hers.

When I looked around for Mom's keys that were supposed to be on the kitchen counter, I remembered she and her car were at a movie. We were stranded.

"Sorry, Ads," I apologized, empty-handed. "I totally forgot my parents went to a movie."

"With both cars? *Great.*" She walked to the front door, like it was my fault she hadn't planned ahead.

I was starting to get antsy. If she didn't leave here pretty quickly, I would miss my chance with Daniel. "Hey, it's only sprinkling now, Addie. I'll get you an umbrella." I stepped outside onto the porch.

"No." She followed me out the door and collapsed into the bench like she had given up. "I'll just sit here and wait until the rain stops."

But the rain didn't stop. It started pouring again, and my patience was dwindling.

"Addie, maybe you should just go right now. You can run super fast–"

"No. I don't want to get wet again," she said, flipping through the book. That was when I figured out Addie's stubbornness was more about getting her way than keeping dry, and there was nothing I could do about it.

The clock was ticking away. Frantically, my mind searched for a solution, for anything except violence or humiliation to get Addie to leave before my precious four and a half minutes rolled by. Convinced she was being stubborn just to bug me, I placed my glasses on the bench, grabbed the book out of her hands, and ran down the steps out into the rain.

"What the...*Claire!* What are you doing?"

"I'll race you!" I yelled, taunting her. There were definitely advantages to having an over-achiever for a best friend.

"What? I don't want to race you!" She stood with her hands on her hips—her famous pose. "Not in the rain!"

"Come on! Just you and me, Addie, and I bet you lose."

The rain had already started separating my hair into a stringy mess, but the water seemed to wake me up, making me feel a little bit daring. I soaked it all in. Addie stood and leaned against the railing as I egged her on. She seemed genuinely shocked when I turned and took off down the dark road without her.

Thanks to a few scattered lamplights, the street wasn't entirely dark, but I was glad to hear Addie coming up behind me so I could follow her lead. She made sure to thoroughly splash me as she passed, and then sprinted the rest of the way. Feigning exhaustion, I slowed to a jog until I reached her driveway.

She stood at the top of the steps, smiling down at me. "You really need to get in shape, Claire."

"Wow," I praised, handing her my book. "I didn't know you had it in you. I'm *very* impressed."

"Why? You never even had a chance."

Exactly.

"See you in the morning," I said, heading back to my house.

"Thanks. I'll probably be up all night. I have a chem test tomorrow, too."

I spun around. "Please don't wake me up with a frantic phone call at two a.m., okay?"

Addie shut the door behind her as I jogged back up the street, toward my house. At the halfway point, I slowed to a stop and stared up at the random droplets floating down, sparkling in the lamplight. They looked like falling stars trickling into my face, and for a second I forgot about everything—even Daniel.

Lightning illuminated the lake, followed by the reverberating echo of thunder. I paused for a second, trying to anticipate the next one. But when I turned back to the road, Daniel was there in front of me. I jerked backward and let out a little scream. "Daniel!"

His laugh was silent, but completely lit up his face.

"Where have you been?" I asked with a smile, wringing out my heavy hair.

He pointed up.

"What, you were in the sky?"

No.

Just not here, I said to myself, getting it. The rain picked up, but I couldn't absorb any more water unless I turned into a sponge, so I didn't care anymore. My underwear was soaked, yet Daniel walked beside me dirt-dry. Talk about surreal.

When something gentle touched my skin, I looked down to find his fingers gripping my arm. It was time again.

Yes.

I let him pull me to him, my own hands around his back. The rain was quickly drenching him now, too, matting his hair to his forehead, and I looked up at him in anticipation, remembering our first kiss, silently begging for more.

Instead, he took my hand and led me away from the road through the pine trees until we stopped beneath a canopy of dripping leaves overlooking the lake. He faced me, his dark eyes intense, like they were trying to speak. I held still…waiting, wondering what was next. It felt like all speech had abandoned me as the tension hovered between us. At last, his fierce, quiet lips found mine, chasing away all apprehension in a single, abbreviated second. I responded instantly, feeling myself go soft in his arms, kissing him back with an unexpected craving that gnawed at my sanity and choked out my breath.

Too soon he stopped.

Before I could protest, he kissed my cheek. Then, as if in slow motion, his lips traveled upward along the edge of my cheekbone, barely touching my skin. At my ear, his warm breath contrasted with the cool air, sending chills screaming through me as his familiar voice, calculating and smooth, whispered like it had a life of its own. "I've been trying to figure this out," he said.

"What?" I asked, dreamily, still lost somewhere else.

"That thing," he said, "You know, in your room last night?"

I shuddered.

He dropped his hands to his sides uneasily then grasped my hands again, as if he'd mistakenly let go. "It's not a *thing.*' It's a…how do I put it? It's something, or someone just like me. Whatever *I am.*"

I pulled back slightly, but he pressed me back to him, and I didn't resist.

"If he's just like you, then why does *'he'* look like a demented piece of string?" I asked.

"Really? That's what he looks like to you?"

"Yes. What does he look like to you?"

"Like he's supposed to. Like a person. The string thing is probably just your imagination," he said, slightly patronizing.

"What?" I asked, a little annoyed. "You think I'm making it up?"

Daniel squeezed my hand. "No, *no.* I just think you're not seeing the same thing I am. Maybe your imagination is getting in the way of what's really there. At least that's what seems to make sense."

I thought about that for a second. "So, he's not some weird science-fiction-looking creature?"

"Um, no. He's just another… *ghost*. Like me, I guess."

"Ghost," I repeated. "That doesn't seem to fit you."

"It doesn't? Then what am I?"

Daniel felt warm and solid and alive. There was no way he was a ghost—at least not right now. "I don't know," I said. "You're YOU. You're the same Daniel I have always known, but without a body. A ghost is something made up for scary stories."

"Boo*ooo*," he whispered, his breath sending chills up and down my neck as he kissed me again, obliterating my concentration. "Your boyfriend is a ghost, Claire."

Boyfriend! He said boyfriend.

My eyes were still closed, my lips tingling when I felt him pull away. I looked up at him—to the old, carefree Daniel with the disheveled, but now soaked, hair falling into animated eyes, a pair of adorable dimples, and a look that meant either adoration or mischief.

"So, who is this *ghost* friend of yours?" I asked, suddenly curious, definitely anxious. "What's his name? How did he die? What does he want? Why does he haunt *me?*"

Daniel seemed to suppress a bit of frustration as he inhaled. "I don't know yet. He's a little…unpredictable. I'm still trying to figure him out."

"Well, figure it out," I begged, squeezing his hands. "I can't stand the thought of seeing it…or *him* again."

Daniel suddenly looked more serious, maybe even worried, which made me nervous. It seemed like he was trying to hide something; I noticed it instantly when he looked off to the side for a second before coming back to me.

"Do you know him?" I asked. "Like, are you guys friends?"

"No. *No.* I don't know him at all. But he seems to know *me.* From before."

"Before?"

"Before I died. He said something to me, about how I..."

"What?"

"Well...for some reason, he thinks I killed him."

"What! *You?* Obviously he has you mixed up with someone else—"

"No, I don't think so. He knew my name. Says we were both the same age when we died. Said a lot of stuff that makes it sound more...personal."

"*Did* you kill him?" I asked, suddenly curious.

"No!" Daniel looked shocked I'd even asked it.

"Okay, okay. Sorry. I just wanted to make sure."

He smiled, almost laughed, and then pulled me closer to him. I thought maybe I had snapped him out of his seriousness, even though my own mind felt stretched out and twisted like a rubber band.

"Did he tell you what he wants?" I asked. "I'm really not that interesting. Didn't you tell him that?"

Daniel continued to smile, but remained quiet.

"What do I do if he comes again? Do you have any suggestions?"

"Not yet. *You* haven't come up with anything?" he teased.

"Me? I'm still trying to get used to the idea of being able to see you, much less a ghost who's trying to suck out my soul."

"Suck out your—*what?*" Daniel laughed again.

I was starting to get self-conscious. "Never mind." I decided to shut up.

He leaned forward until his head was level with mine, our foreheads touching. "Claire, he's just like me. That's not so bad, if you can remember that."

"Kind of like what my speech teacher told us to do when we're nervous."

"Sure," he agreed quickly, then backpedaled as he stood up straight. "Wait, *what?*"

"He said if I get too nervous during a speech I should just imagine my audience in their underwear." A familiar smile emerged as he wrapped his arms around my waist and held me. I wanted to stay forever in his arms. Soon, I felt the touch of his fingers at my neck, and I looked up to find him drawing in close, his lips brushing my forehead, then my cheeks and lips, lingering there until he laughed. "You're kinda funny, Claire. How come I didn't know that before?"

I weakly nodded, balancing up on my toes, tightly grasping his neck as he kissed me again. Just as our lips parted, he whispered, "It's about gone now."

"What?"

"The time."

The rain let up, as if in alliance with Daniel. I clasped his hands, holding them close to my heart while trying to remember their faint, distinctive impression.

In my ear, he whispered, "Don't worry, Claire. I'll keep you safe."

Before I had a chance to answer, his touch and impression, his warmth and heartbeat, all dissolved into nothing as I stood there, seemingly alone in the rain.

Daniel

I knew someone else was there right away. The chills bombarded me as soon as my connection with Claire ended, but I waited until after accompanying her safely home before turning around to face my visitor.

"What do you want?" I asked.

The woman was hovering about fifteen feet off the ground, floating on a tree branch like it was a bench. I wondered if she thought it more intimidating this way. I guess it kind of was.

She smiled.

It was the same lady as before—the one with the crazy hair. Except this time she was wearing some sort of puffy white nightgown, which looked a little graveyard-ghost-*like* from some old gothic novel.

"You still following me?" I asked.

She shook her head, her lips pressed together like she was afraid to speak. But it didn't look like she wanted to leave, either. Her eyes widened as she surveyed our surroundings, and then she drifted downward until we were face to face. Purposefully darting around me, she zigzagged through the trees as if looking for something, and then halted in front of me. With a finger to her lips, she said, "Shhhhh."

"Lady, I really don't have time for this," I said. Okay, so maybe I did, but it sounded much more confrontational when I put it that way.

"I came to warn you," she whispered.

"About what? Why are you whispering?"

She drifted closer until her lips were at my ear, making me just slightly uncomfortable. "He comes after your connection with her."

"He? Who? *What?*"

"He haunts her. You let it happen."

"So…What do you want me to do?"

She still appeared nervous, looking everywhere but in my eyes. "Stop connecting to her, dummy."

"Wait... You *mean...?*" But I trailed off, understanding too well. I didn't want to believe it.

The rain started up again, first a few random raindrops spattering through us, and then a shower escalating to a deafening torrent, drowning out any other sound. I watched her through the downpour, waiting for more. But she seemed finished, and suddenly turned, shooting off through the trees toward the lake.

I chased after her. "How do you know all this? Who are you?"

But she was picking up speed, zooming across the lake and over the rooftops, until all I could see was the tips of her hair, trailing behind her.

I gave up chase, stopping at the far side of the lake, watching her fade into the night.

CHAPTER
TEN THE WICKED TRUTH

Claire

Daniel was gone… Gone to wherever he goes.

I ran through a few puddles to the slippery porch, dripping water across the deck, and then tumbled onto the mostly-dry bench. A bolt of lightning tore through the sky, followed by a loud crack of thunder, nearly startling me off my seat. After peeling off my shoes and socks, I grabbed my glasses, and rushed inside.

A scalding shower soothed my brittle nerves. I probably drained the whole house of hot water, but right then I didn't care. After bundling myself up in a warm towel with another one twisted around my head like a giant Q-tip, I made it back to my room, still shivering. The rain had finally given up, the sound of steady dripping coming from the overhanging trees.

Somewhere down the hall, a door slammed shut. A cold shiver like an icy bead of sweat shot up my spine, bringing back to life my sleeping fear from last night. I tried pushing it away but couldn't. No matter how much Daniel had tried to make my ghost visitor seem harmless, the thought of seeing and hearing that thing again made me anxious.

After dressing in my dark closet where no one or *thing* could see me, I put on my glasses and peeked through the crack of the door, looking for anything that might be lurking out there. So far, so good—my bed was still a mess from the morning, the floor strewn with books, clothes, and the pillow I had thrown at the wall; everything was exactly how it should be. Still, I felt like hiding out in the closet under a pile of blankets for the night, just to be safe.

A gust of wind burst through the window, whisking my curtains inward. I rushed to the window and slammed it shut, then took a deep breath and adjusted my glasses. For some reason those two flimsy lenses felt like an extra layer of protection.

That was before the lights went out.

Great.

My hands trembled, even though the rest of me remained trans-fixed, lost in the dim reflection staring back at me in the glass. *She* looked scared—this person in the window with deep, dark circles under her eyes.

Behind me, I heard a faint creaking sound, like the bedroom door had opened. During one eternal minute of paralysis, I wondered if it was the result of some sort of delayed wind, or if something or someone had pushed it. When I finally turned around, to my relief nobody was there—just dark silence in the corner of my room.

I shuffled across the floor without tripping or falling, wavering at the side of the bed while trying to lasso a little confidence before it shriveled down to nothing. The seconds ticked by, the eerie silence holding me captive until a slight tickle found the inside of my ear, like the wings of a mosquito had brushed up against my skin. Convinced someone was there, I spun around again to find I was still alone, but unprotected and vulnerable, an impossibly easy target there in the dark.

Where was Daniel, anyway? Shouldn't he be here about now?

I looked right…then left…catching only glimpses of patterned shadows on the walls or the glimmer of something reflected in the newly unveiled moon.

Nothing…nothing…still nothing…

And then in an invisible affront, the bedroom door slammed shut, and *it* attacked, sucking the air by my left ear. *"Ssssrooophhhh."*

I screamed, leaping over the bed to the light switch, willing it to work, repeatedly flipping it up and down without success. The dark, ribbony shape advanced toward me, wrapping itself around my wrists like a possessed rope, a slow, cold burning of ice on my skin. The harder I tried to pull it off, the more it stung.

"Get off!" I yelled, finally peeling it away and running out into the hallway where I stopped at Matthew's empty room, trying to decide where to go next. The windows and doors creaked against the wind, rattling my nerves even more. The hallway felt like a tunnel—dark and confining without windows or lights. I peered down the hall, toward the kitchen. A long shadow spread across the entrance, outlining a pale silhouette.

Daniel?

Hopeful, I tiptoed toward it, wondering if my imagination had gotten the best of me, like Daniel had said. I tried recalling his exact phrase, those simple words that calmed me so well an hour ago. I even tried to suck it up and be brave until a thought struck me, holding me back.

What if the shadow at the end of the hall wasn't Daniel? I froze at the bathroom door, the small of my back pressed into the wall, my head tilted upward as I waited there contemplating which direction to go. What if Daniel wasn't here at all? What if the shadow down the hall was waiting for me…waiting to strike?

Not willing to find out, I turned back. My hand shook against the wall as I felt my way backwards, creeping past Matthew's room and my own. My door hung wide open, but I hurried past, afraid to look inside. Counting in a low whisper upon each calculated step, I hoped to distract my mind and settle my nerves before reaching my parents' room at the end of the hall.

Their thick, heavy door wasn't latched, but only opened just a sliver. I placed my ear at the crack, my fingertips lightly touching the door, and listened for any sort of unwelcome noise or movement. All was quiet.

I nudged the door open with my foot, though it only moved an inch as a loud groan echoed through the empty hall. After another push, I slipped in and shut the door behind me, stepping straight into the path of an intruder. He was across the room near the foot of the bed, watching me, his piercing, beady eyes and pale face engulfed by a thick head of jet-black hair. His nose was long and narrow, cheekbones high and defined, and his face almost too delicate in contrast to all that hair and layers of black clothing.

I tried screaming, but my voice was painfully absent as the hot sensation of horror paralyzed me. All that squeaked from my mouth was an amphibian-like croak…and then nothing. I held a hand to my lips, searching for the words that had gone missing as my heart plunged into the bottom of my stomach.

His smile grew as he gracefully floated toward me—which was when I realized this was not a normal intruder. Somehow, somewhere my mind had made the jump from haunted ribbon to real-life ghost—and now I could *see* him. The thought made me lightheaded.

I spun around and attacked the door handle with fury, fumbling with it miserably until it finally gave way and the door opened. Gulping for air, I ran down the hall into the kitchen and stopped at the sink, nearly losing it, not quite sure where to go or what to do.

How do you run from a ghost?

I tried recalling what Daniel had said about *it* being just like him, determined the only option was to face the stupid thing. Except, I didn't have it in me—couldn't even face a fake haunted house on Halloween. This guy was for real…and was now suddenly by the sliding door.

His eyes met mine as he floated effortlessly toward me, a strange look of satisfaction on his face. He stopped a few feet away, almost like he was trying to decide his next move. I gripped the counter, feeling weak and dizzy, trying not to faint.

"What do you want?" I heard my voice squeak, though it sounded nothing like my own. I wondered if the ghost could hear, or speak, or both—if he was anything like Daniel.

His eyes drifted around the room like he was scanning the kitchen for something in particular, and then stopped at the black marble island, where the glowing moon lit up a tall vase filled with drooping white hydrangeas. He drew in close to the flower arrangement, his face level with the vase.

I watched him through the glass, though I didn't want to, my eyes shifting back and forth—from him, to the flowers, back to him, wondering what he was doing. He remained focused, his thin jaw drawn rigidly tight. For a moment, nothing happened, and then he brought his arm forward into the vase, knocking it across the room as it hit a cabinet and fell to the floor, bursting apart into big watery chunks.

I screamed and jerked backwards, trying to comprehend how the bundle of flowers now lay in a pool of water on the floor. Pain signals began radiating from my arm as something warm oozed through my sleeve. I looked down and gasped at the blood, frantically searching for the roll of paper towels by the sink. The pain had doubled by the time I found them, and while whipping the roll around my arm, I realized the ghost was now watching me, his expression cold and malicious.

I dropped the paper towels and ran out of the kitchen, back down the hall, trying the lights as I passed each switch. But they were all still useless. I stopped, breathless, realizing I couldn't keep running away; there was nowhere else to run. The lights were not coming on any time soon, my parents would be gone for at least another hour, and for some reason Daniel was a no-show.

"He's just like me," was what Daniel had said. He's *just a ghost*…not a demon or a monster, not something from my nightmares. Just. A ghost. Like Daniel.

Okay, *Not so bad…not so bad…not so bad…*

My heart felt like it was beating through my chest. I closed my eyes, taking a deeper breath, and exhaling. In-hale…exhale…inhale…until I felt a clear, calm impression pushing its way through the adrenalin.

I thought I could sense the ghost coming up behind me, but I didn't want to move or open my eyes, for fear of losing the stillness I'd discovered. Instead of running away, I tried focusing on the intangible energy stirring around in my mind, reminding me that *I* was alive. That *I* had a body. This was *my* world, not his.

My heart gradually slowed, as if my controlled breathing had convinced it to come back from the edge. Time felt frozen, the circling darkness and quiet the only things moving.

I opened my eyes.

Daniel was in front of me now, watching me. My heart skipped. It felt like I could see warmth and love shoot out from him like a prism of colors...a deep, moody blue trumped by fiery red at the simmering memory of our first kiss just...when was it? Yesterday? I looked down to the silver reminder of Daniel still on my right hand, and twisted it around and around my finger, each turn bringing to the present thoughts and memories of him. Before long, I fell into a different place as the emotions attached to each memory engulfed me. I could feel myself smiling, and exhaled, the shocking relief of peace almost forcing me to my knees.

Daniel was across the hall now, but still eyeing me closely. With a finger on his lips, he motioned to something behind me. I turned around to find the ghost only a foot away, watching me. Now his eyes were wide and roaming, and he seemed slightly confused, maybe even a little annoyed as he drifted through me, down the hall, into my parents' room.

Curiously, I followed him down there, watching as he floated through the room in an aimless circle. He did seem less daunting now, even smaller than I remembered, and I realized I was seeing him exactly how Daniel saw him—just some annoying guy with crazy hair.

Not so scary.

The thought should have cheered me up, or at least given me enough confidence to stand up to him, but he was suddenly moving toward me. When I looked into the cold, endless black in his eyes, I panicked and forgot how *not* to be afraid. Whatever evil or darkness the ghost possessed started seeping back into my mind, like he'd found a crack in my armor.

I backed into the wall as he flew at me and through me, overpowering my senses as an opaque shadow flooded my vision, the horrible screeching noise echoing in my ears and knotting my stomach. *"Sssrooophhhh."* He hovered over me, and I sunk to my knees, squeezing my eyes shut. I couldn't feel his touch when he put his hands on the sides of my face, but there was a strange, sickening sensation that felt like my face was imploding.

I refused to look at him. My heart slipped back into its pounding frenzy, the fear bleeding through and burning my nerves. Somehow, I could no longer run, scream or imagine any warm memories of Daniel. I felt too weak to even try. I was just cold and empty and afraid, and felt myself falling away into my own little black hole.

Everything went dark after that.

When my eyes opened, my body felt weak. I turned over and leaned against the wall, surveying the empty hallway still crawling in darkness. The air felt a little lighter, and I could breathe again, like I was emerging from an airtight closet...or a coffin.

Tucking my damp, stringy hair behind my ears, I looked around for any evidence of my real-life nightmare.

But the ghost was gone.

I expected Daniel to still be there, but couldn't find him. He'd disappeared along with my strength. My breathing was slow and shallow, my eyes felt swollen, and tears stained my face. I crept through the darkness to my room, collapsed into bed, and fell asleep, too exhausted to be scared anymore.

Daniel

Claire looked tired and worried…and beautiful. She was sprawled across her bed with headphones in her ears, reading a book. It was daytime, so she couldn't see me hanging out in the corner by the desk, immersed in her profile.

I felt guilty for having been a no-show for almost a week now. She wasn't very happy about it, either. I wanted to come back, to touch her again, or at least explain what was going on, but was afraid to connect to her after what happened last time.

Her eyes were heavy with dark shadows that seemed to magnify her mood, and her left arm was still bandaged—both evidence of a night gone horribly wrong. It was the vase that really shook me. I was in total shock when it burst. How did he do it? I was afraid to even think about it.

Claire's phone buzzed on her stomach, pulling me back into the room. I could hear Addie's voice through the phone, making me miss my little sister's enthusiasm and the way she was always laughing and making everyone smile.

Claire slid off her bed and wandered down the hall. I drifted through a couple of walls into the kitchen, where she was leaning against the counter, eating a handful of grapes. The conversation was mostly one-sided. Every couple of minutes Claire interrupted with, *"seriously?"* or *"yes,"* or *"I know!"* while discussing obscenely uninteresting things for over a half an hour.

Eventually, she wandered outside and lay on a bench. I zoomed past her, down the hill to a eucalyptus tree. Her voice ambled toward me as my mind ran in circles looking for a connection to her ghost tormentor. It drove me crazy that this wacko had the whole world to mess with, but for some reason he'd chosen to haunt Claire. I wanted to tell him to get a life. Ironic, huh?

At some point Claire went back inside, though I wasn't paying attention anymore. My mind was too busy trying to swallow my new reality—that if I ever wanted to connect to Claire again, I had to take care of an unwanted ghost.

It was time for another Memory Trace. If I *had* killed him like he claimed, then that memory should be in my past, lost somewhere in my subconscious, *right*? Who could forget something like that?

I started to rewind, trying to search for one forgotten moment in a million, combing through every second, every day... turning the clock backward... trying to focus on any memories tinged with danger or anxiety I could've easily suppressed over the years.

He had to be there, somewhere.

"You killed me." His words hovered over me briefly, nearly floating away. I held onto them, trying to remember that voice and face and the look in those eyes...hoping they'd lead me to an answer. He seemed so convinced. Maybe there was some truth to it.

I dove in...

On the very top of the pile were the easy, shallow memories— things that had happened over and over again in the same places with the same people, day after day. Which meant I had to dig deeper, beyond familiar faces of friends and family, past my house and the lake, past school and track meets and mountain biking...even further than that…to a circular playground with a rusted blue spiral slide surrounded by spider-like domes that were perfect for climbing. I saw myself tirelessly bounding to the top in celebration, like a king or a tyrant, my heart pounding in relief…and then I moved along…

To a crowded mall with hundreds of people squishing me with their funny bags and boxes. I try to look up at the gigantic Christmas tree filled with basketball-sized ornaments, but can't see anything above my nose. Then I realize I'm lost, and my heart thumps like a drum. I feel tears falling down my cheeks and I spin in circles, crying for my mom…

Next.

I am running down the shore of a strange beach, the pebbly sand sticking to my soles and in between my toes when a huge wave of salt and sea takes me out. I feel the pull of the monster ocean grabbing for me. As it tries to drag me into its mouth, the rough sand burns my eyes, trapping my ears inside a tunnel. I find my footing and stand up, the water receding, taking with it pockets of sand beneath my feet. Finally I'm free. I run up to the dry sand, shivering and spitting and blubbering all at once…

There was real terror in that memory. However, I felt compelled to move on until something felt strikingly familiar, pulling at me like déjà vu.

I am straddling a bike, speeding along as fast as possible. It's dusk, and I'm riding through a little park lined with shoebox houses trapped between narrow driveways. As I weave in and out of parked cars like I'm leading an obstacle course, my new black and tan beagle, Oscar, runs alongside me as I clutch his leash. We swerve around the towering trees in wide angles before stuttering along the bumpy grass and then on to the bike path leading up a huge, green hill.

Dad and little Addie dawdle together way down at the bottom of the hill. They are much too slow for Oscar and me. Impatiently, I race ahead, feeling an oversized smile overtaking my face. Oscar breaks free from my grasp, and before I know it, he's so far ahead I can't keep up with him. That means trouble. For him and for me.

Oscar is only a few months old and very naughty. Now his leash trails behind him as he yips and yaps at everyone, probably bragging about how he just got away from his owner. I pedal even faster, trying to catch up, thinking I'd better get to him quick—especially after that peeing accident last night (his, not mine).

Without looking or caring where I'm going, I pedal as fast as I can, wondering what's taking Dad and Addie so long. Like a rocket, I fly off the curb and into the street, my eyes focused on catching that crazy Oscar. He's a lot less trouble when he's asleep.

Before making it across the street, I skid to a stop at the sound of a loud screeching. It completely drowns out Oscar's howls. When I realize what's happening, that the horrible noise is coming from a motorcycle headed straight for Oscar, I lose my breath along with the ability to think, or even scream. All I can do is watch the hazy headlight turn in circles around us just before I jump off my bike and run. As fast as I can. For Oscar.

The motorcycle and I reach Oscar at the same time. I pull him into my arms and squeeze my eyes shut at the exploding noise. The motorcycle skids across the pavement as the metal and rubber screech in protest, but somehow miss us. A stinging pain rips into my knee, and I hear the sound of breaking glass and crunching metal behind me as the driver flies off his bike, straight into a tree. I can't see because my eyes are too blurry from tears and my shaking head.

The world goes quiet until Oscar whimpers.

Even though I don't want to, I have to look at the driver all crumpled and mangled beneath the oak tree. Everything about him looks wrong. His head is twisted sideways even though the rest of him is turned the other direction, and his black eyes are wide open, staring straight at me. I see the blood. There's too much of it oozing out through the thick pile of black hair on top of his head, like a slippery sauce spilling all over the ground.

Dad, who has been yelling my name for a long time now, rushes over to me, picking me up in his arms and asking if I am all right. I can't stop crying, even after he keeps telling me everything is okay, and reassuring me that I'm not in trouble.

'Shhhh,' he whispers in my ear over and over again, his warm hands smoothing my head and tickling the back of my neck. It seems like I will never stop shaking or crying. Ever…

Stop.

Wake up.

The sirens faded along with the memory, until everything around me was dark and I was sliding forward through a speeding tunnel of light and color to the present, to Hidden Lake. I felt like I was suffocating, and sunk to the ground, burying my head in my knees, trying to grasp what I'd just seen.

The ghost was right. I *had* killed him, and I thought I was going to be sick. *I created a monster.* My anger suddenly felt much more complicated.

The nausea along with the spinning memory subsided as I scanned the neighborhood, eventually focusing on the glassy water of the lake reflecting blue, dotted with a couple of stray cotton ball clouds. More than anything I felt a sense of relief to be back in the present, away from the contorted, bloody face of the victim I now recognized too well. But I couldn't move. Not now. *I'd killed someone.*

I wondered what it meant for Claire.

As soon as her face registered in my mind, I felt the pull toward her, and shifted to wherever she was—which by then happened to be at school. *Great.* Reluctantly, I followed her around most of the day, mulling over what to do about her, and more specifically this slowly unfolding nightmare.

Claire and Addie ate lunch outside on the quad while I watched everyone hanging out in their little groups and cliques, all talking and laughing, like what they had to say was the most important thing in the world. Just stuff like last night's sitcom or next week's party. I'd never noticed it before, but everyone here seemed so young, so naïve. *Crap,* it wasn't like I was even that much older than these guys. Is that what death did to you? Turn you into a philosopher?

I had to get away from here.

As I made my exit, a spidery chill crawled up my arms—this time more subtle, but definitely still there. When it reached my shoulders and tingled down my spine, I peered through the crowd of familiar faces, trying to find one that didn't belong. But there were too many bodies everywhere, making it impossible to pick out a ghost among a sea of mortals. I focused on my feet as the crowd traipsed through me, and a light wind blew, scattering a mixture of leaves and wrappers and debris until it was impossible to tell the leaves from the garbage.

The bell rang, prompting everyone to get on with life and file back to class. I scanned the vacated quad and spotted the trespasser—the ghost lady with the crazy hair who seemed to be stalking me. She was leaning against the vending machines outside the cafeteria. Everything clicked, and I realized she was the ghost I had seen here just after I'd died. She wore the same pink robe and fuzzy slippers as before, with messy hair that had never met a comb.

Had she been following me around this whole time?

Her lips turned upward, and she looked me in the eye, like she had something on her mind. I drifted nearer, making a point to keep my distance. With a long, bony finger, she motioned at me. "Over here," she said, her voice deep and mellow.

I stopped a few feet from her. And, whoa—up close she was a real mess. Her face was caked with an orangey-glow powdery substance, her eyelids a bright purple like she'd used crayons to color them in, and her lips varied between dark and light pink, each horizontal line on her lips obscenely magnified. Even *I* could do better than that.

She batted her eyelashes, which looked like black, hairy spider legs. "I know something you don't," she said.

"Okay. Anything different than what you told me the other night?" I asked.

"It's about Aden."

"Who?"

"Aden."

"Who's Aden?" I tried not to stare at her peeling face. Seriously, as a ghost she had so many options. Why choose that?

"You don't know much, do you?"

I shrugged my shoulders.

"Well, let me break it down for you."

"Okay?"

"Do you mind if I have a smoke first?"

I wondered if she were as mental when she was alive as she appeared now. "You do realize you don't have any lungs, right?"

"Habit," she said, fishing a cigarette from her pocket and lighting up. She even went through the motions of the whole thing—one big, fake production. I was curious if she also imagined the poison seeping into her non-existent lungs, too. One time, I'd tried eating a hamburger but thanks to my lousy imagination it didn't taste all that great.

She finished. The cigarette vanished into her magenta lips at the same time her pink robe getup disappeared. Now she was all dressed up in heels and a black, sparkly dress, her hair done up, her makeup no longer sliding down her face, her fingernails long and red. It was definitely an improvement. I was speechless.

"That's much better," she said with a deep, throaty breath. "Well, hello there, Daniel. I'm Nico. I don't think I introduced myself last time." She extended her slender, bare arm. I pretended to shake her hand, but it seemed weird. Probably not something I wanted to repeat.

"You know my name," I said, wondering how, but not enough to ask.

"Let's just say I've been around."

Okay.

"Like I said, I have crucial information for you." She looked over my head and behind me, her eyes roving. "But we need to make it quick before he finds out, or I won't be able to follow him around anymore," she said.

I pretended to sit on a nearby bench while Nico paced back and forth in front of me in ridiculously high heels. "How do I even know I want your information?" I asked.

"Believe me, you will. But hold on...*if* I give you this information—*new* information, mind you—then you have to agree to something in return."

"I'm not sure I'm interested," I said.

"That ghost who's been haunting your girlfriend? You don't want to know more about him?"

Fine. "Okay, what do you want from me?" I asked, wondering what her request might be. How bad could it be?

"What are you worried about, kiddo? I just want a little companionship."

My face must have shown the shock I felt because she made a gesture like she was slapping my back. "Oh! I'm not that kind of woman. *Crimony.* I was only talking about a little outing. As friends. In case you haven't noticed, there aren't a whole lot of us around."

An *outing?* Was she serious? I wasn't looking for more friends.

"I like movies," she said.

"Movies. You want me to go with you to a movie."

"You have a problem with that?"

"I guess not." *This better be worth it.* "Why do you care about me...or Claire, anyway? I don't even know you."

She paced to the vending machine and back. "Let's just say I don't like it when our kind interferes with their kind," she said, clasping her hands together. There were about twenty rings and bracelets there now that I hadn't noticed before.

"*Our* kind? *Their* kind? We're not aliens, you know." This lady made my sister look... well...kind of boring.

"So you're that type, huh? No imagination, whatsoever. You're not going to get very far here, you know."

"Um, that isn't really my goal. And I thought you said you had new information. I already stopped connecting to Claire like you told me to, so unless you're here to tell me you made a mistake the first time you warned me, then I think we're done talking."

She sidled up next to me on the bench, her eyes scanning the empty quad. "I thought for sure that would stop him. Really, I did. But Aden figured a way around it. A way to hurt Claire." Her eyes stopped on mine, like they were frozen.

"How do I even know you're telling the truth?" I asked. "Maybe you're working with Aden, trying to keep me and Claire apart. Come to think of it, last time you weren't exactly helpful by leading me all over the place. He *haunted* her while I was away, you know."

Nico looked guilty. Her eyelids dropped and she turned her head away from me, studying a pink-flowered bush, like it was a mirror. Suddenly, she zoomed to the other end of the bench. "I admit it. That was my mistake. For a while now I've been trying to figure out how he haunts her, which, come to find out, is because of YOU. You just happened to catch me following him that night. But you shouldn't have left Claire. That was *your* fault, not mine."

"Why didn't you just come clean instead of running away from me like you were up to something?"

"I was still figuring everything out. Really. I *still* am—which is why you need to trust me," she said weakly.

"Trust you? You're like a circus act. How do you expect me to take you seriously?"

Her eyes bulged. "Ha! That hurts, you know. Have you always been so judgmental and cruel? I wonder what she sees in you."

"Just tell me something I don't already know."

"Fine. But, for future reference, you should work on your people skills. You're not making any friends here with this kind of attitude."

I stared long and hard at her, waiting for her "so-called" information. Finally, she spit it out. "Aden got someone to help him. Someone mortal."

"Come *on*. Who could possibly be helping him? He's a ghost."

"He's done it before," she said.

"Done *it?* What does *it* mean?"

"Worked with a mortal." Her eyes grew wide, and she whipped her head back and forth, like she was looking for something. And then she was fading, the vending machines behind her beginning to show through. "Just keep a closer eye on your girlfriend for now," she said, growing dimmer by the second. "And keep that mortal away from her, too. I have to go."

Back to her pink robe and slippers, to the nutcase look, she slowly disappeared into the lit-up rows of candy bars behind her.

"Wait. You never told me—why do you want to help me?" I asked as the opaque version of her lit up yet another cigarette and inhaled.

Her eyes drooped, as if she were sleepy. "I don't."

"You don't?"

"No. I want to help Claire, not you."

"Why Claire, then?"

"If you must know, Claire-bear happens to be my niece and let's just say I'm not exactly thrilled with all the attention she's been getting lately...especially by some ghost with a vendetta who's out of his mind. Now start thinking of a movie you want to see. And make it a funny one."

CHAPTER
ELEVEN BLIND DATE

Daniel

Claire had a date tonight—a mercy date Addie guilted her into. Mrs. James was probably already sending out the wedding invitations (wait, that wasn't funny). The whole thing annoyed Claire. Me, too.

The sun was just starting to set, but it was still light enough that Claire couldn't see me yet. She had already started getting ready for her date, and I was sitting behind her on the bed, watching as she sat in front of her mirror. She started in on her mascara, her fingers gripping a neon-orange plastic wand as she meticulously dabbed black stuff along her eyelashes. I watched intently—more so than I'd ever watched her do anything...

And then I lost focus to the memory of the motorcycle accident, wondering how I could've blocked out something so traumatic. Over the years I remember a few sporadic flashes of a barking dog or screeching tires, even the sick smell of blood...*that's right*... as a kid, a bloody nose made me nauseated though I never knew why. Until now, I figured those random memories were just bits and pieces of a recurring nightmare...had no idea they were flashes of truth.

My parents probably kept quiet about it, hoping I'd forget. Lucky for them I did, because the memory as a whole was horrifying now. The thought that I'd been the cause of someone's death made me sick, but what could I do about it now? Did he expect me to somehow change the past? Maybe tell him sorry?

I wondered how old I was when it happened. *How old was I now?* When you stop having birthdays, do you stay that age forever, or do you keep counting the years like everyone else?

"Oh my… *Daniel!*" Claire yelled, turning around to face me.

Oops. Who, *me?* I smiled, shrugging my shoulders.

"What are you *doing?*" she demanded quietly, a pointed finger pushing through my chest. I could tell she was mad, excited and annoyed, all rolled into one. "Where have you *been?*"

I wanted to explain everything to her. But right now, all I could do was smile because of the huge black smudge that marred her otherwise adorable face.

"What?" she asked.

Laughing, I motioned to the mirror behind her. She finally understood and turned around.

"It's *your* fault," she said, slightly grinning, before disappearing out the door. A few minutes later she returned with a wet towel, carefully dabbing at her face until her eyes were perfect along with the rest of her. I wandered up behind her, resting my chin at her shoulder as she finished up and put on her glasses. Black ones this time.

"I'll be right back." She pushed her chair backwards and walked through me to her closet, closing the door.

I waited on the bed until she emerged dressed in a long black shirt and dark jeans, a green scarf hanging around her neck. Her strawberry-auburn-gold-*who knows what color it really is*-hair fell in waves across her shoulders and her big, brown eyes watched me strangely. I was thinking her lips looked irresistibly tempting, and realized I was staring at her like an idiot...and turned away.

"Where have you been?" she asked quietly. "Do you realize it's been over a week? I've been wondering this whole time when...*if*...I was ever going to see you again. You can't just disappear like that, Daniel. Not without telling me first."

Over a week, really? I must've missed a couple of days somewhere in there.

I opened my mouth to respond, but remembered it wouldn't do any good. The fact that she couldn't hear me was especially unfair, because I had no way to defend myself.

"*You*" she whispered, shoving her finger in the middle of my face, "are in trouble."

"Sorry," I mouthed.

Addie barged in. "You ready, Claire?"

Claire spun around to face her. "I can't believe you're making me do this."

"Come on, it's just one date."

Claire gaped at her, and I could feel her frustration. I floated over to the bed and hovered across it, my arms behind my head, my ankles crossed. It seemed like a relaxing pose—too bad I couldn't really tell.

"I'm sorry, *really*, I am," Addie pleaded, instantly insecure. "I promise to do whatever you ask, for like a week straight."

"A week?"

"Come on, Claire. I owe you, I promise. It's just I already told Josh you'd go out with him if he got Landon to ask me out."

"I know what you promised, but you didn't ask me first, Addie."

"I know, I'm sorry, really. Josh is nice, anyway. I don't know what the big deal is."

"Fine. He is nice. We'll have fun," Claire conceded, then looked over at me and rolled her eyes.

Addie sat on top of me, and I shifted to the window, trying to figure out my plan, already starting to second-guess myself. Could I risk being with Claire again? *Should I?* Was Nico telling the truth about this whole haunting business, or was she just making stuff up like the way she conjured up all her little costumes? Worse—maybe she and Aden both happened to be screwing with my mind. No, she was Claire's family; she'd want to protect her.

Right now, Claire was the only thing that made any sense at all.

"I think we're just getting dinner and a movie—nothing too horrible," Addie was saying.

"I'm sorry, Addie. I just hate blind dates."

"I know. That's why you're the best." She squeezed Claire and jumped off the bed at the sound of a loud knock at the front door. As usual, Addie's little act worked on Claire, who was once again at her mercy. My sister is the master manipulator. I would know.

Claire followed her out the door, turning around at the last minute to grab her purse. Throwing me a look of desperation, she whispered, "I'll meet you at ten. Wherever I am, I'll figure something out. Just be there, ok?"

That was when I knew for sure I was going to risk it. I *had* to hold her one more time, at least to say goodbye. How I was going to get Claire to myself with some dude hanging all over her when ten-o'clock rolled around—that was the real question of the night.

At 9:55, I still didn't have an answer. Claire was fidgeting in the back seat of Landon's four-wheel drive, sitting uncomfortably next to a dark, curly-haired, loud-mouthed, overenthusiastic Josh. He definitely was not her type. What was Addie *thinking?*

About herself, obviously.

Claire anxiously watched the green-lit numbers on the front dash. I sat in front of her, pretty much in the middle of the front seat, stuck in between the laughter and music bouncing back and forth. It was obvious we weren't going to make it in time.

"Hey Claire, lighten up!" Addie turned around, laughing.

"Yeah, Claire," Josh interjected, putting his arm around her. I wanted to chuck him out of the car.

Claire and I looked at each other, and at the clock again, realizing we still had ten minutes to go before we'd be home. That was when brilliant Claire leaned over in her seat, pretty much right through my lap, and started groaning.

"What's wrong?" Josh asked, suddenly cautious about where he put his arm.

Claire didn't answer. She just kept making a bunch of sick, moaning sounds. I was impressed.

"Hey," Addie grabbed Claire's knee. "What's going on? You okay?"

Claire sat up again, still moaning, "I think I'm going to be sick."

I drifted to the floor and gave her a big thumb's up. The car abruptly skidded to a stop at the side of the road. I shifted outside to wait for her.

"Hurry!" I heard Josh yell. "Get her out of here!"

Claire threw open the door and bolted out into the darkness. Cars sailed by as she crouched behind a tree and pretended to be sick. I couldn't stop laughing. Addie rushed to her side, rubbing her hand over her back. "Are you okay, Claire?"

"I think so," she answered weakly. "It's probably food poisoning or something. I just need a sec, if that's okay."

"I'll wait here with you," Addie offered.

"No, Ad, that's okay." Claire looked back at the car. "I'll be fine in a second. You go wait with the guys. Just give me five minutes, okay?"

Addie hesitated then started walking back. "You sure?"

"Yeah, it's freezing out here! Plus, I don't want to ruin your date anymore. Seriously. I'll be fine."

"Okay. Just yell if you need me."

Addie ran back around the tree to the car. I didn't know how much time we'd already lost, but I still waited for the door to shut before catching Claire's hand.

She practically jumped into my arms.

As soon as we touched, it felt like my heart started beating and my lungs filled up with air. I couldn't breathe and think and smell and touch her all at the same time. It was such a rush, but the seconds were already ticking away from us. Forget Nico and her theories. I wasn't about to miss another night with Claire just because of some nutcase ghost. It would be torture not to come back.

I pressed my lips over Claire's, tasting again the only taste I'd ever missed, drawing her into me, feeling the warmth of her body. Claire looked up at me when finally, reluctantly, I pulled away from her before time ran out.

"This isn't fair," I complained. "Only four and a half minutes."

She squeezed my hands. "Why were you gone for so long? I was so worried about you! What happened last time—you know, after the rainstorm? Did you see him?"

I didn't want to answer or think about that night. I just wanted to hold her and feel her breath on my neck.

She continued, unfazed, rattling off questions one after another. "Did you see him throw the vase? How'd he do that?"

I couldn't think straight, much less speak. All I could do was look at her…memorize her…absorb her. I felt like she was drowning me. "I missed you," I finally said.

She looked at me like I'd completely missed the point, and then her shoulders dropped and she exhaled, like she'd gotten everything out and could relax now. "I missed you, too."

She smiled and bit her lip as I held her warm, familiar hands. I kissed her again, our lips barely touching, until a powerful *something* took over and I couldn't resist her. I pulled her to me, my lips attacking hers, feeling her touch as she kissed me back. Her hands dug into the back of my head, pulling at my hair, and her breath found its way into me as we fell away, lost somewhere else, oblivious to the rest of the world. The seconds were dying fast, so I had to stop and talk to her before it was too late. That was the whole reason I came back in the first place…*right?*

Finally I pulled away. "Claire," I exhaled, trying to calm down. "I need to tell you something."

Lights lit up the inside of Landon's car. I felt the thump-thump-thump to the blasting music. Claire turned her head toward the noise before finding me again while I told her the abbreviated version of my memory of the accident. About Aden.

"It was *him*? My stupid ghost is from your past?" she asked, tapping her fists against my chest.

I nodded my head, still in shock myself, purposely keeping quiet about Nico, afraid details would just scare her more.

"So, he—*Aden*—haunts me because he's ticked at *you?* Ever heard of anger management?"

"Still, it's my fault."

"Daniel! Come on, you were just a little kid," she said, punching me.

"Like that matters to him. I guess it doesn't really matter to me, either. If it weren't for me, you wouldn't be scared to turn off your lights every night. And you definitely wouldn't be standing on the side of the road in the middle of the night, talking to a ghost."

"If it wasn't for you," she said, looking up at me, "I'd be dead, too, because you saved my life. Remember?"

True. *But, still...*

"So, what do we do now? Just wait around for him to come haunt me whenever he wants? I don't know if I can take it anymore."

I grabbed her hands, wondering if I should even say what I was thinking. "You haven't seen him in a week, right?"

"How do *you* know? You haven't been around to notice," she said, frowning.

"I'm serious, Claire. Have you ever noticed the only time he haunts you is right after we connect like this?"

She started to say something, but stopped and bit her lip, then started up again. "What? *No!* Our connection? This?"

"I think it's how he haunts you...but I'm not positive."

"*What?* Why?"

"I don't know. You just might be more vulnerable to the other side, I mean, to *my* side, after this. At least that's a theory."

Claire looked like I'd socked her in the stomach. "No. That can't be right, Daniel. I'm sure he's come before…" But she stopped protesting once she thought it through. "It can't be. It's not fair."

"That's why I stayed away, Claire. I don't know what to do. I want to be with you…but I'm afraid for you."

Landon or his loser friend honked the horn and flashed the lights, making Claire jump. I hugged her even tighter, but could already tell the time was almost gone. Reluctantly, she looked over at the car then back into my eyes, quickly kissing me once more.

"Please don't let him keep you away from me," she said. "I'd rather–" but before she could finish, our time was up.

Our eyes locked on each other as she made her way back to the car. She looked so sad. I wanted to follow her home to make sure she was okay, but couldn't contain the overwhelming depression seeping into my mind.

As Landon's car pulled back onto the road, I shifted to the quiet lake and let the canoe carry me wherever it decided to go. Water lapped the sides, relaxing me, even though I could sense a storm was on its way. Hypnotized by a sky littered with countless stars, I wondered how I was going to do this. Wondered how long we had before Aden came again.

Claire

The night would've been a complete disaster if not for Daniel. Addie definitely owed me. Josh? Okay, so he wasn't so bad, but not particularly great, either. And "dreamy" Landon? Well, hopefully Addie realized how clueless he was after he dropped her off at the end of the driveway. Dropped her off! At the end! Then honked obnoxiously as she made her way up to the door. Alone.

I expected Mom to be eagerly waiting at the door for details, and was slightly shocked to find her in her room. Maybe Dad being home tonight made it easier for her to relax a little.

After changing from too-tight jeans and an itchy shirt into sweats and a t-shirt, I padded through the house in fuzzy snowball slippers, first to kiss a sleeping Mom and Dad goodnight, and then to venture into the dark kitchen for a snack. I flicked on the pantry light and cracked the door a bit while rummaging through the cabinets for some comfort food.

Other than eating, I had no clue what to do with myself. I was too afraid to sleep, always wondering when the onslaught of horror was going to make an appearance. Was Daniel right? Was my ghost tormentor just waiting for this? Waiting to strike?

Ice cream sounded good. I scooped out some Chocolate Malted Crunch while thinking of Daniel, picturing the way he looked at me tonight. The thought sent shivers up my spine. I couldn't stop smiling, remembering our kiss, wishing we had more than a lousy four and a half minutes. I didn't want to believe tonight was really our last together. It couldn't be. I wouldn't allow it.

"Claire," said a quiet voice from behind me.

I whirled around to find Dad standing in a sliver of the dim pantry light, his hair a mess. "I didn't mean to scare you," he apologized half-asleep.

I gulped down my ice cream and shuddered. "*Everything* scares me lately. Did I wake you up? I'm sorry."

"No, it's okay. But it is kind of late for ice cream, don't you think? Is everything okay?"

"I couldn't sleep," I said before letting him swallow me up inside a giant bear hug. "I thought I was being quiet."

"You probably were. I couldn't sleep, either. Guess I'm not used to going to bed this early. How was your date?"

"Nothing too exciting."

He turned on the kitchen lights, blinding me, and then went to the sink for a glass of water. I closed my eyes to block out the light while concentrating on the smooth, cool sensation of cream sliding down my throat, savoring every ounce. For some reason the cold combined with the sweet soothed me, even though I was exhausted.

"Well, try to get to bed soon, okay?" Dad kissed me on the forehead and put his glass in the sink before flipping out the light. "Love you."

"You too, Dad." But, then something at the sliding door caught my eye. "*Wait...*"

Pressed up against the glass was a strange face, watching us. He looked young, maybe nineteen or twenty, with a distinctive shaved head that glowed in the moonlight. At first I paused, confused, my mind not quite registering, and then my heart dove into the fiery acid of my stomach as I pointed at the window. Strange squealing sounds streamed from my mouth as Dad jerked backward at my reaction.

Realizing he'd been discovered, the Peeping Tom reeled backward and disappeared. But Dad was already after him. Stumbling over a couple of chairs, he briefly hesitated to unlock the back door before leaping out into the dark.

He was really there? Dad saw him, too?

I didn't know what was real anymore, and that thought scared me even more. My legs were shaking, barely holding me up as I gaped at the open door, waiting for something else to happen. All I could hear was my own pulse in my ears.

And then that noise again.

"Ssssrooophhhh."

I spun around to find the ghost named Aden hovering right behind me. I stepped backward, knocking into a chair while trying to keep him as far away as possible. He seemed to be beaming with enthusiasm, like he had a surprise he couldn't wait to reveal. Tonight his hair was smooth and tame, like he'd taken extra care to get it just right, and I could see every detail in his face, every button on his shirt. Even the contours of his cheekbones stood out against the deep holes that were his dark, onyx eyes.

He drifted to me, grinning, and put his arm around me. I almost fainted when I felt pressure on my shoulders. But I couldn't let Mom or Dad know what I could see. It would only convince them I needed help. Slowly, I backed away from him, but he followed.

"What do you want?" I asked, trying to exude a little confidence, but mostly just wanting to shrink down into a little fleck of dust.

He reached for my hand. I gasped and pulled it away the moment a cold, burning sensation passed beneath my skin.

"Get away from me," I whispered, looking around the kitchen for some kind of weapon, though I didn't know why. It wasn't like I could attack him.

"What in the world?" I turned to find Mom standing in the doorway, rubbing her eyes, apparently a couple of hours into her beauty sleep. Her usual smooth, dark curls were now matted together into a bed-headed mess. Speechless, she surveyed the mess of toppled chairs and open door, and then reached for the light switch.

Daniel materialized from out of nowhere, standing right next to Mom, an undecipherable expression on his face—something between surprise and concern, and maybe even fear. I wasn't sure. Aden sneered at us both, and then vanished just as Dad barged back in through the door, his hair messy and his cheeks flushed. He leaned against the doorway, holding his side and panting.

"What's going on?" Mom asked, her voice all high-pitched and nervous-sounding as she looked from Dad, to me, back to Dad again.

"I don't know…we saw…Claire and I…" Dad looked at me while trying to catch his breath. "…there was someone outside…watching us through the window…"

Daniel eyed me curiously, perhaps trying to gauge my reaction.

"You saw him too," I said, relieved to know I wasn't alone in this. Dad gave me a rare look of irritation. "I just thought…maybe my scream startled you, or something."

He ran his hand through his thick, dirty-blond hair. "You think I raced outside in the middle of the night because you screamed?"

I ignored his question, skipping straight to my own. "Why was he watching us, Dad?" I looked up, trying to stay calm in front of Daniel, but the fear of a strange Peeping Tom and psycho ghost who wouldn't leave me alone was overwhelming. Dad just shook his head, though he seemed a little calmer now. I couldn't believe he really chased after that guy. I didn't know he had it in him.

Daniel drifted closer to me, possibly for a little mental support, which helped because I was starting to feel faint.

Probably trying to release some of the tension, Dad started picking up and rearranging the scattered chairs. "I have no idea, Claire. I almost had him down by the lake, but then he hopped over Mrs. Thompson's fence, and I lost him."

Mom put her arm around me. "Are you okay, honey?"

"Not really," I admitted, burying my face in her chest, glad she was there, after all.

"It's okay," Mom said, her fingers smoothing my hair.

I gripped her arm for support when the air grew thick and warm. A sudden knot twisted in my stomach and the kitchen started to spin.

"I'm sorry, Claire," I heard a calmer, gentler Dad speaking. But he sounded so far away now…somewhere off in a tunnel…or underwater. Little white specks were floating all around my head, bursting apart like popping bubbles.

The next thing I knew, my head was cradled in Mom's lap and I was lying on the couch. She skimmed her fingertips along the edge of my temple, a light tickling sensation soothing my skin. While resisting consciousness, I clearly heard Dad's quiet voice above me, but I pretended to be asleep.

"I *swear* I saw him earlier at the train station," Dad quietly said to Mom.

"Which station? Here?"

"No. Embarcadero," he said, his voice laden with concern. "I noticed him, because we were the only two in our car."

"Are you sure?"

"Pretty sure." His voice faltered a bit. "I don't know. Now I'm second-guessing myself, but I'm still pretty sure it was him."

"Do you think the police will find him?"

"I don't know…"

Silence. My eyes fluttered, and found the strength to open. Both Mom and Dad stared at me, worry seeping out through their unconvincing mask of calm.

CHAPTER TWELVE WILD GHOST CHASE

Claire

The sun's warmth woke me the next morning despite a chill inside me that refused to thaw. I could hear a buzz of strange voices out in the hallway, and when I opened my door, a small crew of workers with drills and walkie-talkies in hand were wandering around the house.

Once dressed, I strategically dodged them and found Mom and Dad in the kitchen, eating breakfast. They both looked up when I walked in, their faces etched with concern. Even with reassurance that I was okay, Mom kept fretting over me, apologizing for what happened last night, as if she'd caused the whole fiasco.

I changed the subject and asked Dad what was going on. He started explaining the security system being installed. Mom finally seemed to relax as Dad went on and on about codes, beeps, windows and doors. But I had stopped listening, mentally moving on to the Peeping Tom's face—and the fact that Dad had chased him for me. I never expected that.

"Claire, why don't you eat something?" Mom asked, interrupting my thoughts and Dad's long-winded dissertation on how the alarm system was going to make us safer.

Mr. Head Security Guy with noticeably huge sideburns came around the corner with a bunch of questions for Dad, so I grabbed a muffin and a pair of shoes and sneaked out the front door. My own house suddenly felt like a crime scene, and I desperately needed to get away.

At first, I wandered down to the dock and lay out on the splintery boards, letting the sun soak into me while eating my muffin. But too soon, every chirp or bark or creaking tree made me jump, and I couldn't relax anymore for fear of that Peeping Tom sneaking up on me.

I hopped up and climbed the hill, walking past the lake and Addie's house, directly toward Main Street. I had no idea where I was going. I was just *going*.

"Claire-bear!" a very familiar voice echoed from behind just before I reached the entrance to our street. I turned to find Addie half-walking, half-jogging to catch up to me.

"Where you going?" she asked, catching up.

"Nowhere, I guess. Just on a walk. You want to come?"

She shrugged her shoulders. "Sure."

It wasn't quiet for more than three seconds because Addie couldn't stand not talking. "I'm so sorry about last night," she said, walking backwards, facing me. I didn't answer. It was always fun seeing where she would take her one-sided conversations. "Okay, so you were right," she continued. "It didn't really turn out like I imagined. Landon wasn't my type. He's definitely hot, though. Too bad he knows it."

I smiled and pushed the "walk" button at the intersection as we waited to cross.

"Seriously, whatever you want—you name it. I am so sorry you got sick. Do you feel any better today?"

Right. Since the confusion from last night, I'd forgotten about my whole fake-puking-on-the-side-of-the-road-so-I-could-meet-with- Daniel act. I smiled at the thought of it. "I'm fine now. It was probably the hot dogs. I didn't really feel like hot dogs–"

Addie whacked me in the arm. "Can you believe they took us to get *hot dogs?* On a date? Gross!"

The light turned green. We crossed to the other side to catch a biking/walking trail alongside the canal while rehashing all the details of our fabulous night and even more fabulous dates.

Addie turned to me suddenly. "What's up with the security van in front of your house?"

"You're never going to believe it."

"Try me."

A jogger was approaching from behind, and I waited to explain until he passed. Call me paranoid. "When I got home last night, a sicko-Peeping Tom was watching me through the kitchen window."

"Shut *up!*" She hit me on the arm again. I could feel a bruise coming on. "Are you *serious?* Are you *okay?* Who was he? Did you call the cops?"

I didn't feel like delving into the whole story again, but figured she would never let it go until she knew everything. I briefly retold the events of the last twenty-four hours. Addie's eyes grew wide—first with surprise, then worry. I purposely omitted the final detail, about how the

Peeping Tom had most likely followed Dad home. The thought of that still terrified me.

"I'm so sorry," Addie said, hugging me. "Now *I'm* freaking out. I hope the police catch him. And fast."

"Me too."

"Wait," Addie stopped and grabbed my arm. "Remind me why we're walking out here in the middle of nowhere? You do realize how completely vulnerable we are with all these overgrown bushes and total lack of witnesses? Your stalker could easily be hiding right over there, watching us this very second!" She pointed to a wild, prickly blackberry bush on the side of the path.

"First of all, this is hardly the middle of nowhere," I said, stepping out of her grip while dodging a biking family as they zoomed by. "See? Lots of witnesses. And anyway, you forget the stalker was *at my house*. You think I want to be hanging around there right now?"

"True, but I still feel vulnerable out here all by our lonesome. Maybe we should head back, just to be safe."

"Fine," I sighed, not sure I even cared anymore. "But let's cut through the park first."

"Why?" Addie asked, stopping.

"I just want to check something out," I replied, my mind beginning to churn.

Daniel

As soon as they crossed the street by the elementary school and started heading down the hill, I immediately recognized Larkey Park. But did Claire even realize where she was? I wondered if, when I told her about the accident, I'd mentioned the name of the park, or the fact that it happened to be less than a mile from my house. No, I was pretty sure I'd left that out. For a reason.

It seemed strange being here again so soon after my Memory Trace. Everything felt faintly familiar, like an echo. After surveying the area, soaking up as much detail as possible, I was surprised by how much it had changed from the memory I'd visited only recently. The trees were twice as tall, there was a new swimming pool and playground, and an entire wing had been added to the old animal shelter—now it was a wildlife museum.

Claire and Addie continued their conversation about Peeping Toms and dates-gone-bad as the pathway led them to the bottom of the hill. About halfway down, I pulled away from them a little, drifting to the colorful, new playground where a couple of kids were being pushed on the swings. Their laughter filled the air, energy spilling from them like some kind of soothing mist. I didn't want to leave, especially when I felt their joy, like the color yellow, flooding through me.

Forcing my eyes from the calming movement of the swing, I glanced across the path. Over by an old fence, a white-haired couple sat together on a blue-checkered blanket. Would today be their last together, or did they still have hundreds left? The woman had a pink carnation pinned to her blouse, and the two of them were laughing about something. I wanted to tell them to soak it all in before it was too late—to forget everything but the present.

The wind blew a pile of old, crackled leaves across the pavement, distracting me enough to draw away from the happy couple, back to Claire. She had stopped walking, and was looking around, like she'd forgotten something.

"What are you doing?" Addie asked her impatiently. "I thought we were going home."

"I know," said Claire, seemingly lost in thought. "I just…I wanted to look around for a minute."

Guaranteed she'd been here a hundred times since she was little. So had I. However, it never had any significance to either of us until now. Was everything clicking in her head as she put it all together—the street at the top of the hill, the bike pathway leading down the steep hill, and the fact that this was likely the only park I could ride my bike to as a kid?

Addie's complaints lasted for exactly two minutes and eleven seconds, which was how much time passed before the cell phone buzzed to life from her back pocket. With her turquoise phone plastered to her ear, she continued walking on down the hill, leaving Claire still standing in the middle of the path, looking around.

I was about twenty yards away when a jogger with black shorts, a grey pullover sweatshirt and a black ski cap pulled down to his eyes approached Claire from behind. Instead of steering clear of her, though, he ran right into her, knocking her to the ground like he hadn't even seen her. *Idiot.*

Instantly I shifted to Claire. She was fine, though annoyed and probably embarrassed.

Addie turned around. "You okay, Claire?"

Claire waved her off while inspecting a slight scrape on her knee.

"I'm sorry," the jogger said, coughing. He apologized three more times, and then extended his hand to her. She ignored his offer and walked away from him, toward Addie. The whole time I was focused on Claire, trying to gauge her reaction. I never paid much attention to the clumsy runner who insisted on sticking around to help her, but when he turned his head in my direction, I instantly felt my fists clench.

"I'm fine...really," Claire coolly replied when he asked again if she needed help.

"I think you dropped this." His voice was deep and hoarse, like a nasty wad of phlegm was lodged in the middle of his throat.

Claire stopped and turned to face him as he shoved a piece of paper in her hand. "Huh?" Claire said, looking directly at him. Her eyes grew wide as she covered her mouth. The jogger pushed past her, nearly knocking her over again, cutting across the lawn toward the wildlife museum.

Addie stopped talking mid-sentence, realizing that her best friend was *not* all right. Claire was shaking, even starting to cry as Addie rushed to her side.

"What's wrong?" she asked, hugging her. "I thought you said you were okay. Did he hurt you?"

Claire didn't speak—I couldn't blame her. I looked to the pavement where the creased paper lay abandoned at her feet. Her name was scribbled across the front in thick, black ink.

Claire James

Except, it wasn't the paper that terrified her, at least not yet. Claire hadn't even seen the paper. She was still in shock from recognizing the face she'd seen in her window last night—the Peeping Tom. Claire stared straight ahead like the fright had frozen her expression, while Addie kept hugging her, brushing her fingers through her hair and asking her what was wrong.

Leaving them there, I hurried down the path in the direction Peeping Tom had gone. He didn't seem to be anywhere, almost like he was trying to lose me, like he knew he was being followed. What was I going to do if I even found him? But I *needed* to find him, and then figure something out later.

After shifting to a street at the end of the alley, I looked up and down the narrow road lined with a bunch of small houses and a couple dozen parked cars, realizing how easily he could've gone into a car. Or even slipped inside one of the houses. I drifted up and down the street, looking for movement, listening for a car to start, then finally gave up and shifted back to the wildlife museum.

The front lobby was mostly empty except for a heavy, older lady sitting at the front desk, reading a magazine. A glass bowl of bite-size Butterfingers sat at the edge of the counter, reminding me of how much I loved Butterfingers. Beside the desk, stood a nine-foot-high stuffed brown bear with three-inch claws and spear-like teeth, guarding the entrance. A couple of rowdy kids ran through me down the hall, stopping long enough to gaze into glass cases filled with snakes and lizards. Not knowing what else to do, I followed the kids and surveyed the room.

Two snowy owls were perched in open cages near the ceiling while a bunch of random mammals slept in small glass rooms lining the white, lit-up hallway for us to watch their every move. I felt bad for them confined like that—too dangerous for adoption, but too familiar with humans to survive out in the wild. It was like they were in limbo. Some of the animals even looked depressed, their empty eyes gazing out at nothing as I drifted by. I wondered if they could see me—wished I could ask them if they'd seen a guilty jogger run by.

I was just about to give up and shift back outside to check on Claire, when I peered over a balcony and caught the flash of something grayish-black skipping off the last stair of a spiral staircase below. I shifted down there just as Peeping Tom exited through the basement door. He walked across the parking lot, weaving in and out of parked cars as I followed a few feet behind him. Finally, he stopped for a second at a four-way intersection and waited for a car to pass.

I drew in front of him to get a good look, but he didn't seem to see me. Either that, or he was an exceptional actor.

The car passed, and he stepped off the curb, continuing his retreat before slowing down near an old black Saab with rusted rims and a cracked side window. After ducking into the front seat, he slammed the door behind him and, with a few thrusts to the gas pedal, started up the engine. I settled into the passenger seat as he pulled out abruptly and slid into the traffic.

The interior was disgusting. Old food containers and stained wrappers caked with food littered the floor and seat. The torn backseat held rotted remains of half-eaten meals and random pieces of clothing lying around, like the bottom of a closet. Thankfully, I couldn't smell anything.

As soon as he turned onto the highway and headed toward the city, I shifted back to Claire, because I now had Peeping Tom's disgusting car stuck in my head. Lucky for me, I could come right back to this very seat whenever I pictured the image in my head. That's how it worked.

Claire was back in her room, sprawled across her bed, her eyes red and teary. Her mom and Addie were quietly talking about the note that was now sitting open on top of the desk.

"She's positive it's the same guy from last night," Addie said.

But I wasn't really listening. The words on the note seemed to pull me across the room. I stared at the message on the glaring piece of paper, furious. Struggling for control over anger boiling up inside me, I felt trapped without any way to release my hatred for this pathetic waste of a human being.

Not knowing how long before the Saab would find its destination, I took one final look at the message, and then thrust myself back inside the noxious car with the vile driver.

We were crossing the Bay. Peeping Tom listened to nothing. No music, no talk radio—nothing except the thumping sounds of the tires as they methodically rushed along like the beat of a drum across the seams on the bridge. Still, Peeping-Tom-Boy found it necessary to incoherently mumble to himself, prompting me to drift outside the car the rest of the way so I wouldn't have to listen to him anymore. Who *was* he, anyway?

The car exited the freeway and wound its way through congested roads and one-way streets to the middle of a small, neglected part of town with boarded-up windows and graffiti applied to everything like wallpaper. As he downshifted around the next corner, the car screamed such an obscene grinding noise that I looked behind us to make sure the transmission hadn't dropped out.

At last he pulled to a stop alongside an overflowing Dumpster I was certain reeked of the depths of hell, though I'd never been there—at least not yet. He hopped out and slammed the door after him, then found his way through a maze of trash along a walkway leading to a three-story apartment building. Most of the lights had probably burned out months ago, leaving a few remaining bulbs buzzing like electric mosquitoes.

After pulling some letters out of a rusting mailbox, he climbed a flight of crumbling concrete stairs and looked around. At the top, he made a quick right down another dark hall, stopping in front of an ominous brown door with tarnished gold-turned-green letters. It read 213.

The lock seemed stubborn. As he jiggled the handle, I glanced at the mail in his other hand to try and make out a name on any of the obscured address labels, zooming in so close that had he seen me, he would have thought I was a pervert.

Mr. Felix Marz.

His name meant nothing to me. It was just one small part of a bigger mystery, but at least I had a name for the face—a name I could give to Claire. Although, I wasn't sure what she could say that would make any sense to anyone.

The door swung open, and I reluctantly followed him inside, annoyed at the urgency that demanded I follow this loser everywhere when I would much rather be, well, *anywhere* else.

Once inside the crawling walls of his decaying apartment, a piercing chill ran up my legs. Felix trudged forward through the mess into the kitchen, but I stopped in the dark entryway as a couple of flies buzzed in circles through my head. There, standing in front of me, with arms crossed and a beaming smile was the ghost of the guy I'd killed twelve years ago.

He seemed to be expecting me.

CHAPTER
THIRTEEN SURPRISE PARTY

Claire

I could hear the hum of hushed voices at the end my bed, but was afraid to listen because then I'd be forced to face a horrible reality. I hoped Daniel had been at the park with us and seen the runner's face—then he would have seen the paper fall to the ground and gone after him....

But then what? There was only so much Daniel could do for me, which was why I could not seem to pull myself together. I should have never looked at that stupid note. The instant he placed it in my hands I should've just dropped it and walked away. But I couldn't. Not once I saw my name written there.

Addie and Mom were standing over by the desk, scrutinizing the letter as quietly as possible. I was already past scared, beyond hysterics, close to the point of numb defeat. The words written on the paper still made me queasy. I tried to block them out of my head, but like an awful scene from a movie I wish I'd never seen, they kept coming back.

You should have drowned the first time.

Next time, I'll make sure you do.

"Claire, honey," said Mom.

I didn't answer. I had nothing to say.

"Claire," she repeated, now beside me, rubbing my back while sitting on the edge of the bed.

I wondered where Addie had gone, but let it go and turned over to look up at Mom. She looked a little fuzzy, thanks to my tears, but I could tell she was secretly freaking out behind those calm eyes, futilely hiding concern behind her soft voice. She stared at me as I lifted a weak hand up to my puffy eyes. Long past trying to keep up a brave front, I released my hand to my side in surrender.

"The police will be here soon," she said. "I know you're upset, but you have to talk to them. I can't do it. It needs to be you, Hon, as soon as possible, so they can find this guy."

I knew she was right, but still didn't know what to say. Instead, I bit my lip and nodded in agreement as she rested her hand on my arm.

Unable to focus on her anymore, I stared at the ceiling, trying to lose myself in my misery. But it wasn't just misery. I felt so violated, so outraged. Yes. *Outraged.* That was more like it. Who were these people, these sick voyeurs and psychotic ghosts, who felt they had a right to interfere in my life? Didn't they have more important things to worry about—like eternity, hell and brim fire, or something like that? Seriously.

I thought I could feel the subtle sting of something like fire igniting inside me, barely flickering to life, shooting out sparks of emotion that initially fizzled out beneath a wad of self-pity. But the more I thought about that stupid note, the more my pity seemed to morph into anger. I was beginning to feel the urge to punch someone, or at least yell at them like Addie would've done.

"Where's Addie?" I asked Mom, who seemed to jump when I spoke. Addie had mysteriously disappeared without even saying goodbye. That seemed a bit odd.

Mom shook her head. "I don't know. She said she needed to fix a few things, and told me to tell you she'd be back in a little while."

"Fix a few things? Like with a hammer?" I asked, laughing a little, feeling a bit of the heaviness in my chest lifting.

Mom's face gave way to a hesitant smile, her teeth finally emerging from hiding inside a frown. "I don't know. That's just what she said before she left."

"Hmmm," I mumbled, opening up my laptop, thinking Addie was probably up to something, thinking maybe *I* should be up to something, too. Anything but feeling sorry for myself.

"What are you doing?" Mom asked as she massaged my shoulders, sending tingles up my neck. I was glad she was here with me.

"I don't know yet. Just trying to make sense of everything."

"On your computer?"

"I guess." *Long story.* Change of subject. "I'm starving, Mom. Is there anything to eat?" I tried to give her something else to do other than stress about me. She was always worrying...but now I was a little worried about her.

"Sure," she said in an upbeat tone. "I'll start dinner."

When she left, I started Googling every possible word that I thought could have something to do with a car accident at the park I'd just returned from: *Daniel Holland, Larkey Park, boy, dog, motorcycle accident.*

Nothing. Not a thing.

Aghhhhh.

I let my pulsing forehead fall into my lap, and massaged my scalp while trying to think... think... think... until I heard a car pulling into the driveway. I wasn't excited about seeing the police again. They'd come last night, sometime between my fainting spell and the morning, and all I could remember about it now was trying to stay awake while being asked way too many questions.

Two car doors slammed shut, followed by a trail of heavy footsteps scuffling up the walkway. Hoping to find something before I was summoned to my interrogation, I clicked on another website, a local news archive. A soft murmur of voices passed by my window, followed by a heavy knock at the front door as I waited, impatiently begging the glowing computer to give me something to make sense of my nightmare.

There it was.

Some local community newspaper, the kind that comes free in the mail. It had a small article dated from over twelve years ago, about a tragic accident at a neighborhood park involving a little boy and a motorcycle.

MOTORCYCLIST KILLED AFTER BOY SAVES DOG
Posted by the East Bay Gazette
From staff reports

A Hidden Lake teen died Monday after he was thrown from his motorcycle while swerving to avoid colliding with a child on a bike. The accident oc-curred at the northwest corner of Larkey Lane and

Oakdale Drive, just north of Larkey Park, said officer Sadie Covington, a spokeswoman for Hidden Lake Police. The teenager, identified as Aden Sawyer, 18, of 665 Keely Drive, died at the scene.

Sawyer was travelling well over the posted speed limit of 25 mph, witnesses say, as he took the turn onto Oakdale Drive. He lost control of his motorcycle when a young child on a two-wheeler entered the intersection to save his dog from the oncoming traffic. The unnamed child and his dog were not harmed.

An investigation of the crash revealed that the rider, who was not wearing a helmet, had a blood alcohol limit above the .08 legal limit, and had a previous arrest for drug use.

My heart pounded as I read the article. *Aden Sawyer.* Did knowing his full name make him more of a person, less of a monster? Not really. Not when I pictured him coming at me in the dark. I Googled his name, but nothing else came up. Not a single thing. He was as much a faceless name back then as he was now.

"Claire."

I jumped.

Mom was peeking her head beyond my bedroom door.

"The police are here. So, whenever you're ready," she said with an encouraging smile.

"Oh, okay. Thanks."

I stalled at my desk a second longer, trying to decide what to do next, digesting this new information. I wanted to tell Daniel what had really happened—what his memory never told him about Aden's death but didn't know when, or if, Daniel was going to show up again.

The image of Aden's face and the sound of Peeping Tom's voice were still mulling through my mind when I walked into the hallway and smacked right into Dad, who must've gotten home the same time the cops arrived. I jumped. Again.

What was wrong with me? I'd become a walking bundle of nerves. Dad's eyes seemed to smile as he hugged me. "How're you holding up?"

"Barely." I didn't want to leave the safety of his arms. "Dad, will you *please* come talk to the cops with me? I *hate* this."

"Sure," he said, leading me into the living room, where the same pair of cops from last night waited for me—one with a dark, tight ponytail and wad of gum in her mouth, and the other with a scowl and dark shadows underlining his eyes.

Mom and Dad sat on either side of me as I detailed last night's drama all over again, plus the added bonus of what happened at the park this morning. The cops took turns eyeing me while taking notes on little pads of yellow paper.

"Are you positive it was the same man as before, Miss James?" the lady cop asked, snapping on her gum. I looked at them both, suspecting they doubted my credibility because I was so young.

"Yes," I answered, this time fixing my eyes on the other cop, until he looked away with a frown and scribbled something onto his paper.

"I understand you opened the letter?" he accused.

"Well, it really isn't a letter. It was just a folded piece of paper–"

"Which you opened?"

"Yes, but–"

"Did your friend touch the letter?" he leaned toward me.

I looked over at the lady, but her smile had been replaced by a scrutinizing stare. She seemed disappointed in me, like I'd deliberately done something wrong. I shifted around in my seat, staring at my fidgeting fingers. "No, but I–"

"Claire is tired and understandably shaken," Dad said, putting his arm around me. "We appreciate your compassion as you continue questioning her."

"She's only sixteen," Mom mumbled under her breath, reaching for my hand. I squeezed it right away.

"Listen," the cranky cop started to say, but then his buzzing walkie-talkie cut in, and he stood and clomped into the kitchen, ignoring us.

"Why don't you show me the paper?" the lady cop said politely. I really wanted to tell her to spit out the gum. It was driving me crazy.

While Officer Grumpy mumbled back and forth into his radio, the rest of us went down the hall to my room. With gloved hands, Officer Gum-Chewer carefully placed the paper into a plastic bag, like it might explode any second. The reality of it all came back to me, so I excused myself to the bathroom to calm myself while keeping my fingers crossed that Daniel might show up. I stayed in there as long as possible without raising suspicion of drug abuse or another fainting spell, and returned to find the two cops and my parents standing together at the front door. Quietly, I snuck up behind Mom. She turned and put her arm around me.

Officer Grumpy's heavy lidded eyes stared down at me before turning towards Dad. "As I said before. We'll do our best with this evidence, but we may not be able to find anything conclusive."

"Thank you," Dad said graciously as he opened the door for them. He seemed particularly adept at dealing with ignoramuses (probably a lawyer thing).

"Miss James," the lady cop said, her voice sounding a little less severe. "We've already talked to your parents about various precautions you should be taking right now, but I just need to reiterate how careful you need to be. Report anything that seems suspicious, and call us immediately if you see him again, okay?"

I nodded. "Okay."

Mom flipped on the porch light as the cops walked to their car.

"Did you see the way he *looked* at me?" I asked after Dad closed the door.

"He's just trying to do his job." Dad put his hands on my shoulders and led me down the hall.

"I agree with Claire. He *was* a jerk," Mom said. I squeezed her hand, feeling more and more glad she was on my side. "Claire, I'm sure you're starving. Let's eat."

Smells of something homemade and delicious called us into the kitchen, where Dad ladled steaming chicken soup into our bowls. I loved it when Mom was in a domestic mood.

"Being a jerk may be the only thing that can catch a bad guy," Dad said, removing his tie and loosening his collar as we carried our bowls to the table. I rolled my eyes and slurped the soothing liquid while holding my face over the bowl. The steamy mist fogged up my glasses and warmed me from the inside out.

"Or perhaps he's a jerk *because* of the bad guys," Dad added with a smile, but Mom and I just looked at him like he was nuts. "You never know," he said, smiling again.

We slurped our meal for a while in silence, when the faint electronic humming sound of the garage door broke into the quiet.

Mom dropped her spoon with a clink. "That sounds like the garage door."

My heart thudded to a stop, as if the blood had been sucked out of me. Despite my earlier bout of confidence, the rush of fear easily found me again. I stared wide-eyed at my parents, imagining all the horrible possibilities that sound could mean.

"Stay here," Dad ordered, scooting his chair out and heading for the garage door. He stood poised at the door, his eyes focused on the knob. My hands clenched into fists on top of the table, and I felt my muscles tightening. Mom and I stared at each other, then at Dad, waiting for the worst.

Where was Daniel?

I guess it didn't matter, because right then the knob turned and my stomach dove to the floor. When the door swung open, Dad attacked.

Daniel

He was studying me like some sort of science experiment. I looked past him to Felix, who was still mumbling to himself in the kitchen as he kicked through empty aluminum cans and piles of faded newspapers. He made his way over to the filthy countertop, pulling open drawers and cupboards, searching for who knows what.

I turned back to Aden, whose dark eyes seemed to follow mine. He looked pale under the fluorescent lights, even sickly—contradicting his broad shoulders and jet-black mane that made him look something like a rock star.

"Do you like my friend here?" he spoke, almost politely. "Felix is a real piece of work."

I didn't answer, not sure yet whether he'd drawn me here purposely, or if Felix had unknowingly led me. It really didn't matter; I was here, but had absolutely no idea what to do next.

Aden drifted further into the grimy apartment, past Felix, who was now hunched over the stove, holding a small, filmy glass pipe in his hands.

"He's been pretty efficient, you know," Aden said, eyeing Felix.

"You got a crack head to do your bidding?"

He laughed. "Isn't that the best kind?"

I gaped at him.

"*What?* You think you're the only one with special access to the living?" he said, lingering by a barred window off the kitchen.

"What are you talking about?"

"Let's just say he's had one too many overdoses. There are lots of ways to die, you know."

I drifted away from him toward a dark hallway, trying to register the meaning in his words. "Felix isn't dead."

"Neither is Claire. But she was, wasn't she?"

I glanced at Felix, who was stretched across the counter with his eyes closed, like he was off in some other place. "What kind of game are you playing?" I asked.

"Game?" Aden said. "I'd hardly call this a game anymore. Not with what I have planned for your girlfriend."

I whipped my head around as he faded into the window behind him like he was about to shift away. I wasn't ready for him to leave, not yet, and I flew across the room, reaching out just as he disappeared. Instantly, I felt something latch onto me, forcefully yanking me forward, like a magnet.

My vision went blank for a second, and I suddenly found myself in Felix's bedroom. A naked mattress lay next to a bench press and weight rack. I guessed the dumbbells explained Felix's other pastime. Smoking crack and bodybuilding—a little counter-productive, if you asked me.

I turned to Aden, who held onto me like a magnet. His eyes seemed fluorescent as he towed me along with him through the bed, into the closet and out the wall, pausing momentarily while hovering outside the apartment building above a parked car.

"This is fun," he grinned, before fading again, pulling me with him as we shifted back inside to the living room. Felix was now planted in a torn, mustard-colored armchair in front of a TV blaring with static and obnoxious voices. The screen flashed in and out as he mindlessly flipped the channels, his head glowing under the lights.

Somehow Aden released me, and I felt a relieving sense of freedom.

He slid in front of me and extended his hand, like we were meeting for the first time. "I don't think we've ever formally met. I'm Aden."

I stared at him blankly until he finally got the picture, retracted his hand, and floated toward the window. He gazed out through the bars and clouded glass. "I don't think you understand who I am," he said before turning back to face me.

"I know who you are now. I know what happened—"

"Great. Then I suppose we can just skip this part." He clasped his hands together, smiling.

"Look, I know you're pissed off at me for what happened. *I get it.* But what do you expect me to do about it now? I'm dead, too, in case you haven't figured it out."

His smile dissolved into a frown, and he seemed to lose his composure before quickly readjusting and continuing. "The problem is, you want everything to instantly iron itself out without any effort or pain on *your* part. That's how you've lived your whole life—the boy who had everything, who never had to lift a finger."

I had no idea what he was talking about.

His mind seemed to drift for a minute as his eyes bounced back and forth from me to the window to me again. "So let's just get right to the solution. Is that what you want? Some neat little fix so I'll quietly go away?"

I almost said 'yes,' but before I could respond, blurred colors were trailing behind him like contrails from a jet as he flew at me, pinning me to the floor. A flimsy aluminum lamp toppled over, breaking a pile of dirty dishes and throwing a pyramid of soda cans across the room. Somehow Aden had pinned me to the ground. There wasn't any pain, but I could feel a distinct pressure at my shoulders and thighs where he held me. His face, only inches from mine, seemed to ooze outrage. How he was doing it completely baffled me. It was like he was dead and alive at the same time.

A strange squealing noise started coming from the corner by the TV. I turned and caught sight of Felix, who was crouched on the floor and peering around with bug-eyes. He was making a moaning noise that sounded like a mix between an injured dog and an asthma attack, and held his hands over his ears, like he could hear us.

He could.

"You don't want to look at me?" Aden asked through gritted teeth, pressing his face into mine so far that I had to close my eyes because of the dizzy claustrophobia. "You sniveling, selfish brat," he hissed, releasing his grip. "Shut up and pay attention for once in your petty, useless existence."

I sunk to the floor where he'd dropped me, overwhelmed by his power.

"I am Aden," he repeated, like I hadn't heard the first time. But it was difficult focusing now, because Felix was scratching at his arms and mumbling to himself. Aden didn't seem to care or even notice. "Did you hear me?" he asked, waiting for me. "ADEN!" he screamed, leaping forward and through me, the stream of color following him like before, but this time without the force that threw me to the ground.

Felix looked in our direction and pushed himself against the wall, holding his knees, and shivering. He was breathing heavily, almost panting —a high-pitched whistle coming from his throat.

"*You* are the reason I'm dead." Aden's face smothered mine before he pulled away and relaxed into the back of the couch, partially submerged. "You took everything away from me—all because you forgot to look both ways."

"I was just a kid."

"Just a kid," he repeated in a funny high voice, trying to mimic me. "Just a kid…"

"What do you want?" I was suddenly fuming. "If I could take it back, I would. You want me to say sorry? I'M SORRY!" I flew at him, the anger driving me.

He laughed and pulled backward, leaving me panting. "Don't you *feel* it now? *What a rush!* You should feel what it's like after a haunting! It's the only power you'll ever get in this place."

I froze, trying to digest what he'd just said, shifting my gaze to Felix, who was still in the corner with his head buried in his knees. The TV continued buzzing in and out, the reception fighting for survival.

"Power…" I repeated his words, still trying to get it.

"Come on, are you really that stupid?"

I whipped around. "Who's the stupid one? You've been holding onto a grudge for twelve years. Get. Over. It. You are DEAD." I rushed through him and felt the strange sensation of overlapping space coursing between us. I emerged on the other side beside Felix, who had fallen over, apparently passed out.

"So, you think just because you *love* her, that justifies your involvement with her?" Aden asked, keeping his distance. "Get over yourself. We all need something to keep us going, don't we?"

"What's that supposed to mean?"

"Love, hate, fear, guilt—take your pick. It's all just fuel to get what we want."

"So, that's what you want? To haunt a girl…or a druggie?" I asked, looking over at Felix. "That's the big kick you're getting?"

"That, and seeing you suffer, which was my intent in the first place. Now it's a two for one—a rush and revenge. What's your excuse?"

"Excuse?"

"To interfere with Claire's life. At least revenge is a legitimate motive."

"I'm not interfering with her."

"Then what are you doing?"

"Why is that any of your business?"

"You made it my business."

"How's that?" I asked, drifting away from Felix, and toward the window where the last of the sunlight was trying to force its way through the dirt into this hellhole.

Aden laughed out loud, *of course*. So dramatic.

"You still don't get it. How did you not flunk out of school? Education, these days…" He floated right up to my face. "I'll make it simple. One—you killed me. Two—you saved Claire. Three—Claire can see me now thanks to you and I get to scare her, which gives me more power…*la-di-da-di-da*… Shall I go on?"

I suddenly felt the weight of what he was saying, like I had slipped to the bottom of the sea. Claire's aunt *was* right. My connection with Claire had opened up a window, a Pandora's box, or whatever you wanted to call it. And now I didn't know how to close it back up.

Claire

Dad pounced on the intruder from behind, pulling him into a headlock. Mom and I jumped and screamed, tipping over bowls and spilling soup across the table. I was afraid to look. All I could hear was Dad's grunting, along with the muffled sound of the intruder's protests. Strangely, the voice started sounding a little familiar—which was when Mom and I both ran around the table.

"Dad!" I yelled, pulling at his arm.

"Matthew!" Mom said, pulling at my brother's torso.

Dad let go, and we all stood there facing each other in surprise, confusion, and a little bit of deflated terror.

"What the…?" Matthew stepped back, eyeing us in alarm.

"Matthew," Dad breathed, finally recognizing him.

"*Yeah!* Were you expecting someone else? What's *wrong* with you guys?" he croaked while rubbing his throat.

"Matthew," Mom said soothingly, like it was the only name in the world. "I'm *so* sorry. We didn't know you were coming. Why didn't you call?"

"Now I have to *call* to come home?" he shot out defensively, fixing his shirt. His face seemed to soften a bit when he looked over at me. I gave him a weak smile and shrugged my shoulders.

He looked so much older—the months and a tragic past aging him too quickly. His hair, still as blond as ever, was longer than I remembered. He also seemed more hefty, like he'd been working out. The one thing that *did* look the same was the tired, jaded look on his face that took over the night Daniel was killed.

Mom pulled Matthew into a hug lasting longer than normal. "Of course you don't need to call. You can come home any time you want." She finally released him just when I thought he was going to bolt.

"Sorry, Son, it's just…well, a lot has happened over the last couple of days," Dad said apologetically. Matthew waited for him to continue, but Dad seemed almost embarrassed to reveal the details. He was never one for drama. "We thought you were an intruder," he finally admitted, not quite looking Matthew in the eyes.

"I figured that much," Matthew answered, still irritated.

"Are you hungry? Come have some soup," Mom said, as if a bowl of soup could solve the world's problems.

"No thanks. I already ate." Matthew walked to the fridge, eyeing me strangely.

I followed him, uncertain what to say or do. It had been so long since we last talked, that I felt uneasy, like we were cousins or something. It made me sad, because we used to be so close.

"So, what's been going on here?" he asked, grabbing a Coke and popping it open. "Obviously there're some things you haven't told me."

"It's a fairly new development, Matthew," Dad said, a little defensively.

"Well, are you going to fill me in? Or were you going to wait until Christmas?"

Mom and Dad looked at each other briefly, then at me. I kept quiet. "There's no reason to get upset, Matthew," Mom said. "We were planning on talking to you about this, once things settled down a bit."

Matthew brought his drink to the table and sat down, kicking his feet up on another chair. Mom and Dad sat across from him, most likely trying to figure out where to start. I quietly gathered the soup bowls and started cleaning up the mess.

Matthew waited for them to speak. "I'm all ears," he prodded, taking another swig. "Give me what you got."

The dishes kept me busy, though I could easily hear the whole conversation behind me. Occasionally, I turned to peek at Matthew's face, trying to gauge his reaction as Dad explained the events of the last day and a half—a.k.a. my Peeping Tom-turned-stalker, and his threatening note. Matthew acted a little surprised, but his reaction seemed subdued, like he was hiding something. *What*, I couldn't tell just yet, so I kept my suspicions to myself and my eyes and ears alert from afar.

"Are the police even doing anything about it?" Matthew asked.

"They've been here twice." Dad answered.

"And they took the note in as evidence," Mom added. "We're still waiting on that."

Matthew tipped his chair on its heels. "So they're essentially doing nothing."

"What do you want them to do?" Dad challenged.

Matthew fidgeted, his mask of confidence briefly transparent, at least long enough for me to notice. "I don't know," he admitted, standing up and finishing off his Coke. "But, they're useless, if you ask me."

Without another word or glance in my direction, he walked past me toward his room, leaving the rest of us awkwardly staring at each other. No one knew what to say, although we all understood what Matthew was referring to—the police never caught the person who shot Daniel. Though we all pushed it back into the corner of our minds, Matthew could *never* forget.

Later, Matthew brought his things in from the car, including four giant garbage sacks filled with dirty clothes, while I hung out in my room in front of my computer. I wondered what the information in that newspaper article meant to me now. My ghost had an identity. Had it changed anything? Even after finding some of the answers I was looking for, I didn't know what to do with those answers, other than wait for Daniel to show up.

It was already dark, though still early evening. Most people hated the way fall hijacked the daylight, but I always liked it—especially now. The sooner the sun went down the better, as far as I was concerned. Except, I hadn't seen Daniel since last night. What if he truly wasn't coming back like he had said, or if he'd somehow figured out a way to get around my haunting ghost?

There was a knock on my door.

"Come in," I called, still lost in thought.

"Claire?" Matthew said, his voice surprisingly meek.

"Hey." I turned around in surprise, almost blushing. "What's up?"

He slowly walked to my bed, probably one of the few times I'd ever seen him so unnerved. I waited to hear what was on his mind as he sat stiffly at the foot of the bed, staring at me for a second. His hands were clasped together like he was trying to figure out what to say. I turned my chair around to face him.

"First of all, I'm sorry about that creep. I wish I'd been here. *I* would have caught him," he said, not really looking me in the eye.

"I know," I agreed. Really, Matthew probably *would have* caught him.

"So, how come *you* guys didn't call me?" He seemed hurt.

"Everything just happened so fast, and, and… *Wait…*" I just caught the emphasis he'd put on 'you.' "You mean someone *did* call you?

He nodded.

"But not Mom or Dad?"

He nodded again.

"You already knew everything!" I accused, remembering how calm he had been while Mom and Dad explained everything.

He didn't deny it.

"Who told you?"

"Addie."

"*Addie* called you?"

"Uh-huh."

"What did she say? When did she call?"

"I don't know, sometime this afternoon," he said, looking down at his watch. "Just after you guys got home from the park, I think."

I could only stare at him in disbelief. I was pretty sure they hadn't spoken a single word since Daniel died. How did she even get his number?

"Wow, that must have been weird," I said more to myself than to him.

"Yeah, but at least she thought to call."

I felt a little guilty when he put it that way, but I also felt somewhat defensive. "Matthew…you *do* realize we haven't talked…*really* talked…in months?" His brilliant eyes watched me briefly, and then peered off to the side. He still didn't say anything. "What happened–"

"What happened?" he asked, cutting me off. "What *happened?* Come on, Claire, I watched my best friend die. I saw a bullet go through his head!"

It was the first time he had ever spoken of Daniel's murder. I didn't move. The air was uncomfortably tense.

"Sorry," he spoke more softly, looking in my eyes. "I didn't mean to yell at you. That's not why I wanted to talk to you."

"It's okay," I replied, regretting the way the conversation had turned, realizing our relationship might always be strained.

He coughed, and then lay on his back, staring upward. "I couldn't go through it all again. Not with you, too."

"Go through what?"

"When I heard you almost drowned, it really got to me, but I pushed it away. Forgot about it like it never happened, just like with…well, Daniel," he explained reflectively. "But when Addie called today and told me what was going on here, I felt like everything in my life was slipping away, and I couldn't do anything about it. I just can't let it happen again. Not to you, too." He finally took a breath, and then covered his face with his hands like a shield.

I stared at him in shock. Sure, I expected him to struggle, knowing he was hurting all this time, but was entirely unprepared for this naked soul to emerge—the Matthew I used to know and love.

"I'm glad you came back," I smiled, not knowing what else to say. He sat up and looked at me, then shifted his eyes down. An uncomfortable silence followed.

"What are you doing, anyway, getting into all sorts of trouble now that I'm away?" he teased, pulling us out of the uneasiness with his infectious smile.

"You know me," I laughed, "always causing trouble."

"Hardly. Addie, on the other hand…"

I dove on the bed next to him, where we spent the next hour or so catching up. College sounded like it had been the best thing for Matthew, even if we still missed him. He already met a couple of girls, though no official girlfriend yet.

My life, on the other hand, especially over the last few months, was a little more difficult to retell. My mind jumped from one place to another, like I was back in that stream where Daniel had found my ring, carefully hopping over the slippery rocks, trying not to fall in. Part of me wanted to tell Matthew everything, to let him in on my ballooning secret, but the wiser part of me noted that he was the one who had gotten all of Dad's left-brained genes.

Finally, our stories caught up to the present, and I yawned and looked over at the clock. 9:13. No sign of Daniel yet.

"So how long will you be here?" I asked, briefly touching Matthew on the back as he stood up.

"I don't know. I haven't decided."

"What about school?"

"Missing a few classes isn't going to sink me, Claire. I'm a little brighter than that." He smiled, knocking his finger on his temple a couple of times for effect. He made it to the door, then paused and turned back. "Tell me the truth."

"Huh?"

"Are you scared?"

"What?"

"Scared. You seem remarkably calm, considering the last 24 hours."

If it wasn't for Daniel, I would be terrified.

"Yes," I sighed. "But I'm also okay, if that makes any sense."

"I just keep thinking about the note," he said.

"What about it?"

"What did it mean?"

"How would I know? It was just an idiotic threat," I answered, afraid to make the connection.

"But how did this freak know you almost drowned? That was a month ago. Do you really think he's been stalking you this whole time?"

"I haven't had time to absorb everything yet, much less attempt to delve into a lunatic's mind."

Matthew just stared at me, waiting for more, like he knew I was hiding something. But I didn't say anything else. I'd already given the police the spiel—that I had no clue what the note meant or what it was referring to, except for the fact that I *did* almost drown on my birthday—but that was about it.

"Matthew, I…" I wanted to tell him even a little bit about Daniel, but didn't know where to start. It felt like old times, like we were lying out under the stars, laughing about the crazy people in the world (everyone but us). We were untouchable then.

His hand rested on the wall, waiting for me to continue.

"Do you believe in…?" I started, looking up at the ceiling for a second, hoping to gain a little courage before chickening out. "Do you believe in life after death?"

"*What?*"

Oops. Maybe a mistake, but I forged ahead, anyway. "Where do you think Daniel is right now?"

"I don't know," he answered abruptly, looking past me, like I was starting to annoy him.

"Well, have you ever thought about it?"

"No. Why?"

I sighed. Was this really going to go anywhere, other than making me look nutty?

"I just…I…" *Ughhh.* "I'm glad you're back," I said, giving up.

"Just stay safe, okay?" Matthew said as he walked out of the room without waiting for a response.

I collapsed into the pillows.

Daniel

We slowly circled the room, facing each other like we were in a duel.

"I should thank you for saving Claire's life," Aden said, feigning politeness. "If it wasn't for your heroic love, I'd be stuck haunting scum like Felix, here, instead of enjoying the thrill of someone who can actually see me."

"Listen—"

"No, *you* listen. I'm done with you! We've had our little talk. You can quit trying to find me, quit trying to convince me to leave your girlfriend alone. I'm through with you and your little Boy Scout act. I have better things to do with my time."

I shot toward him, ending our rotation, shouting the only thing I could think of. I was out of ammunition. "I've stopped connecting with her. So now where are you going to get your little thrill?"

Aden looked surprised, but just for a second. "Nice countermove from someone who can't even tie his shoes." He laughed. "But you're the one who'll suffer, not me. I have Felix to help me now. Either way, I get Claire. And when I'm done with her, there will always be plenty more to haunt. In the meantime, it's nice knowing I've taken from you the only thing you ever wanted, just like you took everything from me. Touché, don't you think?"

He darted away from me down the dark hallway, but I stuck right on his tail. He shot through the wall into the alleyway where long shadows, cast by the setting sun, buried the street in darkness.

"Now this is more fun!" Aden shouted, rushing into a busy intersection where cars plowed through us. "Come on…where's your spirit?" he taunted. "Don't you want to hear what I think of your girlfriend? Should I tell you how I watch her when you're away…how she tosses and turns when she's asleep…where Felix fits into all of this? Is that what you want to hear? *Is it?*"

He tried fading away, and I lunged at him. Just like before, he somehow pulled me to him, and I was stuck. Again. He shifted with me to another place—a strange city filled with honking cars, glass skyscrapers reaching to the sky, and hordes of people all speaking another language. I looked around anxiously, wondering where we were.

"You like following me?" he asked, seamlessly shifting us away from the foreign city to a dark pier as the waves crashed beneath us. A young couple holding hands strolled right through us just as Aden let go of me. "I'll give you this much, just to watch you squirm."

I lunged at him, trying to grab him the same way he'd somehow grabbed me, but found I was powerless. Next thing I knew, he was shoving his head through mine and holding it there until everything in front of me went muddy gray. I tried pulling away, but it felt like a clamp was forcing my head in place. I yelled out, but couldn't hear myself because something like a movie started to creep into my hearing and vision.

At first I was confused, not sure where or what I was seeing, until I looked across the room and saw part of Matthew's bloody face buried beneath a bunch of moving bodies. Fists were swinging, people were screaming, beer was spilling all over the place as music thumped on top of it all. I must have been back inside my own memory of the night I died, though I wasn't sure how. I didn't remember the fight from this perspective—from across the room like this.

When the back of my own head came into view in front of my present vision, I felt dizzy, like I was going to pass out. At first, I didn't realize the head was mine, until the viewpoint took a new position to get a better look at my face. I watched myself rushing into the fight and throwing punches, and then pulling Matthew toward me, asking him if he was okay. Matthew's head was bloody, his eye swollen, and he seemed to be going in and out of consciousness.

"Watch out!" someone yelled.

Everyone in the room screamed at once, but it was too late. I saw myself turn around to face the barrel of a gun held by someone wearing an oversized black hoodie. I tried to stop what I was seeing, knowing what was about to happen. I even screamed at myself, at the room full of drunken kids, and threw myself into the outstretched arm of the kid holding the gun. But it was impossible to change the memory—*Aden's memory*.

He'd been there the whole time. Aden watched me die.

The blast exploded through the air and I saw my head jerk backward. Everyone screamed. My body fell forward into Matthew's lap as Aden's viewpoint turned toward the guy holding the gun. The killer glanced my way and then shoved the gun into his pants before turning and running out the back door.

Light and color exploded through my mind when Aden pulled me out of his memory. My head felt heavy as I watched him drift backward, smiling. "How's that for a killer ending?" He said, drifting over the black ocean, leaving me alone on the pier. This time I let him go without a chase.

My fight was gone.

It felt like my whole body was shaking, even though I knew it wasn't. Panic seemed to choke me from the unwanted glimpse at my murderer, and I fell over, trying to rid my mind of the killer's face.

My killer. Felix.

I knelt on the dark pier, battered with confusion, my mind a pulverized mess. The waves sprayed all around me as people unknowingly walked through me. I couldn't stop thinking about Felix. And Aden. And how he was probably haunting Felix's mind right now, telling him what to do next. Aden's puppet had killed me without even flinching, point blank. What would he do to Claire? How was I supposed to warn her if I couldn't even connect to her without letting Aden back in?

Maybe it would be better to just fade away from her life and hope everything, including Felix, went away, too. It wouldn't be that hard to find some remote part of the world, some interesting place like the Amazon, and hang out there with the natives, right? *Right?*

No. I couldn't do that. Not to Claire.

I shifted from the strange pier back to Hidden Lake, trying to push away my fears, but it was impossible. And as embarrassing as it was to admit—right then I was scared-of-monsters-frightened; I didn't know what to do. There was no one to talk to. I was completely alone in this. Powerless.

Drifting up the hill, I stopped in front of Claire's house, wondering what to do next. That was when I noticed a familiar black Jeep parked in the driveway, one that hadn't been there in months.

Matthew.

CHAPTER FOURTEEN MATTHEW'S SECRET

Claire

The image in the mirror stared back at me. With my hair pulled into a ponytail and a doublewide headband across my forehead, I scrubbed my face clean. After being accosted at the park, talking with the police, and being surprised—no, *shocked*—at Matthew's return, the day needed to end.

Immediately.

Daniel was apparently a no-show, too. Not a great way to usher in a good night's sleep, but I decided to end my hellish day anyway.

I never realized how much I missed Matthew until he came home. It felt good talking about nothing in particular or important, just hanging out like old times before Daniel's death. It also felt weird having him worry about me so much—this from someone who used to hide behind doors just to scare me. I had to admit I liked this Matthew, even if everything felt different.

After splashing cool water on my skin and burying my face in a warm towel, something brushed against the back of my arm. I dropped the towel, ready to scream until I saw Daniel and then fell into his arms.

"Daniel," I whispered. "I thought you weren't coming back."

He hugged me tightly before pulling back. "We almost missed it."

"*You* almost missed it," I corrected him playfully. But when his eyes drooped and his lips turned down, my excitement fizzled. "What's wrong?" I held his hands loosely. For some reason, he looked like he didn't want to talk. At all. "Were you with us at the park today?"

He nodded.

"So, you saw everything, then? The runner, the note–"

"Yes," he interrupted. "I followed him to his apartment, to some dive in the Tenderloin."

The Tenderloin. I'd been there once, to a little southern diner called Dottie's, but there was a reason it closed at three in the afternoon.

"Do you know why he's been following me?" I asked, afraid to hear the answer.

He took a deep breath and held my arms while looking me straight in the eye. "Because of Aden—your ghost-stalker," he said.

"I figured they were connected."

Daniel looked like he wanted to say more, but hesitated.

"The newspaper!" I remembered. "I found an old article about your accident."

"You did?" he asked, his eyes brightening.

"Yes, and it's not what you think. I'll show you–" I started to move around him for the door, but he stopped me.

"We don't have time. I was late."

"Oh, okay," I whispered, leaning up on my tiptoes and kissing him on the lips, trying to linger up there by his face. He seemed to respond, but not like before. Something was definitely wrong. "Daniel. You *didn't* kill him. You know that, right?"

He was quiet.

I went on. "The article said he was speeding without a helmet when he crashed. And he was drunk. It wasn't your fault, no matter what Aden says."

Daniel's face looked conflicted, the brown inside his pupils trying to focus, but seemingly lost somewhere else. I reached up for a few loose strands of hair hanging over his eyebrows and gently pushed them back, then leaned into his neck, touching my lips to his skin. "Daniel," I whispered, squeezing his hands, trying to get him to respond. "*Aden* started this mess. Not you. Stop blaming yourself."

He finally seemed to wake up from his slump, responding to my words by interlacing his fingers through mine until it almost hurt. Then he pulled his head away from me. It seemed like he'd been able to refocus, but his eyes still looked dismal.

"His name is Felix Marz," he said quickly, like a reporter. "The Peeping Tom. Aden found him…I don't know how…but you have to tell your parents, come up with some kind of story. You need to give his name to the police before anything else happens–"

"What? What's going to happen?"

Daniel looked away. "We don't have enough time to go into it," he said, like he was trying to brush me off.

"*What* does Felix want?" I demanded, this time a little louder. I could feel my hands shaking against his chest, remembering the note.

Daniel wrapped his arms around me and pulled me close to him. I inhaled deeply, wishing I could bottle up his scent.

"Felix just does what he's told. Aden's the one calling all the shots."

"What does *Aden* want, then?"

"At first it was just some stupid revenge against me. You know, because of how he died…because of the accident. But, now he just seems *crazy*. I don't know what his ultimate goal is, really, but haunting you and tormenting me seems to be what makes his world go round. I just don't know how to get him to stop—"

"You don't?"

"Well, except for never being with you again."

"But that's what he wants, isn't it?" I asked. "He gets his revenge by keeping you from me. He wins that way."

"He wins either way, Claire. I don't think we have a choice. If we keep connecting, he'll keep haunting you, each time worse than the last. We have to stop now before…well, before you get hurt. And now with Felix on board, everything is more complicated. I don't know what to do, Claire…"

I couldn't respond. An uncontrollable trembling ricocheted through my body until Daniel lightly caressed the back of my neck, replacing the trembling with shivering. An unwanted tear slid down my cheek, nearly finding its way to my chin. Daniel caught it for me with his finger as I closed my eyes and leaned against him, feeling utterly lost.

"Claire."

I didn't want to hear anymore.

"I think… You need to tell Matthew, now that he's back," he said, his voice a little louder.

I looked up in shock. "Tell him what?"

"About me."

"*Right.*" I said sarcastically, before realizing he was serious.

"You *have* to tell someone—someone who's alive—someone who can fight Felix, since I can't. Someone who will believe you, who can protect you. *That's Matthew,*" he insisted, both of his hands now on my shoulders, his forehead pressed against mine.

"But you saved me, remember? The fog…the lake? *You* can protect me, Daniel."

"I don't think it works like that, Claire. I can't stop someone from hurting you. I've only been able to connect with you. Not with anyone else."

"Then what about the police?" I asked, looking for a saner answer.

"Hopefully they can do something about Felix…but we need to do something *right now.* The police might take too long."

"But, Matthew won't believe me," I sighed, unable to look into his eyes.

"Yes, he *will.*"

"Do you know a different Matthew than I do?"

"He'll *believe* you, Claire." Daniel seemed positive, convinced.

"How?" I asked, almost daring him.

Big mistake.

He rested his head softly against mine for a second, and kissed me on the side of my cheek. Then he started to tell me what happened the night he was killed, forcing me to listen firsthand to the horrible details.

"I didn't die right away, Claire," Daniel was saying. "After I was shot, everything got quiet. At first I couldn't see anything—only black. That was when I heard Matt's voice above me and felt his hands holding up my head, though I don't know how. He was so thrashed…"

I didn't want to listen anymore, but didn't know how to stop him from telling me the rest. When he finished, I pulled him closer, wrapping my arms around him tightly. "I'm so sorry," I whispered.

His eyes looked so empty and tired, so unlike himself, without his signature smile and confidence. He was seventeen when he died, but the way he looked at me now made him seem so much older.

"This might be our last time together–"

"No," I gulped, trying not to cry.

He held still as I squeezed him tight, afraid to let go. Then, his touch and scent dissolved as I watched him slowly drift away from me into the wall. I raced out into the hallway for another glimpse of him, but he had already disappeared.

I wanted to wait until morning to talk to Matthew, but was afraid of losing all courage by then, especially if Aden came in the meantime. Hopefully, with a house full of people he would spare me tonight. Unlikely. Maybe Matthew *could* somehow find a way to help me.

The blaring sound of the TV pulled me into the family room, where Matthew was sitting on the couch, manhandling a mammoth sandwich that looked as if he had thrown in every deli item he could find. He didn't notice when I walked in, and was in the midst of another gigantic bite, his eyes still glued to the screen.

"It's 10:30, Matthew. How can you possibly eat that right now?" I always wondered how guys could eat so much all the time without getting huge. Or sick.

There was no answer, thanks to his mouth stuffed with sandwich and his eyes fixed on the screen.

"Hey, *Matthew*," I said a little louder, leaning against the armchair.

He paused his show and gave me a 'make-it-quick' look. I lost my nerve.

"What?" he asked when I didn't answer.

"I need to talk to you about something." I could feel my neck and cheeks getting warm, and hoped he couldn't tell. He was probably wondering what was wrong with me. How could I do this?

"Right now?" he asked, taking another bite.

"Yes. Are Mom and Dad here?" I asked, looking around.

"Went to bed," he said through turkey and sprouts. I didn't realize I'd have to compete with a sandwich. Still, I moved from the armchair to the end of the couch, trying to get comfortable.

"Whassuup?" he asked, finally taking his last bite.

"I know his name," I blurted out.

"Who?"

"The Peeping Tom. I know who he is."

"What?" He coughed, obviously surprised.

"But before I say how, I need to ask you what I should do about it," I said, trying to be clever. With Matthew, though, that never seemed to pan out. Still, I tried.

"Claire, you're not making any sense." His voice was beginning to sound just like Dad's.

"Just bear with me for a minute, okay?" I pleaded.

"Claire–"

"Please?"

He closed his eyes, like he was trying to force himself into a new persona. When he opened them again, it seemed a veil of patience had descended, if only briefly.

"Okay," I started. "If you knew the name, but wanted to protect your source, how would you go about giving it to the police?"

"I don't know. You could lie, I guess. But I don't really recommend lying to the police."

"Okay, so I could make up a story. That's a thought."

"Claire," he interrupted, already finished with hypothetical. "What are you talking about?"

His eyes seemed to impale me, and I felt my heart accelerating. How was I going to do this? A gulp stuck in my throat. When Matthew reached for his Coke, I finally dove in. "Do you promise to hear me out without interrupting—without listening to the logical, literal, factual side of your brain?"

"You mean, without thinking?" he asked, finishing off the can.

"Funny. No, I just want you to use your imagination a little bit."

"Oh...*kay*..."

"I mean, *really*, Matthew. Like, try to dig deep, way back inside to when you were a kid, back to when you believed in monsters and buried treasure and, and...ghosts."

"Cla–"

"*Please.*"

"Okay, I'll try."

I could tell he was already starting to jump to conclusions, which wasn't helping. I unclenched my hands while trying to untangle the nerves all bundled up inside me. He watched me closely, as if I were presenting evidence to a jury.

"I don't know where to start. It has to do with Daniel."

Whew. There. I said it.

"Daniel? *What?*"

Obviously just saying his name wasn't going to do the trick, but at least I was up and running. I turned my face toward the TV, my gaze getting lost in some actor's magnified face.

"You know how I fell in the lake on my birthday?" I asked, not waiting for an answer. "I never told you or anyone what *really* happened. I kept it a secret."

"What's up with the secrets, Claire?"

"Just listen."

"Okay," he whispered condescendingly. "Tell me your secret."

I wished Daniel were here to give me a little encouragement. It didn't seem fair I was the one to have to do this, especially since it was turning out to be so much more difficult than anticipated. I had forgotten how conversations with Matthew always took twice as long, because his brain refused to work without proof. And I thought my imagination was bad.

"I didn't *almost* drown, Matthew," I confessed. "I *did* drown."

"You drowned," he repeated.

"Yes. I died for a little bit."

"Claire, that's not possible."

"How do you know?"

"Because I know that's not possible. Not without brain damage or death—*permanent* death."

"You're wrong," I refuted, looking right at him, refusing to give in. I knew I was right, and because of that, wasn't apologetic anymore. Well, at least not yet.

"Why do you think you died?" he cross-examined me. "I mean, what did you see that convinced you that you were dead?"

"It wasn't just what I saw. That was only a small part of the whole thing. It was more about what I *felt*, what I *knew*. I wasn't in the lake anymore. Instead, it was like my whole spirit, or mind was alive in everything, like I'd become part of the sky and the stars. I felt so peaceful and free, and didn't want to come back."

Matthew watched me, his eyes like glass as they stared into mine. I could tell my words had floated into his ears, inched up into his mind and were mulling around, trying to find their way down to his heart.

So I went right on.

"But someone called me. I could hear him whispering my name, pulling at me to return and wake up. When I recognized the voice, I decided to come back."

"Who was it?" he asked, leaning forward.

I glanced down at my hands, scared to go on. "It was Daniel," I said, looking up at Matthew boldly. He didn't move, didn't blink, didn't breathe—didn't do anything for an excruciatingly long time as I anxiously waited for a reaction…

"Daniel," he finally repeated.

I nodded my head yes.

"Well, that must've been a nice dream, then," he reasoned dryly, the previous look of interest gone, a shadow of steel falling across his face.

"It wasn't a dream, Matthew."

"Not a dream. You heard Daniel whisper in your ear, but it wasn't a dream? I'm not following."

"I didn't just hear him. *I saw him*. He was there–"

"Daniel is dead."

"I know."

Matthew looked at me like I was being unreasonably thick.

"When everything went black, I *died* for about four or five minutes. Then Daniel called my name. When I woke up, he was still there, right next to me."

"*Come on—*"

"He's the one who saved me, Matthew!" I practically yelled. "It was Daniel. He saved me."

"You hit your head. Maybe you were seeing things, imagining things—"

"No. I know what I saw."

"No you don't! Daniel is dead! I watched him die! I was with him, in case you forgot—"

"I *know* he's dead. That's not my argument. If that's your only reason for not believing me, then—"

"What do you want me to believe?" he shouted. "That Daniel saved you from drowning, or brought you back to life, or whatever? Fine, I'll give you that. I believe that's what you *saw*. But you can't convince me it was not just some strange phenomenon from hitting your head."

"That's not what it was," I said defiantly. But he wasn't looking at me anymore. He seemed to be staring across the room at nothing. "I *saw* him. He was there. I could hear him. I could feel him, and then he vanished."

Matthew turned his head instantly. "So, you're telling me that your little secret is Daniel has come back from the dead? Come on, Claire."

I stood up and paced across the room and back, trying to make him believe me without telling him what he didn't want to hear. "I can *see* him sometimes, Matthew."

His jaw was clenched, his profile harsh, almost angry, like I had disappointed him. But I continued, hoping he would realize I was telling the truth.

"Ever since he saved me, I've been able to see him when it's dark. At the exact same time every night, he comes to life again. I can touch him, hear him, and talk to him for about four minutes. I don't know–"

Matthew stood up. "Stop it, Claire! Just stop," he exclaimed, his eyes wet, his face red. He scared me. Just for a second. "Stop talking like you've lost your mind," he said more quietly. "Do you realize what you're saying? Can you hear yourself? Do you want Mom and Dad to send you to a therapist, to put you on meds or something? Can't you see where this is going? You can't talk like this. You can't say this stuff."

"But, Matth–"

"I'm serious." He placed his hands on my shoulders and nearly shook me. "I miss him too, Claire. I wanted to die that day, I did. I still can't think about him without losing it." A single tear found its way over the edge of his lashes, but he quickly wiped it away, hoping I wouldn't notice. "You *can't* do this, Claire. *Please.*"

I felt my eyes start to water, but didn't care when it trickled down my cheek, clinging to the edge of my lip.

"When Daniel—when he died, I wanted the world to end. I didn't care about anything. The only thing that kept me going was Mom and Dad. I couldn't stand being around you and Addie anymore because it brought back too many memories. I didn't know what to do with myself. It felt like I was about to explode every second, the sound of the gunshot and the image of blood all over his face refusing to leave my head. I tried everything to push it away. *Everything.* But nothing worked." Matthew let go of me and shoved his hands in his pockets.

"I'm sorry, Matthew," I said quietly, carefully.

He didn't answer. Instead, he stood there as if trying to force something back inside him, something too powerful or horrible to face.

"Going away to college was the best thing I could've done. It got my mind off my misery. No one tiptoed around me, and no one reminded me of him. I wasn't choking anymore. When Addie called me yesterday, I almost hung up on her. It's so much easier living a new life and not having to face the old one, but after she told me what was happening here, it sort of woke me up. It scared me. I realized that life really did go on, and it would keep marching ahead, with or without me. That's when I decided I wasn't betraying Daniel anymore—"

"Betraying Daniel?" I asked, amazed that he had thought something so far from the truth.

"He died while I went on living—living a life that could've just as well been *his* life. It seemed wrong and twisted after what he did for me...and...and..." Matthew paused.

"Talk about twisted, Matthew," I interjected dryly. "Daniel would never think something like that."

Matthew threw me a look of irritation.

"He *wouldn't*," I insisted.

"My point," he continued, "is that even though you're dealing with this differently, you obviously need to get away from here like I did. Once he's out of your mind, you can go on with your life."

"I don't *want* him out of my mind."

Matthew fell backward into the couch, and threw his hands up in frustration or defeat—I wasn't sure which. It was silent then, and I didn't know what else to do or say to convince him, except...

He reached for the remote.

"Wait…" I said.

He ignored me and pushed play.

And so it had come down to the one thing I didn't want to say. But I *had* to because I really needed his help.

Matthew looked especially annoyed when I sat on the coffee table in front of him, partially blocking his view. He craned his neck to look around me, hoping I would get the hint.

Deep breath.

"Matthew, Daniel told me about the night he was shot. He said he didn't die right away like everyone said, but that you talked to him for a little bit."

Deeper breath.

Matthew hesitated and then turned off the TV. He slowly brought his eyes to meet mine. "*What?*"

"Daniel told you he was sorry for getting blood all over your new shirt, and then you said, 'It's not your blood, bro. It's mine. You're going to be fine. Just stay with me a little longer…' His last words were, 'I tried to duck, Matt.' He died with his eyes still open, looking right at you."

"Claire…" Matthew said my name quietly, slowly, his voice nearly shaking, just like mine. The remote fell into his lap. I couldn't suppress my heartache anymore, and felt torn apart from having to picture Daniel's death all over again, combined with the burden from making Matthew relive it, too.

"How would I know this, Matthew?" I asked, trying not to entirely lose it as I felt my voice shaking. "Either you told me, or Daniel did."

"I never told anyone."

Matthew stared straight ahead. He was at a total loss—of words, of voice, of composure. And I felt like I was turning a knife into him, driving it deeper and deeper. I put my arm around him as he caved into the tide of emotion that tried to pull him under.

There were no words between us, no sounds. Nothing but pain.

Matthew buried his head in his hands, nearly smothering his voice. "I still haven't figured out how to go on. I can still see his eyes staring up at me. He even laughed when I told him it wasn't his blood. He knew I was lying. He knew he was going to die." He gasped. "Sometimes when I look at my hands, I see his blood all over them."

I didn't know what to do. I was having a hard enough time myself, the image of Daniel's blood on Matthew's hands was too much.

Finally he turned to me. "I still don't know if I can believe it, Claire, despite the evidence. It's impossible."

"I know."

I explained the rest—about ghost-Aden and stalker-Felix. Little by little, things seemed to start making sense to Matthew, and the more we talked, the more he seemed to break out of the static that held him trapped inside a mind that could not see beyond his own rationale.

"I'm sorry, Claire," Matthew said, putting his hand on my knee. "I don't know what to do. I can't think straight right now, because every logical connection in my mind has suddenly dried up."

"I don't know what else to say to convince you."

He was quiet for a minute.

"You should probably tell the police that you remember seeing Felix's name at the park when his wallet fell out, or something like that…" Matthew finally said, already thinking things through.

"Okay."

Suddenly his phone rang, causing me to jump. He looked at me funny, and answered it. For about twenty seconds he didn't say another word, but just smiled, covering the phone. "It's Addie. She says she knows you're home, because where else would you be, and demands to know why you're ignoring her."

He handed me the phone, and then sat at the dining room table, staring intently out the sliding glass door, like he was brainstorming. Right then Daniel drifted into the room, resting casually at the end of the table, opposite Matthew. He turned and smiled at me.

Nice timing.

"Hey, Ad," I said in the phone, smiling at Daniel.

"Hey, Ad? That's all you have?" Her voice carried loud enough for both Matthew and Daniel to hear. They laughed.

I finally found an opening and started telling Addie she had a little explaining to do with her secret S.O.S. call to Matthew—but then Matthew looked like he wanted to choke me.

"He *told* you?" Addie yelled, her voice louder than her normal loud. What had I just gotten in the middle of? "I told him to make up some story, to convince you guys that he had a bout of homesickness, or that he just needed a break from school, or something!"

"It doesn't really matter, Addie," I reassured her and Matthew. "I'm *glad* he's here. *Glad* you called him. *Glad* you went behind our backs."

"Well, that's what I'm here for."

"What, to go behind my back?"

"Sure. Listen," she continued, oblivious to what she had just admitted, "Do you think you've had enough time to, you know, bond, or whatever you guys need to do with Matthew?"

"*What?*"

"Have you brushed everything under the bridge, or however that saying goes? Like, have I given you enough space yet?"

"Is that what you were doing?" I laughed. "Wow, that must have been quite the ordeal for you."

"Tell me about it. So, do you mind if I come over? My parents left for some weekend trip a couple of hours ago, and I'm kind of freaking out a little bit here, with that psycho-stalker lurking around and all."

"Right now?" I asked, looking at the clock on the wall. "It's past eleven—"

"Kay, I'll be there in a sec." The phone was dead before I could respond.

"I've actually missed her," Matthew said with a smile.

"Who wouldn't?"

My stomach growled like it usually did when I stayed up too late, so I wandered to the pantry in search of a snack, finally settling on a strawberry Pop-Tart. While breaking open the package, I sat at the table between Matthew and Daniel.

"So, while you're both here," I said, looking first at Matthew, and then Daniel, before breaking off a huge piece of pastry and popping it into my mouth.

"He's here?" Matthew asked, looking around the room.

"Yes. He's at the table, sitting across from you, actually."

"Seriously?" Matthew's face was skeptical, although belief was definitely trying to break through. It was as if doubt and hope were at war, neither willing to surrender.

"Seriously," I said, chomping on a frosty corner.

"What's he doing?" he asked, looking around.

"Just sitting there."

Daniel lifted his left hand and waved.

"And waving now, too," I added.

"Waving? Sounds a little dorky. Tell him—"

"He can hear you, Matthew."

"Oh. I thought you said he could only hear *you*."

"No, he can hear everything. You can talk to him, but he can't talk back. Well, he can talk, but I can't hear him."

"That's annoying."

"Um. *Yeah*."

"So, how do you communicate then, if you can't hear him?"

"It's not easy. I'm getting really good at charades, though."

"Oh, yeah, that would work," he laughed, probably remembering how uncreative I had always been, and wondering if Daniel was ready to give up yet. "Sorry, man," he seemed to whisper, like he wanted to say something to Daniel, but was too embarrassed.

Daniel shifted closer to Matthew and looked right at him, his eyes overflowing with something like regret filled with gratitude for his best friend. Six months ago, Daniel would've considered that kind of gesture beyond cheesy. Dying must change *every* perspective, even a teenage boy's.

"So, from what you've told me, Aden can only come right after you and Daniel have your connection, right?" he asked, snagging my other Pop-Tart.

"Yes, if that makes any sense..." I looked away, feeling strange talking about it out loud.

Matthew stretched his arms, like he was getting tired. "When was the last time you and Daniel connected?"

I looked at Daniel, then back at Matthew again. "Um…about an hour ago."

"Oh."

"He said it was the last time, though," I said, looking back at Daniel, who wouldn't meet my eyes. It hurt even more saying the words out loud. "Tonight will be the last night we have to worry about Aden haunting me."

"So, after tonight, we only worry about Felix?" Matthew asked, thoroughly missing my underlying remorse.

I nodded my head.

"You can't be by yourself. Ever," Matthew said, slapping his hand on the table.

"Ever?"

"Not until Felix is caught. I'm also not sure how effective Dad's fancy new alarm is going to be with a ghost hanging around, and all. But I guess it's better than nothing."

"What do you think, Daniel?" I asked, but he just kept staring off in a pensive gaze out the window, like he wasn't listening anymore. "Um, he looks like he's thinking."

"Tonight, Daniel can watch for Aden, and I'll keep an eye on you the rest of the time," Matthew said.

"But for how long?" I asked, suddenly overwhelmed by everything. "We can't do this forever. You still have to get back to school, *I* still have a life, or at least I *should* have one. I don't think this is going to work, Matthew. I–"

"Claire," Matthew said, leaning forward, grabbing my clenched fists. "We take it a day at a time. You're right. I have school, we both have a life, but for right now—tonight, tomorrow, I don't know, until it doesn't make sense anymore, this is what the plan needs to be."

I smiled, thankful Daniel made me tell Matthew, because I didn't feel so alone anymore.

Addie arrived close to midnight, and around one-o'clock we all finally went to bed. Dad had already set the alarm four hours ago, but Matthew did it all over again, mumbling under his breath something about how useless cops were.

I was glad Addie had invited herself over, because with her all snuggled up inside the covers beside me, I somehow felt a little safer. Even after she turned her back toward me and mumbled, "Wake me if you hear anything, okay?"

CHAPTER
FIFTEEN DAWN OF THE DEAD

Daniel

When Claire went to bed, I drifted outside to my regular spot beneath the eucalyptus tree and waited for Aden to show up. The black sky pulled me into a daze until the fog began creeping up over the hills, gradually spreading out like a mystical army. I wanted to join the ranks and float away with it, just wandering aimlessly through the sky with no purpose or care in the world—but that wasn't going to happen.

Aden suddenly materialized in front of me, bringing along with him the usual icy chills running up and down my legs. He was smiling, but I didn't want to let on how much it bothered me. I tried ignoring him by looking the other way, like I couldn't care less. But he kept getting in my face.

"I thought you were sick of me," I finally said.

"Yes, well, I just came by to give you an update."

"Then give it," I said, looking past him toward the house.

"You're too late," he announced. I couldn't tell if he was bluffing, and before I could decide, he added, "Felix already has her."

What? How could he already have her? I'd been watching the house the entire time. Was this a trick, or did I somehow miss something?

He hovered beside me, watching my reaction. I was afraid to listen to him, afraid not to. "So long," he said, fading out.

Wait.

No!

I lunged forward, regretting my rash decision a second too late when a magnetic force pulled me to him, like in Felix's apartment. It was a trap.

"Can't help yourself, can you?" Aden said, shifting us away from Hidden Lake, dragging me unwillingly with him.

His first stop was the park where it all started twelve years ago. Long shadows stretched across the road beneath the dim street lamps where we lingered in the familiar intersection, the school across the street dark and empty. Even cars were a no-show this late; it was just a quiet neighborhood in the stretch of a new morning, seemingly unaware of its tragic past.

Aden turned to me. I tried pulling a poker face, though I was never that great at cards. "You are so easy to predict," he said, circling around me, his voice a rollercoaster of soft and loud, fast and slow. "That really is your downfall."

I kept trying to detach myself, but couldn't seem to focus. It felt like he was a giant magnet, scrambling my mind so nothing worked.

"You realize this is all your doing? I never even lifted a finger. You should *think* before you act. Now I've got you."

He was right.

The park was gone in a flash, and next we were in Felix's apartment. This time, only shapes and shadows were hiding in the dark. I tried not to ingest any of the details that had previously disgusted me, but my memory of the place repulsed me as much the second time.

"If you'd thought things through twelve years ago, if you hadn't blindly jumped into the street like an idiot to save a useless dog, neither of us would be here right now. You have no one to blame but yourself."

I looked away from him, wishing he would shut up, trying once more to pull my mind away from his grasp, but it was impossible.

"You'd think by now you would've learned that your impulsive need to act the hero hasn't really worked out for you," he continued.

Shut *up*.

He methodically pulled me from the dark hallway, through the wall into the bedroom, and then out into the hallway again. "Now we wait." He stopped. "Felix needs a little more time."

"You have Felix doing everything for you now? Got tired of making the trip yourself?" I tried not to sound as panicked as I felt.

He laughed, which made me more anxious. "Let's pretend you're not a total moron just for a second. How about that? Because this is the part I've been looking forward to the most."

"You never make any sense," I mumbled, already feeling exhausted.

At that, he pulled me with him back to the park, dragging me through the swings, down the hill, to the empty parking lot. At the bottom, he stopped and looked around, like he was waiting for something. "Where are they?" he muttered to himself, his voice verging on irritated.

"Things not working out how you planned?" I taunted, hoping to distract him long enough to escape.

"Where is he going?" Aden growled.

"All you ever do is blame everyone else for your mistakes. You can't do a single thing by yourself."

"Shut up!" he hissed, pulling at his hair. I felt a slight change in the force linking us together, like tension relaxing from a rubber band. "I'm the one who calls the shots!"

"My point, exactly," I said, encouraged at the way he seemed to be losing focus. I kept going, trying to egg him on. "Felix pulled the trigger because you couldn't do it yourself. Just like everything else you do. You have no real power."

"That's right!" he yelled, pushing me backward through a chain-link fence. "Thanks to you!"

*Wait a second…*this was not where I was heading.

"I was five years old when it happened! FIVE!" My own anger seemed to be working against me as the magnetic force drew me to him again. But I couldn't help myself. "What's wrong with you? You were drunk. Your death was more your fault than mine!"

For a half a second he looked vulnerable, almost sad, like he had an ounce of remorse hidden behind his eyes. Quickly though, the pride/hatred/jealousy or whatever it was that drove him, took over. He threw me across the grass and slammed me through a wall. "*You* took my life away!"

There was no pain, only a dull sensation from the force of the blow, and my mind felt cloudy. Speechless, I nodded at him in silent agreement as he pulled me by the neck, out of the wall. "Let's go find your girlfriend, Romeo."

Next thing I knew, we were hovering above the water at Hidden Lake, waiting for something as the dense fog blew right through us.

Claire

A foreign noise called me back from a dream that had gotten all twisted and confusing. I tried opening my eyes at the sound, but the thickness of the dream pulled at me, refusing to let go. My head felt heavy, and I was disoriented until my eyes finally opened to my dark, moonlit bedroom. I scanned the shadows, wondering what had awoken me.

Addie was still sound asleep, sprawled across the bed, snoring.

I rolled out of the covers and wandered into the kitchen for a glass of water, my heart pounding with every step. Why was I still scared? Daniel would warn me if anything were wrong. Yet, I still practiced deep yoga breaths while filling my glass at the fridge, nervously watching the ominous shadows that seemed to be climbing up the kitchen walls.

I gulped down the cold water in seconds.

Wait.

I froze, the cup still resting on the edge of my mouth. Why was the red blinking alarm light *not* blinking? Why was it solid green?

"Dad? Matthew?" I squeaked, wondering if one of them had gone outside for some reason.

I expected to hear the sound of breaking glass when the cup slipped from my hand, but someone caught it, instead. I turned my head and tried to scream when I saw Felix standing behind me, but he had already slapped his icy, rough hand over my mouth and shoved me against his torso.

Where were Daniel and Matthew?

I tried to run, but Felix pulled me back. "Don't even think about it," he growled.

My heart pounded through my ears as terror engulfed me. Felix's eyes seemed like fire as he craned his head forward to face me. The porch light cascaded across his head, illuminating his deep-set eyes and cracked, peeling lips.

He twisted my arms behind my back with a free hand. "You need to listen to me carefully, Claaaayre," he said, his voice deep and raspy. Unable to breathe or see or think, it felt like I was drowning again. "My demon was right—the things he said about you." He licked his lips, and I squeezed my eyes shut. "You will move very quietly now, do you hear me? Very quietly."

Obediently I nodded, willing to follow any command as long as it resulted in my release. As soon as he loosened his grip, I started forward.

"Now," he whispered. "If you scream or run, you'll regret it, do you understand?" It was then that I felt the sharp point of a knife at my throat, its razor edge slightly piercing my skin. I felt faint, but did as he ordered, despite my wobbly knees.

"We're going to take a little walk now."

I had imagined this moment a hundred times, determined never to be taken by force—to scream, kick, bite, whatever it took, in order to keep from being forced away from safety into the unknown. But that was exactly what I was doing now. All my previous intuition failed me. The knife at my throat along with Daniel's absence had paralyzed me. Not wanting to die, I took the risk of being able to escape between point A and point B, praying Matthew or Daniel would show up any second.

"Slowly...slowly," Felix whispered, pushing me out of the kitchen.

As we entered the hallway, I tried peering back toward Matthew's room, but Felix's rough hand turned my face forward, forcing me to the front door. It was already cracked open, and the alarm somehow disabled.

We silently stepped into the chilly night, the sudden coolness like a breath of fresh air, despite my circumstance. I paused at the top of the steps, but his hand was back at my throat and the knife now against my back. "Move," he growled, shoving me down the stairs.

The tranquility I usually felt in the fog disappeared as soon as Felix spoke, like his words had broken a magical spell. My bare feet felt raw and vulnerable as the hellish night engulfed me. Fog wafted around in wispy puffs, unintentionally providing an atmosphere of terror as it shrouded nearly every bit of light.

All was eerily quiet as he forced me down the road, away from the house. I stumbled over a pothole, and Felix pushed me forward, almost knocking me down. I took advantage of the break by trying to make a run for it, when his hand caught my sleeve and yanked me back. The *Self Defense 101* class Mom made me take last summer finally kicked into gear, and I kneed him in the groin and took off.

Everything in the distance was fuzzy and dim without my glasses, and I wasn't sure which way to turn. The only thing I knew for sure was that the dock and lake were to my left. Thanks to my hesitation, Felix caught up almost immediately, shoving me to the ground. I tried to scream out, but he crammed his face into mine, covering my mouth with his hand.

"Nice try," he said, almost calmly. That was when I started to freak out. Felix didn't even seem rattled.

He jammed his knee in my stomach, holding it there like he was trying to decide what to do next. The weight of his body on mine was suffocating, and I could feel myself beginning to break down. A sob shook my shoulders and ricocheted through my chest until I reined it in, nearly choking on it. He pulled me up by the hair and forced me further down the hill, to the dock where we waited…for *what*, I didn't know.

My muscles tightened in anticipation, and I expected him to push me over the edge at any second. I blinked hard, trying to keep my tears from coming, refusing to expose any weakness, even though the thought of drowning again threw me into a panic. I was not ready to die. Not yet. Not like this.

But he didn't push me. Instead, we just stood there staring out at nothing while his breath obscenely molested my neck.

I started to protest, but he stopped me with a commanding grunt. "Shut up!"

Some kind of movement over the middle of the lake caught my attention. Felix finally loosened his grip on me, and I felt liberated, but then remembered I was trapped at the edge of the dock with nowhere to run. Squinting through the darkness, I wished for my glasses. "What is it?" I whispered, feeling more and more nervous. Whatever it was seemed to be coming toward us across the water.

Any previous thoughts of Daniel swooping in to save the day vanished the instant I recognized the approaching face—Aden. And he wasn't alone. To my horror, I saw that he somehow held Daniel by the neck. I gasped when they stopped a few feet in front of us, hovering above the water.

"Claire–" Daniel mouthed, but just like any other time before or after our four and a half minutes, I couldn't hear him.

Aden was talking, too, though I couldn't hear him any more than I could Daniel. Felix, on the other hand, seemed to be paying close attention, like he was listening to every word. Yet, instead of looking at Aden, his eyes roamed back and forth across the lake. Felix suddenly twisted me around and forced me back up the hill to the road while Aden and Daniel circled around us. Aden closed in abruptly into Felix's ear, and Felix pushed me to the ground, the cracking sound of my knees smashing into the pebbly concrete.

I cried out in pain. Daniel futilely reached out to help me, but Aden launched him backward across the lake. A screaming, twisting sound trailed after them, and they were gone.

Felix yanked me up to him again, anchoring me stiffly against his torso as we waited in silence until Aden and Daniel returned a few seconds later.

"Let's try this again." Felix said, pressing the knife into the base of my ear, running it up and down along the side of my neck, puncturing my skin. I screamed and jerked at the pain, then forced my eyes shut when Felix's mouth brushed the side of my cheek.

"Where were we?" His lips touched my skin. "My demon says this is where your boyfriend gets to make his choice. What'll it be? You going to keep up your little connection, or not?"

Aden dragged Daniel upward so his face was right in front of me. His eyes met mine, wide and afraid—so far from the inviting, soothing brown I was used to.

"Last chance," Felix said, scanning the darkness, like he was waiting for some kind of sign. "Do you want to keep her, or can I have her? She's real pretty."

I looked at Daniel. His mouth was still, but now his eyes were fuming.

"Well, okay then," said Felix as he twisted me around and pushed me down the road...away from Hidden Lake...away from safety.

Daniel

I tried a million times to break free. But I was Aden's prisoner as we circled around Claire while Felix forced her down the deserted road through the fog.

"Having fun yet?" Aden sneered.

Claire turned her head briefly, catching my eye. "*Go*," I mouthed to her. "*Run.*"

She understood perfectly, turning sharply and jerking Felix backward. The knife slipped from his hands and fell to the side of the road as she ran away from him, down to the hill. As I silently cheered her on, Aden's grip on me slackened long enough for me to escape. Before he could react, I'd already shifted away from him, straight to Matthew's bedroom.

Matthew was sound asleep, the covers pulled up tight around him. I had absolutely no clue how to wake him—poltergeist-type activity being new to me. Getting right up in his face, I tried pushing my thoughts toward him. But nothing seemed to be happening other than a lot of snoring.

Aden poked in through the wall separating Claire and Matthew's room. Only his upper torso and head were visible as he peered in, like he'd been searching each room in the house. When he saw me, he rushed forward, but I dodged him and he careened straight through the foot of the bed, creating enough of a draft to move Matthew's covers. Matthew stopped snoring, and turned over to his side before falling back into heavy breathing.

I slid across the bed, purposely provoking Aden. "So, what's your plan now, Aden?" I taunted, dancing around Matthew's bed. "Your Felix wasn't so great out there, after all."

Aden careened toward me again, this time right on target. He tagged me and took me with him as we flew across the bed, creating enough of a draft to topple a lamp. It landed on the floor with a thud. Matthew's eyes popped open.

"What the...?" he moaned.

Aden stopped when he realized his mistake, but it was too late. Matthew was already sitting up, scanning the room.

The door flew open, and Addie flipped on the light. "What was that?"

Aden glared at Addie, then at me, and vanished.

"What?" asked Matthew, still in a daze.

"Where's Claire? She's not in bed...not in the bathroom...and why is your lamp on the floor?" Addie asked, looking down.

"I don't know. It felt like someone opened the window or something..." His eyes grew big and he leapt off the bed to the window, checking. He was finally awake. "*Wait*—Claire's gone?" he asked, his face losing color.

"I don't know. But she's not in her bed."

Matthew ran out of the bedroom and down the hall, flipping on the lights as he tore through the house. I shifted outside to Claire. She was scrambling along the edge of the lake, only a few yards ahead of Felix, who was momentarily lost in the fog behind her. But Aden seemed to be leading Felix right to her.

Back at the house, Matthew was still running up and down the hallway, still calling for Claire. But I needed him to hurry and get down to the lake. I shifted back to Claire, then back up to Matthew, trying to decide where I was needed most.

I took a gamble, and went back for Claire.

She was hurrying her way through the fog, across a narrow ledge over a steep embankment, stumbling across rocks and boulders that lay stacked atop each other among the grass and cattails. It was the same spot she'd fallen in on her birthday. Hopefully, she hadn't noticed.

But she wasn't fast enough. Felix's hand caught her foot and pulled her to the ground, slamming her against the rocks. She screamed as Felix flipped her over and jumped on top of her, smothering her with his body. "You're not getting away again, sweetie."

Aden was right behind him—both he and Felix staring at Claire wildly, regarding her like a piece of meat or a means to an end. Furious, I dove in, trying to push Felix off of her, trying to yank her out of there. But I couldn't do it.

Felix slapped Claire across the face and she screamed. Aden turned to me. "See what you started?"

Just up the hill, I heard familiar voices.

Finally.

Claire tried to scream again, but Felix shoved his hand over her mouth, and she seemed to choke.

"Hold on, Claire," I said to her, hoping she could read my words, but she didn't seem coherent. Her eyes were glazed over; she was already going limp, giving up.

Footsteps were coming…running down the hill….

Felix looked up at the sound, then clasped his hands around Claire's neck. I instinctively flew at him, trying to pull his gigantic paws off of Claire's body as Aden yelled in Felix's ear. "Don't kill her yet, you idiot! Pick her up. Let's go!"

But Felix wasn't listening to his demon anymore. He seemed possessed by something else—something inside his own head.

Claire's eyes opened again, finding mine just as a dark shape approached from behind Felix, pummeling him in the head.

Matthew!

He launched Felix off of Claire, shoving him to the ground. Claire flipped to her side and began crawling out of the way while Matthew continued his assault, slamming Felix's head into a rock, shouting at him furiously. It was a Matthew I had never seen.

I drifted backwards, hovering beside Claire. Aden held back, watching me, watching Matthew and Felix, probably wondering what to do next. I could only imagine what was spinning through his mind as he watched his plan disintegrate.

Claire lay there in a daze, gasping.

"Claire!" Addie was suddenly beside her, pulling her to her feet, squeezing her tight. "It's okay, Claire-bear," she said over and over again.

Claire's parents emerged from the fog, calling her name as they ran down the hill. Relieved to see more faces, I looked up just as Felix broke free from Matthew. He dove straight for Addie and Claire, knocking both of them over a steep ledge. Right into the lake.

CHAPTER SIXTEEN SUBMERGED

Claire

The impact was so hard that I felt the wind go out of my lungs just as Addie landed on top of me. Water rushed in my ears and up my nose. Everything was melting together into one big watery mess as I struggled to untangle myself.

My head popped out of the water to a rush of cold air. I gasped and kicked, trying to keep afloat. Something brushed by me, and I twisted around to find Addie right behind me.

"Addie!" I yelled, reaching for her, but she wasn't swimming. My heart nearly quit when I realized what that meant. I threw my arms around her and swam toward the shore. About halfway there, something pulled at my ankle, jerking me away from her. I kicked, trying to get away. Frantically, I swam toward the voices calling my name...toward Dad...toward his fingertips touching mine...

Like quicksand, I was sucked back down before I had a chance to grab his hand. The watery world enveloped me and the darkness returned, until everything was quiet.

Daniel

Claire's parents made it down the hill just as Claire and Addie hit the water. Claire's dad immediately jumped in the lake, leaving her mom on the shore, crying and blubbering into her cell phone, screaming for help.

Aden was down by the water, likely trying to figure out how to fix his botched plan, while I hovered near Matthew and Felix. They were still pounding fists into each other, when Felix suddenly flipped around on top of Matthew and started smashing his head into the ground.

"Matthew!" I yelled, drifting in close by his face. He was in trouble, and Felix wasn't stopping any time soon. "Mrs. James! Someone!" I yelled, but nobody could hear me. No one was even close by. They were all down at the shore, still focused on Claire and Addie in the lake. The world was falling apart around me, and I was helpless.

Matthew's eyes fluttered closed—I could tell he was losing it. Felix pounded his fist into Matthew's stomach, and then brought his other hand to his face, swinging hard. Blood sprayed from a slit beneath his eye.

This was not happening. I couldn't let Matthew die.

I looked into Felix's crazed face smeared with dirt and blood, then back down at Matthew's bleeding head. It took me back to a different night, to an explosion ringing in my ears, expanding through my head. Matthew was screaming for me, holding my head in his lap...I could feel the slick warmth spilling out of my head. I tried to wake up, to keep my eyes open, but the world was so dark, the pain was too much, Felix had killed me...was killing Matthew...

No.

NOOOO!

I dove full-force at Felix, creating a gust of air that seemed to knock the wind out of him, a whistling sound coming from his throat. With a look of confusion, he pulled himself off of Matthew and looked around, his wheezing quickly getting worse. "Who's there?" he asked, shaking. Maybe he thought Aden was attacking him.

Flying at him again, I drove straight through his chest. He shivered, shrieking, "Get away from me!"

I rushed him again, and he stumbled backward, landing in the lake with a loud splash. Hopefully, he couldn't swim.

I turned to Matthew. Blood was smeared across his face, his nose gushing. He was limp. Quiet. *Too quiet.*

"Matt, wake up, Bro."

Nothing.

"Matthew!"

Screaming. Sirens in the distance.

"Matt, come on! You're going to be fine," I said, shaking him, trying to ignore whatever was happening in the water, hoping somehow Claire was okay. I couldn't leave Matthew yet. "You have to help Claire now. You have to live for her. *Please.*" Something like a sob was climbing up my throat. "I need your help. Claire *needs* you, Matt. Felix…*Felix* is still after her. Felix was the one who shot me. You have to *hear* me. Wake up, Matthew *please!*" I begged, somehow placing my hands on his face and pulling his head into my lap.

Matthew's body jerked and he inhaled, slowly crawling to his knees. He turned his head and looked up, his eyes blinking and then widening. He froze, like he was afraid. *Afraid of what?* Matthew wasn't afraid of anything. Then I realized he was staring at me, looking me straight in the eyes.

I didn't know what to do. I just watched him watch me, wondering what was going through his mind. He sat up, holding his head, hesitantly reaching for my arm, his fingers gripping me solidly. A faint smile emerged from his bloody face. "Daniel," he whispered.

There was a shout from below. Something was still happening in the water. We both turned. Addie was standing at the edge of the lake, screaming.

Matthew jumped to his feet, but almost toppled over. "Dizzy," he said, still holding his head.

"I'll help you." I draped my arm across his shoulders and walked with him a few steps, his weight leaning into mine. Suddenly, I lost hold of him as my arm sailed through him, and he fell. "Matthew?" I asked, in front of his face.

He just looked at me, like he was trying to read my lips. "Help me up," he said, his hand extended.

I reached for his arm again, but our connection was gone. I shook my head as he hobbled over to the rocks, down to the edge of the lake, tripping a few times, but still managing to reach the shore.

Addie turned and ran to Matthew when she saw him, throwing her arms around his neck. She quickly pulled back, her eyes wide. "Your face, Matthew! Oh my gosh. And your eye...you're bleeding. Are you okay?"

"I think so," he said, looking past her to Mrs. James, who was standing in about two feet of water. "What's going on? Where's Claire?"

"She's still under the water," Mrs. James yelled hysterically. "Your dad dove in to find her."

Matthew was already splashing through the water, stumbling over the rocks and picking himself up each time he tripped. He seemed to be regaining strength with each step. Spinning lights and sirens were making their way down the hill, but Matthew wasn't waiting for anyone. As he swam, I shifted beneath the surface to search for Claire. The water was hazy and dark, but the moon glowed through the fog, softly illuminating shadows and a fighting Claire.

She was near the bottom, still holding her breath while trying to break away from some kind of whirlpool that appeared to be keeping her under. Just behind her, a faint outline rippled through the water. I zoomed closer to find Aden there, his arms extended in front of him, somehow using the water's force to hold Claire under.

I shifted back to the surface, where Matthew had met up with his dad, their heads bobbing up and down in the moonlight. Just as I reached them, Felix came out of nowhere and jumped on Mr. James' back, pushing him under the water, leaving a pool of bubbles in their wake.

"Get Claire," Mr. James choked out to Matthew when he resurfaced, his arm around Felix's neck in a chokehold.

While Mr. James grappled with Felix, Matthew turned my way, his eyes catching mine. Everything seemed to stall, like the world was crawling, when he looked at me and pleaded, "Do you know where she is?"

I nodded, moved by the intensity in his eyes. "Follow me."

He dove under as I led him down to Claire. She was still caught in the freak whirlpool, which Matthew was already trying to breach. No matter how hard he kicked, he couldn't break into the vortex of water that encaged her. Her eyes had lost focus, and I could tell she was out of air. Matthew knew it, too, and propelled himself forward again. I looked for Aden and rushed at him the same way he'd attacked me—but he remained unfazed as I flew through him.

Circling to try again, I turned around just as a flash of red zoomed by, knocking me off balance. The water rippled as the light barreled straight into Aden, knocking him backward several feet. The whirlpool instantly dissolved, releasing Claire. She weakly kicked for the surface, but stopped. She'd run out of breath.

I went to her and tried pulling her up, but she floated through me—her body limp and her eyes empty. Matthew's watery scream matched what I felt seeping out of me, floating through the lake around us. He pulled Claire to him and raced to the surface, leaving me all alone. Claire didn't need me this time. She needed *them*.

Feeling the pull of the water glide through me, I drifted through the lake in search of Aden, or for some explanation for what had freed Claire. Making out a faint outline of something in the distance, I drifted closer, soon recognizing the face belonging to all that hair.

Crazy Hair Lady. *Nico*. Claire's aunt.

She was still under the water, floating a few feet in front of Aden, wearing a red floral dress, her eyes swirling turquoise and yellow.

Aden was seething. "Why did you do that? You ruined everything!"

They were facing another, circling like animals. Nico seemed to be enjoying herself, a triumphant smile forming on her lips. "You need to quit bugging the *living*," she said, flicking her hand against Aden's shoulder and shoving him backwards through the water. "It's not very fun when you're the one getting pushed around, is it?"

Aden tensed his shoulders and crouched low, making some sort of strange growling noise. Then he rushed at her, like he was going to wring her neck. "You need to mind your own business, Witch!"

Nico turned and winked at me just before he reached her—and this time I saw it coming. *For once.* I felt myself smiling when I heard a soft metallic *clink* the second Aden made contact with her.

"You need to learn to *think* before you act, Aden. Now I've got you," she said, mimicking Aden's earlier words to me, making me wonder if she'd been eavesdropping the entire time.

Aden fought. He punched. *Screamed.*

"Hopefully now you'll realize you can't change the past," she said, pulling him with her as they began to drift away. "Next time try focusing on the future. It's much easier."

Aden's shrill screams flooded the watery world. I tried covering my ears, but the noise reverberated through the lake, the water magnifying the sound waves, multiplying and engulfing my senses.

Finally it stopped.

Aden's broad shoulders slumped in defeat. He turned to Nico and whispered, "Where are you taking me?"

"I'm going to teach you a few lessons."

They started to fade away. Just before the water appeared to swallow them up, Nico turned back to me and winked. Her eyes were a cool green. "Don't forget our date. How about this Thursday night at the Galleria? Eight-o'clock, sharp. I'll bring the popcorn."

"Wait. Do I…?"

But they were gone, and the lake was suddenly quiet.

I shifted to the shore, where Claire's cold, pale body lay in the mud. Compared to the still quiet beneath the water, the rest of the world seemed alive and angry, sound waves bouncing around me like a rubber ball—sirens, walkie-talkies, voices yelling, screaming, or crying.

Felix lay face down on the ground, his arms cuffed behind his back. The paramedics surrounded Claire and pumped her chest as Addie, Matthew and her parents huddled over her, crying, calling her name, begging her to live. I drifted through the circle of people surrounding her, and sunk next to the guy trying to save her life.

Matthew looked up at me, then grabbed Claire's hand and leaned into her ear. "Claire. Claire, it's me, Matthew. You have to come back. For Mom and Dad, and Addie. For me. For *Daniel*. Please, Claire, you have to come back."

We waited, but she still didn't move. Matthew gasped, choking hard before he found me again. I could see panic inside his eyes as they pleaded with me to save his little sister. That was when I realized Matthew needed Claire, and she needed Matthew. And because of that, I was going to be okay. She was going to be just fine.

I kissed Claire's forehead, and placed my head on her chest, hoping the soft rhythm of her heartbeat would start. At the first muted thump, I looked up at the swollen lump of serrated flesh beneath Matthew's blood-shot eye, the purple and black patches spreading like a disease beneath his skin, and I smiled—because *he* was going to be all right now, too.

I turned back to Matthew's little sister and whispered in her ear, "Claire. I love you. I think I always have."

Claire

I could feel my heart beating and the rush of blood waking me up. Slowly, I opened my eyes to a crowd of strange faces looking at me, to the feeling of wet and cold seeping through my skin into my bones.

My skin…my bones…

Startled, I reached out for Daniel. He was there, somewhere. I could feel him near me, but couldn't find him.

"Claire," I heard familiar voices talking amidst the swirl of commotion encircling me as Matthew came into view, followed by Addie and my parents, the neighbors, and a bunch of other strange faces.

"Daniel," I called out weakly, trying to sit up as a dozen hands pushed me back down into the grass.

"Take it easy, there," said a deep voice.

I wanted Daniel, but the overwhelming mass of faces smothered me. I finally located Matthew's face, and looked at him hopefully. "Daniel?" I squeaked out. Matthew only smiled, his relieved eyes hiding any answers.

Everything felt upside down as the crowded world spun around me like a merry-go-round, my eyes growing heavy again. When I tried to lift my arms or move my body, I felt constrained like there was a weight pressing on my chest, and I sunk back to wherever I'd been…

…*back to Daniel.*

CHAPTER
SEVENTEEN NOT THE END

Daniel

The moonlight shone down on us as we lazily drifted around in circles, her head resting against my chest as I held her, one arm along her waist, the other brushing her hair.

"This isn't so bad," she said, looking up at me.

I leaned down and kissed her forehead, letting my lips linger on her skin. She reached for my hand, her fingers interlaced through mine.

"I never said it was bad."

"Then why don't I just stay?"

"This isn't a place where you should stay, Claire—you know that."

"But I don't want to leave you." Sitting up suddenly, she gasped, "My ring, Daniel! Where's my ring? It must have fallen off in the lake…"

"Shhhhh," I hugged her…. "I'll find it for you."

Dusk or dawn filtered in through slatted shades, sending blurry patterns across the room. People came and went—some familiar, some not; some with flowers, some with cards or hugs. Claire's face looked so peaceful on the pillow near mine. For hours at a time, I would get lost in her silhouette while dragging my fingers across her eyelids, then along her cheek, pretending I could feel her again.

When she had company, I usually stood off in the corner, burying myself in a small patch of sunlight.Even though no one could see me, I still felt like an intruder. Sometimes she would stir, her moaning cause for excitement as they all eagerly waited. When she didn't wake up, their faces and heads would droop as they all tried to hide their disappointment after she eluded them once again.

"You can't keep doing this to them," I told her the next time she came to me.

"But I'm not ready."

We'd found refuge at Hidden Lake again. The leaves were falling around us as we stood at the edge of the dock, this time in the shadow of a golden sunset. We faced each other as I brushed my hands along the sides of her arms. Her skin felt so delicate, though my memory could never do it justice. Soon, I was holding her face in my hands, closing my eyes, and letting my head fall forward until our noses were barely touching, her cheek grazing mine as our lips met....

"Claire. *Claire,*" we could both hear her mom calling her. "I'm so sorry, honey. Please come back..."

Claire's lips stayed on mine.

I pulled back.

She hesitated, a look of confusion on her face.

"You need to go," I urged, for her sake.

"But I'm happy here with you."

"I love you, Claire," her mom's voice broke in.

Claire looked at me, her eyes sad, then scared, then uncertain. "I don't want to leave you, Daniel," she sighed, looking out across the lake.

"Say hi to Daniel for me," Matthew's voice intruded. "And then you need to wake up."

Claire gulped.

I held her hand, even though I could only feel subtle pressure. Looking down, I tried to imagine or remember what it felt like to hold her. The memory weakly returned, but I couldn't make it last. Suspecting the same for her, I squeezed her fingers as tightly as I could, and then released them.

"We'll have our time." I attempted courage. "Just not right now."

Her eyes told me tears wanted to fall, but here they only brimmed with sadness. "I know." She bowed her head, unwilling to look at me anymore, but still unable to let go. "I know," she repeated.

Lifting her chin with my finger, I forced her to look at me, and then kissed her one more time, trying to remember how she felt in my arms, as numb as I was, insistent on retaining one final memory that would have to last years, or decades, or more.

And then she left me—to return to her life that still waited for her, to the life without me.

I was glad it had been her decision, and not mine.

Claire

Day and night blurred together, composing a continuous span of dripping, fading time. Mom and Dad were there when I opened my eyes. I first heard Mom's gasp, then looked up to find Dad's crooked smile.

"Claire," he sighed in relief and squeezed my hand, his eyes brimming with emotion. Mom smothered my face with kisses and tears, and I felt my heart growing warm.

I'd missed them.

Over the next few days my foggy mind fought for awareness, unable to keep track of time. My life consisted of never-ending visits from family and friends who peppered me with a million questions interspersed with long naps and bland hospital food, both, which left me exhausted. I felt paper thin, my lungs weak as a butterfly at first, my mind shouting from the inside for my body to move. Eventually the beeping and whirring of machines were abandoned until all that was left were a few annoying needles I begged to have removed.

The only thing I couldn't get rid of was my insomnia. Night after night I tossed and turned, sometimes only sleeping an hour or so, my daydreams blurring with reality, thanks to the various drugs taking up residence in my mind. Visions of Daniel seemed to come and go. As long as I was dreaming he was never far away, so I wanted to sleep as much as possible.

Everyone was afraid to speak of that night; they all avoided it—even Matthew, though occasionally he looked at me like he was bursting inside. The doctor had probably ordered everyone's silence. That was fine by me, because not only did I prefer not to have to think about Aden and Felix ever again, but I also didn't want anyone to see me cry. Being stuck half-naked in a hospital bed was bad enough.

After almost a week in the hospital, I finally got to go home. It felt good being surrounded by familiar walls, smells and sounds, and even better being fattened up by Mom's cooking. She pretty much made whatever I wanted whenever I wanted, which opened it up to just about anything when your mom could make absolutely everything. I never really noticed before.

I had been home only a few days, and was sinking my teeth into a warm pumpkin scone slathered in butter, when Matthew invited himself in my room and sat beside me on the bed. He still looked pretty bad, with two huge bandages on his face and head, and another on his arm. At least his eye was almost down to its normal size.

"How are you doing?" he asked, smiling.

"Okay, I guess. Addie updated me on all the drama at school." I laughed, taking another bite.

"Good. Important stuff," he said, bringing his hand down on my knee.

"So have you officially dropped out of school?"

"No. I just worked a few things out with my professors," Matthew said, looking out the open window that was letting in a cool breeze Mom thought would give me pneumonia, never mind it was 65 degrees outside.

"Mom and Dad might kill me for doing this," Matthew said, "but we *have* to talk about what happened—about Daniel."

Hearing Matthew say Daniel's name out loud sent my heart racing. I swallowed hard and looked up at him, not sure where things were going.

"I know," he apologized profusely, afraid to look at me directly, "It sucks, Claire, but–"

"It's okay," I interrupted. "Really, I'm fine. You're the only one who understands, anyway."

He shifted back and forth on the bed, like he wasn't sure how to begin. Every time I thought he was going to say something, he'd close his mouth again and look out the window.

What was going on?

"Matth–" I started, but he interrupted.

"I saw Daniel, Claire."

I dropped what was left of my scone, and sat up. "WHAT?" Matthew nodded, his deep ocean eyes overflowing with excitement. "*How?*"

"I don't know. But he was there. *I saw him.* I couldn't believe it, either. I kept trying to convince myself it was a dream, but Daniel really *was* there. And then he was gone."

"This is *insane!*" I said, leaning forward. "Did anyone else see him?"

"No. I mean, I don't think so. I'm pretty sure it was just me."

"I don't get it. There has to be some reason you saw him. You really don't know why?"

Matthew looked away for a second, almost like he was hiding something, but then he laughed, and punched me in the side. "Nope. I thought *you* would have all the answers."

"I don't get it *at all.*" I tried coming up with some kind of explanation, but my mind was blank.

"What about you?" he asked, almost apologetically. "Have you seen him…since then?"

I shook my head, feeling a lump forming in my throat. "No. I think he's gone now. I mean…I don't really know where he is…I definitely can't see him anymore."

Matthew leaned over and hugged me, apologizing like everything was his fault. "I'm sorry, Claire."

"It's okay." I kissed his cheek and hugged him back. "Thanks for listening, and for believing, and for *everything*. I don't know what I would've done without you, Matth–" but my throat caught, and I couldn't finish. Instead, I just held onto him, grateful for his solid, unmoving, predictable existence.

Cautiously, he whispered into my ear, "What about Aden?"

"He's gone, too," I answered, leaning back and settling down into the covers.

"You sure?"

"Yes," I answered confidently. "That was the deal, you know—no more Daniel meant no more Aden."

"Are you okay? Do you want to talk about it?"

"No. I'm fine," I said, quickly dumping the thought, before adding, "How's Dad feeling?"

"He's better."

"What about Felix? I hope he looks worse than you."

"I don't know. They carted him off before I could get another look at him. Probably a good thing, though, because not even the cops could have stopped me from killing him."

"Thinking about him still gives me the creeps. I never want to see him again."

"I'm pretty sure he won't be bothering you—or anyone else for a long time," Matthew answered, smiling, a hint of *something* in his words. "Attempted kidnapping, attempted murder, assault, drug charges, oh, and even a handful of parking tickets, too," Matthew chuckled. "I think he's pretty screwed."

I felt a wave of relief rush through me, even though I hadn't worried much about Felix once Aden was gone. It was just comforting to know Felix was fully incapacitated in as many ways as possible.

"Plus," Matthew said, hesitantly, like he was afraid to look at me, "someone called in an anonymous tip to the police."

"About?"

"They just announced it on the news today."

"Announced *what*?" I asked. Matthew stared at me, his jaw clenched, his muscles tight. He looked angry again. "Tell me, Matthew," I said, afraid for the answer.

Matthew took a deep breath. "Felix was the one who shot Daniel."

"WHAT? Are you sure?" I asked, leaning forward, dumbfounded.

Matthew just nodded, like he was done talking.

"I can't believe it…"

"Claire," Matthew said, looking down at my other hand clawing his leg.

"Oh, sorry." I leaned back and tried to relax, still not knowing how. "How do they know it was Felix? Who tipped off the police?"

"Claire!" Addie barged in and shoved her way past Matthew before diving on the bed beside me. "So, what have you two been talking about?"

Matthew slid off the bed and mumbled something about Dad, then left us alone.

Addie fell backwards, sighing dramatically, and then grew uncharacteristically quiet. I hooked my arm through hers and stared at the ceiling.

"You okay?" I asked her.

"I don't know," she said. "Did Matthew tell you about Felix?"

"Yes."

"But…" she paused. "It still doesn't change anything. Daniel isn't coming back, you know." Her eyes were glossy.

"I know, Addie."

"It just brought everything back so suddenly, like a tsunami. You know, so quiet and unexpected, and then all of a sudden—WHAM!" she slapped her hands together. "And it hits you, just like that."

She turned toward me, our faces inches apart. Remarkably, for once she didn't hide behind wit or sarcasm or her boisterous personality. Instead, she simply smiled, and her blue eyes lit up momentarily until the grief she'd never been able to release finally exploded, taking even her by surprise. I grabbed her hand, as the weight of sorrow enslaved by weeks of silence seemed to lift from her, like rain was washing it all away.

"Daniel loves you, Addie," I said, pushing away her dark mane of hair hanging in her face, and looking into her shimmery eyes.

She whispered, barely loud enough for me to hear, "I know."

CHAPTER EIGHTEEN SUNRISE

Claire

The strange sensation of having just missed something nagged me each time I awoke. I couldn't seem to brush it off, and finally accepted it as a side effect from too much medication.

Matthew was busy getting ready to go back to school after having been given a few extra weeks to finish his assignments and finals. He hadn't even left yet, and I already missed him. *He was my hero*. He had listened and believed me when I had nowhere else to go, despite his doubts.

The night before he left, I asked him about the strange feelings I was still having, hoping for some logical insight, since all rationality had left me weeks ago. He surprised me by suggesting I was still able to sense Daniel. Since, I'd lost that ability, the idea of it didn't make sense anymore. Why would I just suddenly be able to sense Daniel again, after he'd already faded away for good?

Early the next morning, when the sun was just peeking in through the window, I awoke suddenly, like the breath had been sucked out of me. Sitting up, I looked around the room, and then slipped out of bed, blindly making my way to the bathroom.

My reflection in the mirror was pathetic. In addition to persistent dark circles under my eyes, I was still covered with greenish-yellow bruises and gnarly-looking scrapes. I looked like a Halloween mask. A bad one.

Depressed, I turned around and moped back to my room. Just as I pulled back the covers, my eye caught something on the nightstand, something that hadn't been there two minutes ago.

Lying on its side, reflecting in the sunlight, was my lost ring.

How did he find it?

I felt my knees go wobbly as I picked it up and turned it around in my shaking hand before sliding it back on my finger. Smiling, I fell backwards into bed, wondering how in the world Daniel managed to bring it back to me.

I whispered *thank you*, hoping he could hear me.

Wondering if I would ever know.

Daniel

They were all together, *really together*, the first time since my death. Matthew was home for winter break and the three of them were biking up in the hills, for old time's sake. I followed along—an invisible fourth wheel. I liked to think of it as my last hurrah.

Addie and Matthew threw their bikes down as soon as they reached the opening by the muddy pathway, though Claire looked a little hesitant before following them through the bushes.

"I think I'm too old for this," Matthew complained as he gripped the rope and stood out over the edge of the branch.

"Wimp." Addie pushed him from behind before he could protest anymore. He fell forward like a lead brick, swinging back and forth while yelling at the top of his lungs.

"Not bad," I applauded, though no one could hear me.

It was Addie's turn on the rope and, just like before, she forgot to let go in time, and found herself stuck in the middle of the stream. She dropped into the water when no one came to her rescue. "Thanks a lot, you guys," she pouted, wiping herself off as best she could.

"I figured there was no way you'd make the same mistake twice— so, sue me for having a little faith in you," said Matthew, laughing.

Claire went last again. She closed her eyes and held her breath, then leapt off the branch. Her body sailed smoothly across the stream and back to the tree again. But instead of stopping, she planted her feet against the tree trunk and pushed off again…and…again…and again, letting one hand go while leaning backward, her head hanging down, her hair flying through the wind.

When the sun hung low in the sky as nighttime approached, Matthew took the lead down to the stream as they nostalgically hopped from rock to rock. Claire stopped, plunging her hand into the water where I'd found her ring. Addie and Matthew stood back, watching silently… waiting.

Claire looked up at them and smiled. "This is where Daniel found my ring," she said, pointing. They nodded, probably not knowing what to do or say.

I smiled—glad I'd found it for her again, though this time wasn't quite as easy. It was a good thing I'd had a little help. I looked at Matthew, who was leaning against a boulder behind Addie and Claire.

Claire turned around and hopped over a fallen log. "Addie, what did you call this place last time? You gave it some kind of name."

"That's right. What was it?" Addie asked, thinking. She stopped for a minute, leaning against an old tree stump. "The Secret Walk," she announced with a dignified look on her face.

"Which I still say sounds stupid," Matthew said, dodging a spray of water Addie kicked up on him.

"No one asked *you*," Addie laughed. Matthew threw his arm around her waist, and she screamed as he boosted her up over the log.

When they made it back to the rope swing, Claire turned to face them, a giant smile on her face. "Let's keep it that way," she said. "A *secret*."

Matthew remained quiet, probably not willing to become another target with Addie still close behind.

"No one else will ever know about this place," Claire added mysteriously, her eyes lit up.

"*Ever*," Addie emphasized, always loving a secret.

"Just the four of us," Matthew said under his breath.

"Just the four of us..." Claire whispered back to him, smiling.

I led the way out.

Acknowledgements

The idea that I should be able to put into words my gratitude for everyone involved in the creation of this book is an overwhelming thought. I look back on the path leading me to this point, afraid of overlooking influences and inspirations that carried me here. How do I say thank you in a way that means as much to ears on the receiving end as it does to me in my own head? How do I embrace my heroes and advocates through a few lousy words printed on paper?

I guess I just try.

Thank you to my husband, Greg, and my four children who didn't laugh at me three years ago when I began carting my laptop around everywhere, and for allowing me the guilt-free indulgence of writing whenever I could. Though, now they make fun of me and will probably forever remember me being attached to my computer. Sorry.

To my parents, Rand and Joyce King, who didn't allow video games or much TV when I was a kid, which forced me to be creative; who always pushed me and never let me give up; who even now aren't afraid to tell me they love me; and who make the best food on the planet. I am me because of you.

To my big sister, Kristin Johns. Thank you for being my first-ever reader, fan, editor, pseudo-agent, and for leading the story in the right direction whenever I veered too far off the path. Thanks for keeping it real; I admire your honesty and sincerity, and I needed it! I owe you a trip to Hawaii, but tell Bob that for right now you'll have to settle for your names in print here at the back of the book.

To my little sister, Caroline, who never fails to deliver the latest musical inspiration, for exuding uber-coolness and style nearly all of the time, and for her snazzy design skills when I've lost mine. Justin, for your wife and her enthusiasm at all the right times.

To my early readers Donna, Aunt Helen, Anne, Jody, Brett, Aly: thank you for seeing the diamond in the rough, and for telling me what I needed to hear. Brett, for telling me it is the best book you ever read (whether it's true, or not).

To Stan Soper and his much-needed guidance, for believing in this story, and for convincing me not to give up when it seemed like I should.

Thank you, Elena Kalis, for your gorgeous photograph that miraculously captures the essence of On the Fringe in every way possible.

To my editors Lisa Paul and Heather McCubbin, and formatter Kimberly Martin, and to Lisa, for taking a chance on me. I am indebted to you for a thousand and one things…for your expert eye, for saving me from the 'I's', for trusting in me, for keeping me focused, for putting up with all my questions and my amateur editing process. Mostly, thank you for loving Daniel and Claire as much as I do.

Lastly, I cannot express or define the gratitude I feel for an infinite heritage spanning time, for invisible heartstrings that bind us all together, and for grandparents and ancestors whom I still feel with me, whispering in my ears that we are all connected.